ARROW'S EDGE MC

PRAISE FOR FREYA BARKER

Freya Barker writes a mean romance, I tell you! A REAL romance, with real characters and real conflict.

~Author M. Lynne Cunning

I've said it before and I'll say it again and again, Freya Barker is one of the BEST storytellers out there.

~Turning Pages At MidnightBook Blog

God, Freya Barker gets me every time I read one of her books. She's a master at creating a beautiful story that you lose yourself in the moment you start reading.

~Britt Red Hatter Book Blog

Freya Barker has woven a delicate balance of honest emotions and well-formed characters into a tale that is as unique as it is gripping.

~Ginger Scott, bestselling young and new adult author and Goodreads Choice Awards finalist

Such a truly beautiful story! The writing is gorgeous, the scenery is beautiful...

~Author Tia Louise

From Dust by Freya Barker is one of those special books. One of those whose plotline and characters remain with you for days after you finished it.

~Jeri's Book Attic

No amount of words could describe how this story made me feel, I think this is one I will remember forever, absolutely freaking awesome is not even close to how I felt about it.

~Lilian's Book Blog

Still Air was insightful, eye-opening, and I paused numerous times to think about my relationships with my own children. Anytime a book can evoke a myriad of emotions while teaching life lessons you'll continue to carry with you, it's a 5-star read.

~ Bestselling Author CP Smith

In my opinion, there is nothing better than a Freya Barker book. With her final installment in her Portland, ME series, Still Air, she does not disappoint. From start to finish I was completely captivated by Pam, Dino, and the entire Portland family.

~ Author RB Hilliard

The one thing you can always be sure of with Freya's writing is that it will pull on ALL of your emotions; it's expressive, meaningful, sarcastic, so very true to life, real, hard-hitting and heartbreaking at times and, as is the case with this series especially, the story is at points raw, painful and occasionally fugly BUT it is also sweet, hopeful, uplifting, humorous and heart-warming.

~ Book Loving Pixies

ALSO BY FREYA BARKER

ON CALL SERIES (Operation Alpha):
BURNING FOR AUTUMN
COVERING OLLIE
TRACKING TAHLULA
ABSOLVING BLUE
REVEALING ANNIE
ROCK POINT SERIES:
KEEPING 6
CABIN 12
HWY 550
10-CODE
NORTHERN LIGHTS COLLECTION:
A CHANGE IN TIDE
A CHANGE OF VIEW
A CHANGE OF PACE
SNAPSHOT SERIES:
SHUTTER SPEED
FREEZE FRAME
IDEAL IMAGE
PORTLAND, ME, NOVELS:
FROM DUST
CRUEL WATER
THROUGH FIRE
STILL AIR
LULLAY: A CHRISTMAS NOVELLA
CEDAR TREE SERIES:
SLIM TO NONE
HUNDRED TO ONE
AGAINST ME
CLEAN LINES
UPPER HAND
LIKE ARROWS
HEAD START
STANDALONE BOOKS:
WHEN HOPE ENDS
VICTIM OF CIRCUMSTANCE

EDGE
OF
FEAR

FREYA BARKER

Copyright © 2021 Margreet Asselbergs as Freya Barker
All rights reserved.
No part of this publication may be reproduced, distributed, or
transmitted in any form or by any means, including photocopying,
recording, or by other electronic or mechanical methods, without
the prior written permission of the author or publisher, except in
the case of brief quotations embodied in used critical reviews and
certain other non-commercial uses as permitted by copyright law.
For permission requests, write to the author, mentioning in the
subject line: "Reproduction Request"
at freyabarker.writes@gmail.com
This book is a work of fiction and any resemblance to any person
or persons, living or dead, any event, occurrence, or incident is
purely coincidental. The characters and story lines are created and
thought up from the author's imagination or are used fictitiously.

ISBN PAPERBACK: 9781988733623

Cover Design:
Freya Barker

Cover Image:
Golden Czermak (FuriousFotog)

Cover Model:
Scott Benton

Editing:
Karen Hrdlicka

Proofing:
Joanne Thompson

Formatting:
CP Smith

ACKNOWLEDGMENTS

First and foremost I'd like to thank my readers. Both my loyal followers who eagerly await each new release, and those for whom this was the first book of mine they tried. I thank you all for taking the time to read my words. It's a humbling feeling that never gets old.

I especially want to thank the members of my fabulous Barks & Bites reader group. These folks lift me up, cheer me on, and support me on a day-to-day basis.

My group is very welcoming, so if you enjoy my books and would like to join, we'd love to have you: https://www.facebook.com/groups/FreyasBarksandBites/

Next I have a veritable laundry list of amazing people without whom there would be no books. Writing is only part of what it takes to bring a story to you, the rest of the work is done by my amazing friends: Karen Hrdlicka, Joanne Thompson, Deb Blake, Pam Buchanan, Petra Gleason, Krystal Weiss, Debra Presley, Drue Hoffman, CP Smith, and my agent Stephanie Phillips of SBR Media.

Finally, I have to mention my husband who is probably the most tolerant person I know. He puts up with a lot when I'm in the writing zone, and given that's where I spend most my time, he deserves a best-husband award. He couldn't name you even one of my book titles, but he picks up the groceries, does the laundry, keeps the house clean, and runs every errand, just so I can focus on writing the next one.

I can't imagine another partner who would be as quietly supportive as he is.

Love you all.

EDGE OF FEAR

1

SOPHIA

"I SEE HERE you have experience in the food industry. Where did you work before?"

The barely twenty-year-old fidgets in her seat.

"McDonald's."

Of course.

I did my own creative résumé writing when I was younger, eager to bolster up my meager qualifications to land a job, but for the Backyard Edge it's simply not enough.

The restaurant has only been open a couple of weeks and already I've lost a few of my waitstaff. I'm told it's not unusual to have a high turnover at first, but I find it a little discouraging. Especially since I'm new to this type of business.

I spend a few more minutes talking with the girl before I get up and hold out my hand.

"I appreciate you coming in, Crystal. I'll be in touch."

Unfortunately that will be to let her know she didn't get the job.

"No luck?"

I turn around to find Bernie, one of the sous-chefs, wandering in from the kitchen. He's here early to start on prep.

"Afraid not. Too young, too inexperienced." I run my fingers through my short hair. "I need to add at least two reliable servers and I can't even find one."

"I was thinking, I may know someone. A girl I worked with at my previous restaurant before it closed down. She may not have found anything else yet. I can give her a call, if you like," he offers.

"Yes. Please do."

"I can't make any promises, but I can at least get the word out there."

"That would be amazing, thank you."

Temporarily putting the staffing issues out of my mind, I disappear into my small office and dive into the orders I need to place.

That's more my strength, paperwork and budgets. Other than a part-time job at a fast-food joint when I was still in school, I have no experience in the restaurant business. In fact, three weeks ago I was still doing payroll and accounts payable for a small manufacturing company in Denver.

I was in Durango in May, attending the wedding of

my best friend, Kelsey's father. Kelsey and I both worked for the same military transport company in Denver, until last year when she discovered our boss was involved in illegal arms deals. Unfortunately, that knowledge cost Kelsey her life and put a target on my back as well. I ended up with a gnarly scar on my left leg, from a bullet wound, but survived. My bestie did not and left behind an infant son, who ended up living with her father.

Brick, his new wife, Lisa, and her two young grandkids took Finn into their home without question. I'd be lying if I said part of me wasn't disappointed—I love that baby like he was my own—but I'm not sure a single, and at that time unemployed, woman would've been best for him. He's better off with them, as part of a family. A family I seem to have been adopted into as well.

Brick runs the auto shop at the Arrow's Edge MC compound, where Lisa basically runs the clubhouse. The club is not at all what I would've expected. It has a strong focus on family, provides a safe haven for troubled boys, and owns a growing number of legitimate businesses in Durango. The latest of which is the Backyard Edge.

By merit of being Kelsey's friend, I was taken into their protection last year. Protection that was taken a little too seriously by two of the brothers, which is why it was Ouray, the club's president, who gave me a ride to the airport last month.

I'd flown in to attend Lisa and Brick's wedding for a few days and had to rush back to Denver because my boss was an asshole. On the drive I'd mentioned to Ouray my job in Denver wasn't shaping up the way I'd hoped, and I was looking for something else. Even considered moving closer to my sister, who lives in Oregon with her family. He brought up the Backyard Edge, a more upscale venue than the microbrewery the club also owns. Then he offered me a job, asking if I'd be interested in managing the new place.

That took me by surprise. I'm a numbers girl, always have been, but he assured me that was part of the reason he offered me the job. That and the fact I'd give the place some 'class.' I'm not too sure about the last, but the offer was intriguing to say the least. It was a challenge, a new opportunity, and a chance to be closer to Finn.

Back in Denver I thought of little else the following week, and after yet another frustrating day at work, I ended up calling him.

Three weeks ago, I drove here with just a couple of suitcases. The rest of my stuff was temporarily stored, until I could find something more permanent than a spare bedroom over the garage of the mother-in-law of one of the club members. Like I said, it's all about family with the Arrow's Edge MC.

Then this past week, I was talking to a couple who came in for dinner, and the woman mentioned she was looking to rent out her place. It sounds amazing and I'm excited to go take a look after the weekend. From what Meredith tells me it's a rustic, one-bedroom A-frame with a full wall of windows looking out on the mountains.

"I've got your keg."

Wapi, one of my self-assigned protectors, sticks his head in the door. He mentioned he'd bring by a fresh keg from the microbrewery for the tap.

"Good morning to you too," I tease him.

"Sorry," he mumbles, an embarrassed blush staining his cheeks immediately. "Mornin', I'm just here to hook it up for you."

"That'd be awesome, thank you."

He reminds me of my brother, is probably about the same age as well. Except, the way Wapi looks at me is far from brotherly. I feel bad; I don't have any feelings for him that go beyond friendship. Even though he's handsome, probably one of the kindest, most softhearted men I know, and would be good to me, there are no sparks on my part.

Not like the ones I feel around another Arrow's Edge MC member.

Unlike his club brother, Tse is dark, smoldering, cocky, and would undoubtedly break my heart. The two men have come close to exchanging blows, a few times, with me in the middle. Not a place I particularly want to be.

I've managed to avoid the club and Tse since I came back to Durango—I haven't seen him once—but Wapi has been here almost every night since we opened. Helping me get settled in behind the bar, sitting on a stool keeping me company, or jumping in when we're shorthanded.

Tse has been pointedly absent.

Maybe he's found someone else to toy with, which would be a good thing.

So why is it I'm disappointed he hasn't shown his face?

Tse

"Ravi, grab your shit, kid."

The boy drags his ass from the edge of the creek where he's been skipping rocks since breakfast.

"Do we gotta go?"

"Yeah. Time to go home."

Ravi is the youngest of the kids Paco and I brought up here. Even after having been with the club for over a year, the boy was having trouble fitting in, which is why we ended up taking him, even though he's not quite fourteen.

This trip to Glenwood Springs was an opportunity to teach the boys some responsibility, some basic skills, and hopefully be a team-building exercise. We have two sixteen-year-old boys in the club's care, who regularly feel the need to measure their dicks. It was high time to teach each of them a little humility.

I'd been looking for an excuse to get out of town for a while and found this two-week Habitat for Humanity build in Glenwood Springs. When I mentioned it to Trunk, our resident child psychologist, he came up with the idea to bring Elan and Maska.

Ravi had been an afterthought. He's mature for his age, which is probably why he's not really jelling with the younger boys, and the older ones ignore him.

The five of us have been camping at Elk Creek for the past two weeks and the kids have come a long way. Ravi still seems to prefer his own company, but he seems less out of place. He held his own working hard on the build during the days, and shared equally in camp duties with everyone else. He's proven himself equal to the older boys, who seem to have found a balance as well.

Yesterday was the final day on the four-home build. We stayed for the barbecue organized and donated by local restaurants and watched the new homeowners take possession. That had left an impression, especially on Ravi, who hasn't said much since last night, which is why Paco suggested he ride home with me. He left ten minutes ago with the others.

The kid seems to have taken a shine to me, following me around the construction site and asking a million and one questions about the carpentry work he was helping me with. Maybe without the other kids listening in I'll be able to get him to tell me why he's so quiet.

"All your stuff in the back, Bud?"

"Yeah."

"Then close the gate and let's get on the road. See if we can beat those other guys home."

That earns me a little grin. Ravi is as competitive as I am.

"You think we can?" he wants to know, getting in the passenger seat and buckling up.

"Beat them? Heck, yeah. Paco drives like a grandma."

I smile when I hear his chuckle and floor the gas the moment the tires hit hardtop.

It's been a good couple of weeks. Work, eat, and sleep for the most part, but we did get a few hikes and some fishing in. Life boiled down to simple basics was a welcome change.

I don't mind the physical work; it keeps my hands and therefore my head busy. I've always been good with my hands; I like building things. Something tangible to show for your efforts. It gives me a sense of purpose I was lacking most of my life.

We'd just finished adding a wing to Lisa and Brick's cottage when Ouray asked me to build a bar for the new restaurant. That was a fun project, using only repurposed wood, and I'm proud of the result.

Unfortunately, I haven't been back to see the whole place finished. I skipped the official opening of the Backyard Edge and kept a low profile at the club. This Habitat for Humanity build provided a good excuse to get out of town for a while, but that's come to an end. Going home it'll be tough to keep my distance.

Fuck, I about lost it on Ouray when I found out he'd asked *her* to manage the restaurant. Sophia: the woman who almost caused a rift between brothers.

I knew she was trouble when she first walked into the club last year. The kind of trouble that would pit brother against brother. Not that she had any intention of doing so. Hell, if anything, she kept both of us from getting anywhere with her.

One look at that woman—all legs and ass—one husky word from those pouty lips, one blink with those large doe-like eyes, and I wasn't the only one having a come-to-papa moment. Never mind I'm almost a decade too old for her. My brother is almost a decade too young and it didn't stop him from falling ass over teakettle either.

It had been almost a relief when she headed back to

Denver after Christmas. I figured it would be out of sight, out of mind, but then she came back for the wedding last month. Any headway Wapi and I had made to settle our differences went flying out the window.

I don't get it, Ouray was the one who ripped us a new one, only to turn around and announce he'd not only asked her to come back to Durango, but also offered her the job at the restaurant. Safest option was for me to stay away, even if it goes against every last fucking instinct.

"Boys seem good."

Trunk steps up beside me at the bar in the clubhouse.

"Yeah. Nothing like manual labor and forced proximity to forge a brotherhood," I suggest.

Elan and Maska would be graduating high school next year and both kids have apparently expressed an interest in prospecting for the club. Except in the Arrow's Edge MC a prospect is known as a cub. Grunts, who can earn a place in the brotherhood by placing themselves in service to the club. After they've had a chance to show what they're made of and have proven their loyalty, the brothers will take a vote to make them a full member.

Ironically, the last vote we had was for Wapi and that was a couple of years ago. It took longer for him to get patched in because he'd made a few serious errors in judgment in his younger years, and it took him a while to win back the trust of the club.

"And you? Clear your head some?"

Trust Trunk to see right through to the core.

"Time will tell, brother."

He claps a hand on my shoulder and leans close.

"Prepare then. I have a feeling you're about to get tested."

I turn to look at him but he's already walking away, passing Ouray who is heading in this direction.

"Good trip?"

"Yeah."

"Get your head straight?"

I drop my head and groan. What the fuck is this with everyone up in my business? The good mood I was in when I sat down for a beer, after that long drive, is fading fast.

"What the fuck do you want?"

I throw him a pissed glare when I hear him chuckle.

"Plumbing problem that needs fixin' before the dinner rush."

"Here?" I ask hopefully, but the feeling in my gut tells me I won't get off that easy.

"At the Backyard."

"Send Wapi."

I turn back to my beer and take a hefty swig.

"No can do," Ouray says, humor in his voice. "He's off to Farmington, picking up some parts Brick needs for tomorrow." He lifts a hand when I open my mouth. "And I'm not about to call a fucking plumber when you can do it. Can't avoid the woman forever, brother. Time to man up."

Oh, I'll man up all right. That's exactly what I'm afraid of.

2

SOPHIA

OF COURSE THIS would happen today.

The one day Wapi is not available to help out.

I should've just called a plumber, but I was trying to save money and figured he'd probably be by anyway at some point.

I was wrong, and now is on his way here, according to Ouray.

"Sophia? Do we have a separate gluten-free menu?"

"Yes, check the shelf under the register."

Today is also Mandy's first day on the job. She's the friend Bernie mentioned last week and happened to be available on pretty short notice. A bit of luck seeing as I've been going nuts plugging holes on my schedule, mostly by working them myself. I would've just liked to have a day where I could focus on training her instead of being dragged into ten different directions again.

Right now I'm on my knees in the kitchen, soaked to the skin, trying to mop up the flood coming from the bottom of the industrial dishwasher. It's almost six o'clock on a Saturday night—arguably the busiest night of the week—and we have no running water in the kitchen.

"I can't work like this!"

The outburst comes from Chris Boone, our chef and barbecue guru, who has all the earmarks of a culinary prima donna. The man is an absolute god when it comes to cooking but unfortunately that attitude shines through in his personality, which leaves much to be desired. Already in the restaurant's short existence I've had to navigate several threats of mutiny by both kitchen and waitstaff.

"I have someone on the way, Chris," I call out, but I'm pretty sure it'll fall on deaf ears.

Can't do anything about that, I have my hands full trying to mop up the small lake that has formed. I'm more concerned about the slipping hazard right now.

I freeze when a pair of boots stops in my line of view, splashing water every which way.

"Hey!"

"Oops, sorry, Fee."

"The name is Sophia," I snap, directing my eyes up Tse's body until I meet his hazel eyes.

Damn man looks too good. Boots, ratty jeans that fit him just right, a long-sleeved white Henley under his cut, and those signature shades clinging to the tip of his nose. His beard has grown since I last saw him, streaked with silver, which only adds to his appeal.

I scramble trying to get to my feet, but slip on the slick floor.

"Whoa, careful."

He reaches out and I reluctantly grab hold, retrieving my hand the moment I'm solid on my feet.

"The dishwasher's leaking."

"I can see that. You're wet."

Of course he would point that out. Not that it's hard to notice, my favorite linen pants are plastered to my legs and I do a quick check to make sure I don't inadvertently have other attributes on display. Luckily only the bottom of my shirt is wet where it dragged in the water when I was mopping.

"Cut off the water?"

I throw him an annoyed look.

"Of course, but it cuts off water to the entire kitchen. Whatever idiot installed this thing didn't put in a separate shut-off valve."

He grins and shakes his head before pulling the spare trays from the cabinet beside the dishwasher and reaching a long arm inside.

"The valve is right here…" he looks up at me, "…and I'm the idiot who installed it."

"Oh." Embarrassment washes over me and I can feel my face flush. "Well, I'll leave you to it then."

Tse is clearly amused when I scurry off to the other side of the kitchen to warn Chris he can turn the water back on. Then I disappear to my office for the change of clothes I keep there. I learned my first week that accidents happen all the time, when I ended up wearing roasted red pepper soup and had to run home to get something clean to wear. Ever since I've made sure to always have a spare set of clothes in my office.

Mack is behind the bar when I walk into the restaurant.

"Everything under control?"

He slides a couple of glasses on a tray that is already full of drinks.

"These need to be delivered. Tables three, seven, and twelve. The long wait for food is making some of the guests grumpy."

"Comp each table one round of drinks on their bill. Food should start coming out soon."

I grab the tray and carefully balance it as I move toward the first table. I don't have any more clean clothes if I make a mess now.

Half an hour later the customers are eating. I'm behind the bar rinsing glasses, while Mack is on a smoke break out back, when Tse comes walking out of the kitchen. I'd like to say I almost forgot he was there, but that'd be a lie. I've had half an eye on the kitchen door the entire time, and that annoys me.

He pulls out the stool where Wapi usually sits and leans his elbows on the bar.

"All fixed."

I wipe my hands on a towel and turn my body toward him. Time to eat some crow.

"Thank you and I'm sorry I was snippy earlier. I had

a dining room full of people waiting for their food and a chef who wouldn't cook without running water, so I was a little stressed."

"Didn't even notice it," he lies with one of his charming smiles.

"Drink?" I offer.

"Whatever's on tap is good. How's business been?" he asks, when I go to pull him a draft.

"Not bad. Weekends are pretty busy." I pour myself a glass of water, just to give my hands something to do. "Have you eaten?"

"I'll grab something later," he says, just as Mandy walks up to the bar.

"A draft, a dry white, and a cosmo for table seven."

She casts a curious eye in Tse's direction.

"Mandy, could you ask Bernie to put together a plate of brisket for Tse while I get these?"

"Sure."

She heads to the kitchen but not without thoroughly checking him out in passing. I can't blame her, but it annoys me all the same.

"You didn't need to do that."

"This is a restaurant and you just fixed our dishwasher. We can feed you, unless you're suddenly allergic to meat?"

His chuckle is deep and a little raspy. "Not a chance of that."

I get Mandy's order ready and it's waiting for her when she appears from the kitchen and slides a steaming plate in front of Tse. He rumbles his thanks and digs in.

A moment later Mack walks in from the back, takes over the bar, and I can slip to my office, where I spend the next hour or so working on payroll and hiding out. Still, when I finally surface, I'm disappointed to see the empty stool at the end of the bar.

We have a pretty effective routine closing the restaurant at night. One where everyone chips in to get the place open-ready for the next day. It doesn't take long before the last person has left.

I slide the till in the small safe in my office, turn off the lights, and lock the door. Then I grab the trash bag by the back entrance someone forgot to take, step outside, and lock that door as well, before tossing the bag in the large bin.

My vehicle is the only one still in the parking lot that wraps around the side to the back of the restaurant. As I make my way toward it, my eyes automatically scan the shadows where the lights don't quite reach. It's not until I hit the unlock button on my key fob, I notice movement near the rear where the parking lot meets the property behind us.

I keep my eyes on the two figures sliding into the shadows as I get behind the wheel.

Then I hit the ignition, shift in drive, and peel out of the parking lot, my heart pounding in my chest.

Tse

Man up. Asshole.

I glare at Ouray, who is hanging out at the bar when I

walk into the clubhouse.

It's a miracle I was able to peel my ass from that stool and walk out of there. Heck, I'd probably still be sitting there, gagging for a glimpse of her, if not for that waitress paying me a little too much attention. Mandy. The woman made sure there was no doubt in my mind she was game for a hookup.

Not even a year ago I would've been all over that, wouldn't have thought twice about following her into a bathroom or taking her behind the building. Quick and easy has always been my MO. I've always been honest about that too. Never made promises to call or handed out my number, and every woman I've been with knew the score.

Then I met Sophia.

"Didn't expect you back so soon."

I take the stool beside Ouray and notice Wapi sitting with Nosh on the other side of the bar, glaring at me.

"Was easily fixed," I dismiss the chief before motioning to Shilah, who is tending bar. "Hit me up."

"Would'a thought you'd make better use of your time than that," Ouray mumbles beside me, and I turn in my seat.

"I don't get you. Last month you basically told me to back the fuck off, and now you're shoving her in my face."

His face cracks into one of those smug smirks that get under my skin and I close my fist around the bottle Shilah slides toward me.

"Letting you yahoos figure this out on your own

wasn't working, so I figured I'd jump in. The kid had a month to try and get somewhere without you horning in, but it's pretty clear he's spinning his wheels. Thought you'd welcome the opportunity to try."

"Jesus, man. You matchmaking now?"

"Fuck no, but this tug-of-war between you two is a drain on my goddamn club. One of you better piss or get off the pot when it comes to that girl or it'll never end."

"Been easier to leave her in Denver," I grumble, tilting the bottle against my lips.

"Not like she wouldn't come to visit, and I don't wanna deal with you guys pissing all over each other every time she does. Time to settle this once and for all."

I drain my bottle and lift the empty at Shilah, who nods his understanding and goes for a fresh one.

"Not sure I could give her what she deserves," I admit.

"Then tell Wapi the road's clear for him."

The thought makes my blood boil and I hit Ouray with an angry glare.

"Like hell. The kid barely knows how to tie his own shoes, let alone look after a woman like Sophia."

That infuriating smirk is back on his face as he gets to his feet, claps a hand on my shoulder, and leans in close.

"Might as well give in, brother."

Then he walks to the door, throwing the guys at the other end of the bar a two-fingered salute, and disappears outside.

Arrogant asshole.

I spend the next ten minutes nursing my beer, and staring off into space, before getting up, and without a word head to my room at the back of the clubhouse.

I've just come out of the shower and flip on the TV to watch the late-night news when a knock sounds at my door.

"Got a minute?"

Paco is leaning against the doorpost, his arms crossed over his chest.

"Come in."

He saunters in and plops down in the only chair in my room. I grab a bottle of scotch and two tumblers from my dresser drawer, pour each of us a couple of fingers, hand him one, and take a seat on my bed.

"I need your help."

"With?"

He takes a fortifying sip before he speaks.

"I wanna build a house. Got a parcel of land off Lightner Creek Road I bought ten or so years ago."

Paco has lived at the clubhouse as long as I've been here, most of the single brothers do. It's not until they find a woman, start a family, that they find their own place and those numbers have grown over the years. I always took Paco to be like me, destined for the single life, and I've never once heard him mention land, so this comes as a bit of a surprise.

"That Habitat for Humanity build got me thinking maybe I could do it myself. With some help," he adds.

"No shit, huh? You got a woman you're keeping to yourself?"

"Why does everything have to be about a woman? Is it against the law for a guy to have a place of his own?"

I lift my hands defensively at his spirited response.

"Whoa, brother. Just asking, that's all. What kinda house are you looking to build?"

By the time he walks out of my room it's close to two in the morning, my bottle of scotch is almost empty, I have a rudimentary idea of what Paco wants, and I don't have a single doubt he has a woman in mind.

No man I know cares about spare bedrooms, soaking tubs, or walk-in closets.

3

SOPHIA

"REAGAN HAS A boyfriend."

I almost choke on my granola.

"A little young, don't you think? She's only eleven," I remind my sister.

Bianca usually calls early Sunday morning when John and her girls are still in bed. It's the only chance she gets for some privacy and both of us have always been early risers. Even though we haven't always been as close as we are now.

Just two years apart—Bianca is older at thirty-seven— we weren't exactly friends in our teenage years. We hung with different crowds and had different interests. It wasn't until I was in college and she got married to John that we started getting along. It only took both of us moving in different directions: me to Denver and Bianca to Eugene, Oregon.

Our parents still live in Arizona where we grew up, but even our baby brother moved over state lines first chance he got, shattering their lifelong dream of a family commune. That's why we all scattered; Mom and Dad are remnants of the sixties and seventies and don't believe in personal space or boundaries of any kind. They don't see the need for them, which made for an awkward adolescence.

"Mom says I should embrace the fact Reagan is becoming a woman," Bianca shares with appropriate disgust in her voice. "Yesterday I had to break up a fight between her and Avery over crayons for crying out loud. A woman?"

Bianca's disgusted snort makes me laugh.

"Who's the boy?"

"A kid in her class. Connor. Cute boy, super shy, and about ten inches shorter than she is. They hold hands on the bus."

"Aww, that's kind of cute."

"Yes, except, on Friday another boy on the bus was bullying Connor, and Reagan felt it necessary to jump in."

"And that's bad?"

"It is when the principal calls me because my daughter swung at a boy two years older and broke his nose."

"No! For real?"

I try to keep the grin out of my voice because I have a feeling that won't go over well. Inside I'm giving my niece a high five. I hope that kid will think twice before picking on someone again.

"Oh, shut up," Bianca grumbles. "You're grinning ear to ear, aren't you? And I'm stuck here with a grounded, prepubescent holy terror."

"Mo-om!" I hear my niece's cry in the background.

"Oh for Pete's sake, can't I even talk to my sister in peace?"

"Is that Auntie Soph? I wanna talk to her."

There is a rustling as the phone transfers hands and then I hear Reagan's voice, sweet as punch.

"Auntie Soph? Can I come live with you?"

The next twenty minutes I spend listening to my niece rant and attempt to talk some reason into her. In the end, I have her hand the phone back to her mother so I can say goodbye.

"You know, I could put her on a flight this morning," Bianca offers with a hint of a plea.

"Oh, Sis, wish I could help, but I work crazy hours. Maybe later this summer I can take some time—"

"I'm just kidding," she interrupts. "We'll be fine."

We say our goodbyes and I carry my bowl to the small sink.

I like the apartment, it has the basic things I need, but I'll be glad when I have some more room to move about. A bigger kitchen where I can prepare actual meals instead of the hotplate and small microwave I have here. Sandra is wonderful, she's Jaimie's mother, who is married to one of the MC brothers, Trunk. She reminds me a little of my mother, but without the boundary issues.

Last Monday I was finally able to meet up with Meredith and Jay, the nice couple I talked to at the restaurant a few weeks ago, to see the rental property. I fell in love with the A-frame on the spot. Exposed beams, massive windows, an awesome loft with a bedroom and bath. The kitchen is one I can see myself spending a lot of time in when I'm not sitting out on the deck, enjoying the stunning view.

It'll all be mine in a month.

Oh, yeah, I can't wait.

I take my time applying my makeup and getting dressed for work. I've always worked a nine-to-five job, so these restaurant hours took some time getting used to. Especially working evenings and weekends. But Monday is a day off because the Backyard is closed, and Ouray insisted I take one additional day a week.

So far I haven't yet, I felt I had too much to learn, but maybe this week I'll take Tuesday as well. It'll give me a chance to call a mover and book a date to move my furniture here, and maybe do a little shopping. I'd like to pick up a few things now that I've seen the place. Meredith offered to leave some of her furniture for me to use, which was very kind, but I really want to put my own stamp on the place. Make it mine, even though I'm just renting.

I wave at Sandra, who is weeding her flowerbeds in front of the house, as I get into my Jeep. I'll sure miss our occasional chats when I leave.

It looks like Bernie beat me to the restaurant; his car is parked at the edge of the parking lot. We are always the first two to get here. Bernie is often already inside by the time I arrive. He's responsible for the food prep, but more so he likes to be here for the food deliveries in the morning. I like to get an hour or so in on paperwork before the interruptions start with the arrival of the rest of the staff.

I pull into my spot—a little closer to the building— grab my bag and get out.

It's not until I'm a few steps away, I notice the back door isn't quite latched. Bernie must not have pulled it shut all the way.

"Morning!" I call out as I step inside, but there's no response.

I pass by my closed office door and head straight for the kitchen. The moment I round the corner I know something is wrong.

The kitchen is a mess. Boxes of the produce delivered daily are toppled over on the floor, which is littered with vegetables. Then I see a pair of legs sticking out from behind the prep table.

"Bernie!"

He's facedown and the back of his head is bloodied, but when I touch his neck to feel for a pulse, I hear a soft moan.

"Hang in there, Bernie. I'll get help."

With shaking hands I pull out my phone and dial 911.

TSE

"SO THE FRONT is facing north?"

Paco points at the concept drawings I made him.

Apparently, his land at one time had a building on it and he wants to use the remaining foundation as the footprint for a house.

"Northeast actually. That's a good thing, you'll get the most out of your sun-hours at the back of the house."

We're sitting in front of the clubhouse at one of the picnic tables, having a coffee and soaking up the sun. It's the quietest place we could find to spread out the drawings since the clubhouse table is filling up with late risers eating breakfast.

"Is that a second deck?"

"Yeah, off the master bedroom. That whole wing is the master suite. The main deck is off the kitchen at the back."

"Gonna cost."

I chuckle. "Yes, it is, but this is just a concept, you don't need to build that second wing. You can go smaller, if it's just for you."

I look at him with an eyebrow raised but he stares me straight in the eye, not flinching. He's not biting.

"How long?" he finally asks.

"Brother, that depends on a lot of things, but using that existing foundation is gonna save a chunk of time. Still, even if you can find an architect who can draw up these plans on short notice, you'll still need a crew who can start right away."

"I've got brothers."

"Yeah, and I'm sure everyone is gonna chip in, but you'll need someone in charge who can manage a construction schedule. Have you checked with Jed Mason?"

"Not—"

"Tse, Paco, saddle up!"

Ouray comes barging out of the clubhouse, Wapi on his heels.

"What's goin' on?"

I get to my feet as they head straight for their bikes.

"Trouble at the Backyard."

I'm right behind them when they hit the bottom of the drive and the first chance I get I pull ahead.

I haven't been back to the restaurant in two weeks. Not since talking to Ouray that night at the clubhouse. I was going to, but Wapi's bike was missing and I figured he was probably over there. Whatever he and I have to sort out, I didn't want to do that at her place of work.

Ah, who the hell am I kidding? I chickened out. There's no denying I want the woman, but she deserves more than a quick fuck, and I don't know whether I have more in me to give. What if I try and mess up? I don't want to hurt her, and not just because I'll have to face the wrath of my brothers. This is a woman who is already woven into the fabric of our club.

But none of that matters as I weave my way through traffic, driving way too fast to get to the restaurant. To her.

Trouble at the Backyard.

Fuck. I'll never forgive myself if something happened to her.

I see three cop cars, a fire truck, and an ambulance in

the parking lot. Along with Sophia's Jeep. I pull up as close to the back door as I can get and hop off my bike, just as EMTs wheel out a gurney.

"What the fuck happened?" I bark at the fresh-faced uniform trying to stop me.

I vaguely register the sound of motorcycles behind me, but I only have one focus.

"This is a crime scene, sir."

The young kid puts a hand on my chest to hold me back, but I easily brush it aside and catch up with the EMTs as they start loading the gurney into the back of their rig. It's some guy I don't know, not Sophia. I immediately turn and head for the back door when Ramirez steps out. He's a detective with the Durango PD and a decent guy.

"They're fine," Ramirez calls out to the uniformed kid, who is now trying to hold back Ouray and Wapi. "She's in her office," he tells me, as he steps to the side so I can get in.

She's alone, sitting at her desk, her head resting on her arms. In two steps I'm around to her side and crouch down, putting a hand on her back.

"Hey, Fee."

Her head snaps up and she turns my way. Then she twists in her seat and throws herself in my arms. I hear rustling at the door and just catch Ouray pushing Wapi out of the office, pulling the door shut. The kid didn't look too happy.

"Seriously," she mumbles into my neck before pushing herself upright. Her face is pale and her eyes large, but there are no tears. "I'm cursed. You guys are gonna regret you gave me this job. Every time I show up, shit seems to hit the fan."

"What happened?" I ask. I reluctantly get to my feet and sit down on the edge of her desk.

Her body does a head-to-toe shiver and I reach out and place a steadying hand on the side of her neck.

"I have no fucking clue. I came in and found Bernie bleeding on the kitchen floor. Someone hit him over the head."

The next few minutes she fills me in on what she found when she walked in.

"Anything taken?"

She shakes her head.

"No. They didn't even come into the office. It was still locked when I got here."

The door eases open and Ouray peeks inside. Seeing Sophia is not having a meltdown, he steps inside.

"You okay?"

"I'm so sorry."

Ouray snorts. "Hardly your fault, darlin'. I was gonna suggest we call Chris and put a notice on the door."

"But we have a bunch of reservations for tonight."

"We'll call them. Comp them with free drinks for the inconvenience when they're next in. It'll take some time before the cops are done here and then we'll need time to clean up the mess."

She seems to ponder that and finally nods, moving her chair back. I get to my feet and out of her way as she rounds the desk, pulling open a file drawer.

"Okay, I'll make the calls but then I need to get to the hospital. Detective Ramirez said he would get in touch with Bernie's next of kin, but I think someone should be there."

"I sent Wapi after the ambulance," Ouray informs her.

I can see from the stubborn set of her chin; she'll still be heading to Mercy first chance she gets. That's fine, I'll be right behind her.

Forty minutes later all staff is contacted, reservations cancelled, and Sophia is heading for her vehicle.

"She's not going home, is she?" Ouray observes beside me as we stand by the bikes, watching her get in the Jeep.

"Nope. I'm gonna stick with her until we have some idea what the hell happened."

"Figured you would," he says with a shake of his head. "Tell Wapi to head back here. And for fuck's sake, try to use some tact. Last thing I need is you two getting into it in the middle of the hospital."

"I'll be gentle," I mock, as I swing a leg over the seat and start my bike.

He snorts. "Yeah, right. And, Tse?"

"Yeah?"

"Make sure you see her home safely."

I mock salute him.

Then I follow Sophia off the parking lot.

4

SOPHIA

I GLANCE IN my rearview mirror and clench my jaw.

He's still stuck to my bumper. Has been since I pulled away from the Backyard. I should've guessed as much.

These men, they don't ask if you need or want help, they simply take over. All of them: Brick, Ouray, Tse, and even Wapi, although he's less annoyingly in-your-face about it. They assume the role of protector; never mind I've looked after myself for the past fifteen-or-so years.

By the time I pull in a parking slot at the hospital, I have myself worked up into a nice head of steam. I pointedly ignore Tse parking two spots down from me and march right by, my eyes fixed on the door.

"I'm looking for Bernie Wilson?" I ask the woman

manning the information desk. "He was brought in by ambulance maybe an hour or so ago?"

I try not to notice the looming presence of Tse closing in behind me as she scans her computer screen.

"I don't have him listed here yet, but he's probably still in the emergency department. Just follow the signs and check in with the desk."

"Thank you."

Behind me I hear her ask, "Can I help you?"

"I'm with her."

The rumble of Tse's voice has me clench my hands in fists, but I keep my tongue until I'm directed down a quiet hallway. There I swing around on him. I have to tilt my head back to look at him since he's much closer than I expected. Somehow that takes a little of the wind out of my sails.

"Why are you following me?"

"Don't think you should be alone."

"That's not your call to make," I snap. "Maybe I want to be alone. Maybe I *need* to be alone, have you thought of that? No. You haven't, because you assume you know better. I'm so sick of—"

I'm shocked silent when he suddenly grabs my upper arms and swings me around so my back is against the wall. I'm about to lay into him for manhandling me when an older gentleman with a walker slowly passes by, grinning as he winks at Tse. I press my lips together but a soft growl escapes, which Tse apparently finds amusing.

"Right," he says, giving me a little shake, "before you give yourself an aneurism, have you stopped to consider that whoever knocked out the cook might not have been there for him? We don't know that. We don't know anything yet and until we do, I'm sticking close."

All my indignant anger evaporates on the spot and I hate that he makes a good point.

"Sous-chef," I mumble stupidly.

"Sorry?"

"Bernie is a sous-chef, not a cook."

Tse drops his head back and looks up at the ceiling, as if asking for divine intervention.

"Did you hear anything else I said?" Exasperation is clear in his voice.

"I did," I grudgingly admit, and his eyes come back to mine.

"Hell, Fee, it wasn't that long ago I had to carry you bleeding into the clubhouse."

"Don't remind me."

He hooks a finger under my chin and lifts my face to his.

"Then don't give me a hard time for wanting to avoid another scenario like that...please."

His plea is genuine and I find myself a little embarrassed. I'm throwing around attitude because I feel controlled and undermined, when in effect these guys— *this* guy in particular—is trying to keep me safe. Getting shot was probably the most terrifying experience of my life, but I clearly remember Tse scooping me up off the ground and running through gunfire to get me to safety. He even got winged by a bullet himself, but that didn't stop him from getting me safely inside.

"Okay," I promise contritely.

But a few minutes later, when we're directed into the waiting room where we find Wapi, my resolve is quickly forgotten.

He shoots up from his seat and reaches for me, lifting a hand to my face.

"Are you okay?"

"I'm fine. Have you heard anything?"

"Not yet, I'm still—"

"You need to go," Tse interrupts the younger man, who drops his hand like he got burned.

"Tse!" I snap. "You're being an ass."

"What? Ouray wants him back at the restaurant," he says defensively.

"Oh, I give up." I throw up my hands. "I'm sick and tired of this, you know? You're putting me in the middle of something I didn't ask for. I'm going to see if I can get some information, and you two…" I point a finger at each of them, "…can sort this shit out without me."

Then I stalk out of the room and go in search of someone who looks like they belong.

A woman in surgical scrubs hands a file over to the nurse behind the desk and I zoom in on her.

"Excuse me? Could you tell me anything about Bernie Wilson? He was brought in—"

"Are you family?" she interrupts.

"No, but I'm his boss and I'm the one who found him. Police are still trying to locate any next of kin, but for now I'm all he has. Please?"

She gives me a long hard stare before her face softens.

"Very well. As you likely will have noticed, he had a large laceration to the back of his head. That was easy enough to fix. More serious is the skull fracture underneath, which is considered a significant head injury. He was able to answer a few basic questions when he first came in, but has been in and out of consciousness since. For now we wait and see; our first concern is possible swelling of the brain. Should that happen, we may need to relieve the pressure."

"You mean surgery," I conclude.

"Yes. That's a possibility, but as I mentioned, we'll monitor him closely."

I hold out my hand.

"I appreciate it, Doctor…"

"Morozova. And your name is?"

"Sophia Vieira."

"Okay, I'll have you added to his file as contact for now."

"Thank you."

I'm halfway back to the waiting room when I bump into Detective Ramirez.

Tse

THE MOMENT SOPHIA leaves the room I turn to Wapi, but he speaks first.

"I care about her."

I have to give it to him; he gets straight to the point.

"I know."

"She sees me like a brother."

I didn't know that, so I keep my mouth shut and wait him out.

"Do you know how I know?" I'm not sure he's expecting an answer and simply shrug. "I don't get her fired up. Oh, she tolerates me, maybe even likes me, but I can't get under her skin. Not like you do. It fucking sucks."

His observation startles me. I never looked at it that way, but now that I think about it, almost every couple I know gets up in each other's face from time to time. Didn't exactly have any good examples, growing up in homes and foster care. When I was older, I was only interested in getting laid and paid little attention to any subtle signs or signals. I looked for blatant come-ons, easily recognized and leaving little to the imagination.

Turns out, my brother has more sense than I had at that age.

"Sorry, kid."

His eyes flash anger at my use of that tag—something I do without thinking—but then he shakes his head.

"Not gonna shut her out, though."

I suppress the smile that wants to surface at his defiant tone.

"I'm not asking you to."

I would've insisted he keep his distance from her if he hadn't just shown himself the bigger man.

"And if you hurt her, you're gonna have to answer to me."

Fuck, fifteen years younger, but definitely the bigger man.

"Expecting nothing else."

He narrows his eyes on me for a moment, before he turns away and heads for the door.

"Later."

"Later, brother," I call after him.

Not long after he leaves, Sophia walks in with Ramirez in tow.

"Any news?"

Sophia sits two seats down from me and Ramirez fills us in on Bernie's condition.

"Did you talk to any family?" she asks Ramirez.

"Finally got hold of a sister. She's on her way, driving in from Shiprock. She shouldn't be too much longer."

I lean forward with my elbows on my knees.

"Do you have an idea what happened?"

"Beats me. Until we can talk to Mr. Wilson, your guess is as good as mine. It wasn't theft, nothing looks to be taken, or even attempted. The only place that shows any disturbance is the kitchen. Whoever did that must've just walked in, or maybe Wilson let them in himself. Crime scene techs are going over the place with a fine-tooth comb, but I have a sneaky suspicion they won't find much."

"What about Clover Produce?" Sophia suggests. "Could their driver have seen something? Those boxes must've just been dropped off. "

Ramirez grins at her. "That's my next stop. I'm heading to Farmington to meet up with local law enforcement. I should probably get going. Dropped in hoping maybe I could ask our victim a few questions, but it doesn't look like that'll happen today." He walks to the door and turns back. "If you think of anything else, let me know?"

Sophia nods and then suddenly freezes.

"Wait. This is probably nothing, but a few times over the past couple of weeks I've seen people hanging out at the edge of the parking lot when I locked up. Not seen them so I couldn't identify them, nothing but shadows, really, but I noticed them three, maybe four times."

I sit up straighter and so does Ramirez.

"How many?"

"Hard to tell, they were right by the trees. Two, could've been three."

"Same people every time?"

"I wouldn't be able to tell you. Like I said, it was dark, and it may not mean anything."

"Anyone else mentioned seeing people back there?"

Sophia shakes her head.

"Nobody's mentioned anything and I haven't asked. Should I?"

"No." Ramirez is firm. "I'll take care of that. You call me if you remember anything else."

"I will."

"Good." His eyes slide to me. "Be careful. I'll be in touch."

The moment he's gone, I get up and move over to a seat next to her.

"Did you chase Wapi off?"

Straight for the attack. It won't be hard to figure out when I piss her off, she doesn't seem to hold back on her anger. Just on everything else.

"No. We cleared the air." She snorts derisively. "I'm serious," I insist. "Actually, he did most of the talking and I listened, but we each know where the other stands."

She turns her face my way.

"And where would that be?"

I lean toward her and note she doesn't back away.

"Can't speak for Wapi, that's not mine to share." I drop my voice low. "But I'd be happy to tell you where my mind is at."

She sucks in a sharp little breath.

"Forget I asked. I'm no longer sure I wanna know."

"*Coward*," I whisper.

She shoots to her feet.

"I need some coffee," she mutters. "Or a stiff drink."

"You sit. I'll go. Not sure they serve hard liquor, but I'm sure I can rustle you up a coffee."

"Some cream and—"

"Two sugars," I finish for her. "You like it sweet. I know."

The cafeteria is not hard to find. I doctor us up a couple of coffees and take them to the checkout, bypassing the food they have on display. It's probably been there all day and if she gets hungry, I'll just get one of the guys to drop something off.

When I've paid and make my way back down the hall, my phone rings in my pocket. Juggling the two cups in one hand I use the other to fish it out of my pocket.

"Talk to me."

"How are things?" Ouray says without introduction. Not that he needs one.

I tell him what I know, which isn't a whole lot.

"You gonna stick around?"

"His sister is on the way; I imagine Sophia will at least want to wait for her. I'll see her home."

"Good. I talked to Benedetti. He'll keep an eye out."

Benedetti is Police Chief Joe Benedetti, who happens to live right across from where Sophia has been staying. The house she stays at actually used to belong to Benedetti's wife and since she had some trouble a few years back, it is outfitted with good security.

"Sounds good."

"Okay. See you later."

I tuck my phone back in my pocket and resume walking.

Truthfully, I'd feel better keeping an eye on her myself, but something tells me I won't get very far. Not yet, I'm not going to force the issue after the day she's had, but soon.

When I enter the waiting room, Sophia is talking to a platinum blonde woman dressed head to toe in black leather. Biker babe is the first thing that comes to mind.

"Tse, this is Liz, she's Bernie's sister. Liz, this is Tse."

The blonde turns around and unapologetically checks me out top to bottom.

"Tse? I'm liking the name." I grunt. I'm not interested in a conversation with this woman. I know her type. I know it all too well.

I'm spared when a nurse walks in.

"Ms. Wilson?"

"That's me," the blonde says, facing the nurse.

"Your brother just woke up. He's asking for you. If you'd like to come with me?"

Liz turns to me and runs a lethal-looking, bright red fingernail down the front of my shirt. I have to curb the urge to snap it off.

"You gonna wait for me?" she purrs.

I step out of her reach and pull a rigid Sophia to my side.

"We'll be heading out. I gotta get my woman home."

With that I firmly steer Sophia out of the room and down the hall. Halfway to the front door she manages to slip from under my arm.

"I'm nobody's woman," she fires at me.

"Not yet."

I let her dart outside in front of me and get on my bike as she gets in the Jeep.

Then I follow her home.

5

SOPHIA

NORMALLY ON MONDAYS I do some laundry, clean, run any errands, and grab a few groceries. Today I haven't gotten much further than hanging around on the couch, sipping coffee, and streaming Netflix on my laptop.

I did call the hospital first thing this morning to find out how Bernie made it through the night. As it turns out, not so good. When he woke up, he became incoherent and combative and they suspect his brain may be swelling. I guess that would mean surgery, as his doctor had indicated was a possibility.

I wish I'd had a chance last night to exchange numbers with his sister. The woman is alone in town and I could've given her a call, even though she's already not my favorite person. She'd been borderline hostile to me yesterday, before Tse returned and whisked me out of the waiting room, but maybe that had been the stress of finding out her brother's condition.

Yesterday was exhausting and I'd almost immediately rolled into bed when I got home. Of course, that was after Tse annoyingly insisted on following me, parked his bike alongside my Jeep in the driveway, and walked me to my door.

There was a moment I wondered whether he was going to try and kiss me. It wouldn't have been the first attempt, he tried it once last year and I rebuffed him. Last night though, I'm afraid if he'd tried I might not have stopped him.

The man tempts and infuriates me in equal measure and it makes me feel off-kilter when I'm around him. He's like chocolate, you know it's bad for you if you make it part of your daily diet, but you tell yourself all you want is a little taste. Except, one taste leads to a constant craving.

My phone rings and I grab it off the coffee table. It's Lisa.

"Hey."

"Just heard what happened yesterday, are you all right?"

"I'm fine. It was a bit of a shock, that's all."

She makes a humming sound.

"Mm-hmm, I bet you are. How about you come here for a bit of lunch? I know Brick will wanna see you."

I look down on my ratty old yoga pants with the torn

seam on my inner thigh. The most comfortable piece of clothing I own and I was hoping I could spend the rest of the day in. I'd have to get dressed.

"Oh, I don't know…"

"Get your butt over here before my husband decides to come knockin' on your door to see for himself you're doing okay. Besides, Finn's first birthday is next month. We need to plan."

I grin. Not sure how much planning a birthday for a one-year-old requires, but her mention of Finn awakes a different kind of craving. That little boy has my heart and it's been weeks since I've seen him. He's the only man in my life I'd ditch these yoga pants for.

"Oh, all right. Give me an hour. I'm not dressed yet and I want a shower."

"Fine. We're in the clubhouse."

I don't get a chance to change my mind because she's already hung up.

The clubhouse. I assumed she meant lunch at their place. I should've asked before agreeing. I don't feel like running into Tse, or Wapi, for that matter. The last few times I was at the clubhouse you could cut the tension with a knife.

Maybe they won't be there. It's the middle of day on a Monday; surely those guys have work to do. A girl can wish.

I drag my ass into the bathroom and take the next half hour to get ready. Then I grab my purse, check my wallet for some cash for the dessert I want to pick up on the way, and head downstairs.

I lucked out at the City Market downtown. They had a dozen pastéis de nata left. Mom makes those Portuguese custard tarts for special occasions and despite trying my hand at them for years, I can never quite get them right. The ones they sell at the bakery in the City Market are the closest to my mother's recipe I've ever tasted, and I'm craving a little comfort food.

Only a few motorcycles are parked in front of the clubhouse when I drive up and I sigh a breath of relief. Looks like most of the club is out, which suits me just fine. Don't get me wrong, I appreciate the sanctuary the club offered me last year, but the testosterone runs so thick in there sometimes it felt like I couldn't breathe.

"Sophia!"

My name is called as soon as I get out of my vehicle and when I turn I watch Brick walk toward me, wiping his hands on a rag. He must've been working in the garage and seen me drive up. As soon as he's close enough, he pulls me in for one of his bear hugs. He smells of motor oil and mountain air, and for a moment I linger in his arms. Every time I see him he greets me like he hasn't seen me in years, instead of a few weeks at most.

I get it. When I lost my best friend, Kelsey, he lost the daughter he had been estranged from. He welcomed me, gave me the special part in little Finn's life the boy's mom had awarded me, and I gave him the second chance at a relationship he never had with his daughter. We both recognize the gift in each other.

"You're gonna piss Lisa off with that." He points at the bakery box in my hand.

"It's just dessert. My favorite taste of home; custard tarts."

He smiles his crooked grin at me as he guides me to the clubhouse, his arm slung around my shoulders.

I barely have a chance to give Lisa a hug because Finn is about to bounce out of his high chair at the sight of me. I pluck him out of his seat and soak up his slobbery smile sporting four perfect little teeth, two at the top and two at the bottom.

"Look at you."

"Bah!"

He slaps a hand on my face and immediately grabs for my lip. Ever since his own first tooth broke, he seems to have a fascination with teeth.

"Gotta be gentle, buddy," Brick cautions him and reaches for him, but Finn clings on for dear life, burying his face in my neck.

"It's okay. He'll be gentle, right, Finn?"

His head lifts and I'm rewarded with another smile as his head bobs. I grin back; this is the kind of attention I could handle all day long.

I take a seat at the kitchen table, Finn on my lap, and catch up with Lisa as she dishes out lunch. The baby briefly protests when Lisa picks him up and firmly seats him in his chair so I can eat, but he's quickly distracted with some food. Typical boy.

I'm about to dig into the tarts Lisa grumbled about, but put on a plate anyway, when Tse walks into the kitchen. He grins wide when he sees me.

"Miss me already?"

TSE

SPENT THE MORNING with Paco, picking up where we abruptly left off yesterday.

By a stroke of luck, Jed Mason was available to sit down with us and we left my concept drawings with him. He has an architect he works with he said he'd get in touch with, and he was going to drive up to the site to have a look at the existing foundation.

We talked about potential timeline, his availability, and the possible labor the brothers could contribute. He offered to crunch some numbers and would get back to Paco with a cost range.

Paco and I came back to the club to talk to Trunk about my idea to get some of the kids involved with the build. Give them something to work on during the summer. But when we pulled up, I didn't see his bike.

What I did see, however, was Sophia's Jeep, and I was already grinning when I walked into the clubhouse.

The only person there is Nosh, who has news on TV while working on his daily crossword, a common sight. I know Ouray and a few of the guys were supposed to head out to the Backyard to clean up and install a few security cameras before it opens up for business again tomorrow, but I can hear voices coming from the kitchen.

Her face is priceless when I walk in and I can't resist.

"Miss me already?"

Her lips thin with annoyance but before she can say anything, Lisa gets up.

"You hungry? There's plenty of soup and I have some

frittata left. Pull up a chair."

The only empty seat is the one on the other side of Sophia, with Finn's high chair wedged between. The kid already has his arms out to me.

"Bah!"

Ignoring his sticky hands, I lean over and kiss the top of his head.

"Gotta eat first, buddy."

Over the top of the baby's towhead, I wink at Sophia as I take my seat.

"You heading to Moab this weekend?"

I turn to Brick.

"Been thinking about it. You?"

He grins at his wife, who rolls her eyes in response but doesn't quite manage to hide the smile as she turns to the stove.

"You bet. Lisa's coming with me. The old lady's taken to the back of my bike of late."

"That so?"

Lisa sets a plate and a bowl in front of me.

"Yeah, I like it. It's too bad my husband insists on ticking me off and risking a fork in his eye for calling me his old lady."

"I hear you," Sophia contributes. "I had the same impulse when Tse called me his *woman* yesterday. I'm not sure what pissed me off more: the presumption or the label. Either one is barbaric."

"And stabbing someone in the eye isn't?"

Brick looks in mock horror at his wife, who snickers as she takes her seat beside him.

"Would you've preferred girlfriend?" I ask Sophia innocently.

"Nice try," she fires back, her eyes narrowed on me.

"Old lady?"

"Get real."

"Don't diss it until you've tried it," I tease her, the thought of her on the back of my bike very appealing. "You should come. To Moab. On the back of my bike."

"Me on a bike?" she snorts. "Don't forget I've been in a car with you, you drive like a maniac."

Brick starts laughing, the bastard. I may have a bit of a reputation as a speed devil. I turn my upper body to Sophia and put my hand over my heart.

"Swear I'll be on my best behavior. I'll even let Brick take the lead, he doesn't go any faster than a lawnmower."

"Hey. Just because—"

"Hush, honey," Lisa interrupts him with a pointed look my way. "Don't let him goad you." Then she turns to Sophia. "Or you," she adds. "Having said that, I think it's a great idea. You should come, that way I won't be the only odd one out. It's my first rally."

I try not to grin when I see Sophia bulge her eyes at Lisa, who pretends not to notice.

"I have to work."

"We don't have to go both days," I suggest. "Take one day off. Sunday's the better day anyway and you have Mondays off, right?"

Her eyes dart around the table until they land on Finn.

"Don't you need someone to look after the kids?"

"Yuma is sittin' this one out," Brick informs her. "He

and Lissie are taking them. They're covered."

I used to love going to rallies that would quickly turn into weekends of drinking and debauchery, but in recent years they lost their shine. I like the ride, don't get me wrong, but the partying is getting old. Or maybe it's me who's getting old. Not that the club frequents meets like that often anymore. A lot of the brothers have families, the club runs legitimate businesses, and we always have a handful of boys in our care.

Long gone are the times when the entire club would be riding out to two, sometimes three, events for each of the summer months. These days we stick closer to home and hit two, maybe three for the season.

The Moab rally is put on by a local club, the Mesa Riders, and their president, Red, is a good friend to Ouray. Moab is only a three-hour ride, but it's a pretty one going from the lush green of the Rockies to the red rock formations of Arches National Park.

I reach across Finn's high chair and grab one of Sophia's hands.

"Come with us. You'll have a good time, and I promise I'll be on my best behavior." Brick makes a laughing sound and I kick my boot out, hoping to catch him in the shin. "Not helping, old man."

"Who are you calling old? I'm not even ten years old than you are."

I ignore him and focus on Sophia, who seems to be looking at Lisa for answers. I give her hand a squeeze so her eyes come back to me.

"Come on, Fee," I plead. "Have a taste of the life. I

swear, just a nice ride and a few drinks with good friends. No strings attached."

I throw that last line in hoping that might convince her. I'm not going with the expectation something will happen, but that doesn't mean I won't be trying hard.

When she says, "I don't even have a helmet," I know the battle is won.

"Lots of helmets around, you can borrow one," Lisa says.

I make a mental note to hit up the Harley store this week to pick her up her own lid. I plan for her to spend more than only this one trip on the back of my bike.

I fucking hope she likes it.

ARROW'S EDGE MC

6

SOPHIA

"HEY, BOSS?"

Emme sticks her head around the door.

"There's someone here to see you."

"I'll be right out."

Emme is my second bartender and a complete opposite of the preppy-looking Mack. I liked her right off the bat: direct, brutally honest, and completely comfortable in her skin. Skin that is covered in colorful ink.

She works hard, doesn't take shit from anyone—not even from Chris, who has most of the staff shaking in their boots—and doesn't hesitate to lend a hand where needed. Doesn't matter whether it's bussing, helping in the kitchen, or cleaning the bathrooms.

She and I are the same age, but as different as night

and day. Her uniform is jeans or cargo pants and a T-shirt, while I try to get some wear out of my former office wardrobe. Her blonde hair hangs straight down to the small of her back, while mine is dark, cut in a short bob, and wavy. The only ink I ever got on my skin is the small tattoo on my ankle depicting two peas in a pod. Kelsey had one of those too. We had them done right before she discovered she was pregnant with Finn.

I miss my girl so much.

Lisa is becoming a good friend, but she's at a different place in her life than I am. Most of the women at the club are, and I haven't really had a chance to make new connections here. Not that that was ever my forte; making friends.

Kelsey and I developed a friendship in the break room at the company we both worked at. Workplace friendships make sense, given that I spend most of my time at my job and have never been a barfly. The women who work here are either unapproachable—like Lauren Harris who works with Chris in the kitchen—or a different generation, like most of the waitstaff. I could see Emme as a friend, though.

I sure could use one right about now. In three days I'm supposed to climb on the back of Tse's bike and head for Moab for a biker rally. Talk about being completely out of my comfort zone. Heck, I don't even know what to wear. I haven't seen him since the clubhouse on Monday—Wapi showed up every night, though—and am hoping maybe he forgot about it, but something tells me I won't be that lucky.

Entering the last item on the liquor order form, I send it off to the supplier, close my laptop, and head to the dining room to see who's looking for me.

"Hey."

Lea Hemmingway, wife to Kaga, who is Ouray's second in command, is sitting on a stool at the bar. She quickly gets up and smooths her hands on the black slacks she's wearing before reaching out to shake my hand. I don't know her well, other than an introduction at the clubhouse at Christmas and seeing her around at Lisa and Brick's wedding in May.

"Sorry to barge in unannounced," she says, appearing a little nervous. "I was hoping to have a word, but if you'd prefer me to come back another time…"

"No, no, not at all," I reassure her, as I quickly look around the restaurant. We're between lunch and the dinner rush so only two tables are occupied. Since my office is small and not really outfitted to receive guests, we'll probably be more comfortable in a booth. "Would you like to sit down?" I point at a booth in the corner where we'd have privacy.

"If you're sure."

"Absolutely. Would you care for a drink? Or a coffee?"

"Coffee would be nice."

I look at Emme, who apparently heard us because she gives me a salute before I can even ask.

I wait until we're both seated before asking, "What brings you here, Lea?"

"I was wondering if you have any openings. I'm looking for a job, now that—" She stops when Emme approaches with two cups of coffee and waits until she returns to the bar.

"Go on," I prompt when she hesitates.

"Well, with my boys in high school and driving themselves, I've got too much time on my hands. It was Kaga's suggestion, actually. He said you guys had some staffing issues and he was gonna talk to Ouray, but I wanted to do this on my own." She grins. "He's not too happy about that."

I can see why. Her husband is just like the other men at the clubhouse, protective and more than a tad controlling. The only difference is the other couples all met later in life when the women already had careers of their own. From what I understand, Kaga and Lea were high school sweethearts.

"I bet, and yes, we're still a little shorthanded on waitstaff."

Mandy—my latest hire—came to me on Tuesday and offered to work in the kitchen. She apparently has previous experience as a prep cook. Bernie has been improving since his surgery, but I don't see him coming back to work any time soon. But with Mandy now filling Bernie's spot on the schedule, I'm once again short in the dining room.

I'm not sure if that's what she's looking for, though.

"It's waiting tables, though," I tell her. "The kitchen is covered, so is the bar, but I don't have enough servers."

"That's fine."

"Okay. What do you have by way of experience?"

Not that it really matters, I wouldn't dream of

turning away a club wife when the club owns the damn restaurant, but since it appears to be important for Lea to do this under her own power, I'm going to treat her like any other applicant.

"Well, before I got pregnant with the boys, I worked part time at a diner in town. After they were born I stayed home, but I helped Momma out at the clubhouse a lot."

I've heard about Momma. She ran the clubhouse before Lisa. She was Nosh's wife and Yuma's mother.

"If you can handle that clubhouse, I'm sure you can handle the dining room. There's not much that changes about serving."

"Actually, that's my one concern. I'm not very computer savvy and from what I've seen everything is done on computers these days. Taking orders, taking payments. I'm being honest here, it intimidates me."

I reach across the table and put a hand on her arm.

"That's easily learned," I reassure her, but she still wears a dubious expression. "And if not, it's easy enough for Emme or Mack—that's the other bartender—or me, whoever is handy, to put in your order for you. But I don't think you need to worry about that, the system we have is very simple."

"Simple is good."

I smile back at her. "Drink up your coffee and we'll head to my office and have a look at the schedule. When can you start?"

The dinner rush is just starting by the time she leaves with a few Backyard T-shirts and a printout of the new schedule with her name added. I watch her get into her

SUV and am about to close the back door when I notice movement.

There, right at the edge of the parking lot, under the same trees. This time, though, there's a security camera aimed in that direction.

I rush inside, pull up the feed on my computer, and dial the detective's number.

TSE

"WHERE ARE YOU off to?"

I swing a leg over my bike.

"Backyard."

Paco grins and shakes his head.

"You still chasing that piece?"

My knuckles turn white as I clench my hands around the handlebars.

"Her name is Sophia," I grind out.

Not intimidated in the least, Paco laughs out loud.

"Guess that's a yes."

We just spent most of the day with Jed and some of his guys on Paco's land, digging up the old septic tank, which has to be replaced. A job I never want to repeat in my life. I had to shampoo four fucking times before the stench was out of my hair and beard, and the smell is still stuck up my nostrils.

I'm already in a pissy mood and Paco is not helping.

We're supposed to have the plans back from Jed's architect after the weekend and Ouray has a contact with the city, who promised to expedite the permits we need.

Fingers crossed, with a bit of luck we could be framing sometime next week.

I've had a few late nights helping Brick in the garage while Wapi held vigil at the restaurant, but tonight, come hell or high water, I'm heading to the Backyard, and not just because of the killer brisket.

There are a fair number of vehicles in the parking lot, but the one catching my attention is the police issue Explorer. It could mean nothing—maybe just a follow-up visit—but I quickly park my bike and rush inside anyway.

No sight of Sophia or the cops, but both the bartender—a pretty blonde covered in art—and a young waitress are leaning on the bar; their heads turned my way.

"Hey!" the blonde calls out when I walk right past them and start down the hall. "Where the hell do you think you're going?"

I look over my shoulder and see she's followed me, a baseball bat in her hands. I almost laugh, the woman doesn't even reach my chin, but her expression conveys she means business and I'm not about to test that.

"Here for Sophia. Name's Tse."

She tilts her head, scrutinizing me from the shades I pushed up on my head down to my boots.

"Yeah? That supposed to mean anything to me?"

I don't bother fighting the grin; this is fun. I like this chick. She's got balls.

"I'm her man.

I can see that shocks her but it doesn't take long for

her eyes to narrow to slits.

"Bullshit. Aside from the fact she's never mentioned your name, you're definitely not her type, and I've never seen your ass in here before."

"Better get ready to see a lot more of me, darlin'," I drawl, purposely goading the pint-sized ballbuster with a wink in her direction.

"What is go—" Sophia sticks her head out of the office and catches sight of me. "Tse? What are you doing here?"

"Ah shit," the blonde mumbles before turning back to the bar.

"Tse?"

I face Sophia and am about to answer when Ramirez steps up behind her.

"Come in, I want you to see this."

He disappears back into the office and I step up to Sophia, who stands frozen in the doorway. Leaning down I drop a kiss to her forehead.

"You heard the man, Fee."

She abruptly moves aside, color flushing her face.

Ramirez waves me over. "Have a look."

I get behind him and direct my attention to the computer. The screen shows the feed of a security camera, from the angle I'm guessing it's the one I know Ouray and the guys mounted over the back door earlier this week.

The picture is of the east side of the parking lot where it backs onto a run-down property, separated only by some brush and trees. The boarded-up house is on the next street over and faces the railroad tracks and the river beyond.

The first guy approaches from the south, moving in the shadows along the line of trees. The second figure suddenly appears at the back of the neighboring building. I'm not sure whether he actually came from the house or from the narrow alley on the side. With the tree coverage it's difficult to see. They appear to talk for a minute and then exchange something before each of them heads back in the direction they came from.

"Looks like a drug transaction," I suggest.

"That was my take. And in broad daylight. We were just going back through the feed and it looks like that wasn't the first deal of the day."

"Not a bad location for it," I point out. "From what I recall, that building," I tap on the screen, "is condemned, and from there it's easy to disappear in the overgrowth along the railroad or the river. Lots of businesses along this side to park a car unnoticed and walk under cover of those trees. It's less obvious than stopping at a street corner or parking in a back alley somewhere."

"That's what I figured. This doesn't look like some kid selling a bit of pot on the side. Too many transactions and too well thought out. It looks professional and organized."

He turns his head and looks up at me.

"You boys wouldn't still have an ear to the pavement, would you? Maybe heard of any new players in town?"

Sophia, who's been quiet so far, makes a small sound in the back of her throat as her eyes flit to me. But I focus my angry attention on the cop.

"Go fuck yourself, Ramirez. You know damn well that's ancient history."

It's been at least a dozen years since we had anything to do with drug trade in this city, and the fucker knows it. Not a part of my past I appreciate being broadcast in front of Sophia.

"Relax. All I'm asking is whether anyone's picked up on any chatter. People are more prone to talk around you than they do around us."

As fast as my hackles went up, I calm down again. I hate to admit he's got a point.

He pulls a flash drive from a port on the computer and gets up, tucking it in his pocket.

"Taking a copy of the feed with me, but it would be helpful if we could monitor traffic remotely. It's currently on a closed network."

"I can ask Paco, he knows about that stuff," I concede.

"Great. I'll be in touch."

With a nod to Sophia he's on his way, leaving us alone in her office.

"There was a time when the club was involved in the drug business, weapons trade, a lot of illegal shit I'm not particularly proud of," I volunteer softly without looking at her. "That was over a decade ago, before Ouray took the helm."

"Drugs?"

Now I look up at her expecting to see judgment, but other than maybe a hint of concern there's little else showing in her expression.

"Among other things. Ouray's plans for the club met with some resistance at first—money had been good and the brothers didn't want to give up on that, some of them left for other clubs—but over the years he made good on his word we could make decent money going legit."

"Oh."

She folds her arms in front of her and doesn't appear fully convinced, so I take a step toward her and put my hands on her shoulders.

"Those of us left from the early days and stuck it out are happier for it. I won't say there aren't times the boundary of the law isn't tested, but what I can guarantee you is that not one of us has regrets leaving that life behind us."

Large, honey-brown eyes look up at me, searching for the truth in my words. I know she's found it when her features finally soften into a faint smile. My gaze is drawn to her lips. Pink, soft, and full.

Fuck me.

"Okay," she whispers.

The next moment my mouth is on hers.

At the first taste of her I groan softly. The urge to claim her is strong, but instead of plunging my tongue in her mouth, I slick the tip over the swell of her bottom lip before lifting my head. Her eyes flutter before they open on mine, her pupils dilated.

Any other time, with any other woman, my hand would already be down her pants, interested in only one thing. Sophia is different—she's more.

I don't want her to see me as the proverbial bad boy.

I want her to see *me.*

1

SOPHIA

"PUT THIS ON."

He hands me a helmet and it suddenly gets real.

The helmet is similar to his—little more than an inverted bowl—although I see this one looks a bit more padded and has a bright red stripe running front to back.

"This looks new," I observe.

"It's yours."

I'm not entirely sure what, but I get the sense when a biker buys you a helmet it means something. My hands are shaking when I put it on my head and try to fasten the strap under my chin. Unsuccessfully. His steady hands brush mine aside and he tilts his head down to see what he's doing. I notice his thick dark eyelashes, the slight bump on his nose, and the crease that runs down the center of his full bottom lip.

"There," he mutters, as his eyes come up and lock on mine.

"Thank you."

For a moment I think he might kiss me, but then he straightens up and I try to hide my frustration.

He hasn't touched me since he kissed me in my office on Thursday. Not that he hasn't had a chance; he's been around enough. He waited around that night and followed me home on his bike again, watched me get inside, and drove off. Friday night he walked in around nine to see me home.

Same routine last night. Except last night, he'd called out to me to make sure to pack light. That resulted in a bit of an argument since I hadn't clued in to the fact this would be an overnight trip. I don't know why not, it makes sense it would be. I've had so much stuff going on, I just didn't pay close enough attention, but that didn't stop me from blaming Tse for tricking me.

That made him laugh and he told me, in no uncertain terms, when the time was right he wouldn't need to trick me into bed. Then he drove off and I spent the night restlessly rolling in my bed, the implication of those words keeping me awake.

Then at eight this morning he was back in the driveway, smiling as if nothing was wrong, this time to pick me up.

The modest bag he told me to pack is already strapped to the back of the seat, which suddenly looks very small for the two of us. A change of clothes, a few toiletries, and at the last minute I stuffed a pair of winter pajamas in there that would cover me neck to ankle. I'm not sure what our sleeping arrangement will be, when I asked, Tse only said it was taken care of, but I don't want to make assumptions or create expectations.

He confuses me.

When he swings a leg over the bike and shows me how to get on, I take a reinforcing breath and climb on behind him. We're wedged tight, his hips cradled between my legs. It's almost impossible not to be plastered against his broad back.

"Relax," he coaxes over his shoulder, before reaching for my arms and pulling them around his waist.

Then he revs the engine—the vibrations shoot straight up through my body—and peels out of the driveway.

It's a beautiful morning, but the first ten minutes while we're weaving through city streets to get out of town, I barely notice. After we leave the city behind, though, I become aware of the sun on my shoulders, the fresh air, and the beautiful views as we slowly leave the mountains behind.

Tse rides at a decent clip but not ridiculously fast, and he handles his bike so easily, his confidence is starting to rub off on me. By the time we pass Mesa Verde, I'm feeling the last of the tension leaving my body.

We're stopped at a traffic light in Cortez when he turns his head.

"Hungry?"

I didn't manage much more than coffee and a slice of toast at six this morning when I was too wound up to sleep any more.

"I could eat."

I figure he'll stop somewhere in Cortez, but instead he turns onto a county road. After about ten minutes we pass through a quaint little town and on the other side, he pulls off to the left into the small parking lot of a place called Arlene's Diner.

It's Sunday morning, probably around nine o'clock, and the parking lot is full. Glancing in through the windows I notice the diner looks busy. I have my doubts we'll be able to get a table, but Tse doesn't appear deterred. He stores our helmets under the seat, grabs my hand, and leads me to the entrance.

We've barely crossed the threshold when I hear a loud woman's voice call out his name.

"Oh hell, look what the cat dragged in." The woman behind the counter is older—I'm guessing in her fifties—tall, with short blonde hair, and a scowl on her face. "Seb!" she yells over her shoulder and behind her a man steps out of what I assume is the kitchen.

Silver-streaked dark hair and arms covered in tattoos that would have Emme drooling, the guy—Seb, I take it—grins wide when he catches sight of Tse and makes his way around the counter. My hand is released so he can greet Seb with a man hug and bone-breaking slaps on the back, only to be grasped firmly in his again after.

"Been too long, brother," Seb, who is dressed in a large white apron, voices.

"I know. Been busy."

That's when the man glances over at me, his grin

widening.

"I see that."

"Quit your drooling," the blonde snaps, pouring two mugs of coffee. "You're gonna get your bacon burned."

Tse bursts out laughing as the other man turns his grin on the woman.

"You love my bacon and you know it, Arlene. Besides, you know I love only you."

So she's the owner of the place and maybe Seb is her husband?

"Whatever," she huffs.

"Arlene, Seb, I'd like you to meet Sophia." To me he says, "Arlene makes the best coffee and Seb does a killer breakfast griddle that makes you wanna come back."

"Not bad enough, clearly," Arlene mutters.

She tucks a couple of menus under her arm and grabs the two mugs as she moves around the far end of the counter. With a jerk of her head, she indicates for us to follow her.

"Never mind her," Seb says with a smile. "It's not you, she was born in a bad mood. Nice to meet you, Sophia."

"You too," I manage before Tse pulls me along, weaving through the diner to an empty table where Arlene is already waiting.

"You can pick from the menu or trust me to order for you," she says when I take a seat.

With the intense way she scrutinizes me, I get the feeling this is some kind of test.

What the hell, I'm already living on the edge today.

"Sure, you pick."

She doesn't say anything but gives me a tiny nod before turning to Tse.

"You're lucky I still remember what you like."

"Missed you too, Arlene," Tse calls after her, as she makes her way back to the other side of the diner.

Her hand appears over her shoulder, the middle finger clearly extended, and I start laughing. It feels like I've landed in a sitcom.

Tse is grinning when I turn to him.

"I know it's hard to tell, but that woman has a heart the size of an ocean."

"How do you know them?"

"Years ago I was on a ride, saw this place and stopped for a bite. Got to talking with Seb about ink, mostly."

I look down at his hands where tattoos cover even his fingers. I can't help wonder what the rest of his body looks like.

"Food was great, so whenever I was in the neighborhood I'd make a stop, we'd talk. Turns out we know some of the same people," he explains.

"Small world."

"It is, especially in this neck of the woods. Everyone knows everyone."

The way he says that makes me think maybe he's not originally from here.

"Is your family from here?" I ask, curious to learn a little more about him.

But when I notice the way his eyes drift outside and his expression becomes closed off, I'm not so sure he's willing to share.

Tse

Not sure if I'm ready to get into the whole fucked-up childhood thing with her just yet, but maybe I can give her the basics.

"Not as far as I know," I tell her, keeping my eyes on the road outside. It's easier. "I was told I was maybe two months old when I was found in a trash can at a roadside stop along Highway 25 south of Pueblo, and still showing signs of drug withdrawal." I hear her suck in a breath, but keep talking. "Grew up in the system. Homes, foster care, you name it. Don't remember much of those early years, but I was a teenager when Nosh and Ouray picked me up and took me in." I risk a glance at her and find those luminescent brown eyes full of emotion. "My life started here, the first family I knew was the club, so I consider Durango and this whole area home."

"I'm sorry I asked," she says softly, putting a hand on mine.

"Don't be. It's not something you bring up casually, but I don't see the point of hiding it either. Quite a few of my brothers have a similar background. Heck, it's the reason we take kids off the street. Most of us have been there."

I flip my hand over and close my fingers around hers, rubbing my thumb over her knuckles. A delicate hand with long fingers and blunt nails that looks out of place folded in my broad callused one. I hang on to it anyway.

"Spinach, bacon, and Gruyère skillet for you." Arlene slides a steaming cast iron skillet in front of Sophia, forcing me to release her hand. "And Tex-Mex for you."

The one she sets in front of me already has my mouth watering. Hash-brown potatoes, scrambled eggs, beans, tomatoes, bacon, grated cheese, jalapeño peppers, and salsa.

"Oh my God. This looks amazing," Sophia comments, and I catch the little satisfied smile on Arlene's face.

That was a good call by Sophia to let her pick. Arlene is mostly bluster, kind to people she cares about, but she can get downright mean if she doesn't like you.

I'm grateful for the distraction breakfast brings. It's a temporary reprieve from the questions I expect Sophia to have about my past. Instead, she switches topics and asks me about the rally, curious to know what to expect.

We spend the next half hour making our way through breakfast while we chat, until Sophia sits back, her hand on her stomach, and groaning deep.

"I'm stuffed. I can't eat another bite. I'll be lucky if I still fit on the back of your bike."

I chuckle at her dramatics.

"You'll just have to squeeze a little closer."

"Don't say words like squeeze," she moans. "How much longer?"

"Three hours, give or take."

Her eye pop open wide. "That long? I thought you said three in total."

"Yeah, but we took the long road. It's prettier and I couldn't resist having you plastered against me longer. Besides…" I wipe my mouth with a napkin and dump it in the empty skillet in front of me, while watching that easy blush color her cheeks. "…nothing much will be going on until after the noon hour. I'm pretty sure everyone is gonna need some time to recover from partying last night."

"Okay, well, let me go splash some cold water on my face and we can get back on the road," she announces, getting up from her seat.

I watch her move through the diner, taking in her long legs and hourglass figure, which look even better in the rare pair of jeans she's wearing. When she disappears into the bathroom, I get up, pull out my wallet, and head to the counter to settle up with Arlene.

"Pure class, that one," she says, handing me my change, which I promptly stuff in the tip jar. "Never thought I'd see the day."

"Neither did I."

WE STOP TWICE more.

Once at the Mobil station in White Mesa, and then again at Wilson Arch where I convince Sophia to climb up to the sandstone arch with me and have a lone hiker take a picture of us with my phone.

I think I have a handful of pictures on my phone that aren't bikes, cars, or the Habitat for Humanity build, but that may change.

Our destination is Arches National Park, but first I want to stop off at the cabin just outside of town I was able to rent. They'd had a late cancellation and I lucked out because Moab is nuts during the rally. The place is modest, a two bedroom, but it's right on the Colorado River and has beautiful views. We'll drop off our stuff and freshen up a bit.

"This is so pretty!" Sophia yells in my ear when I turn onto the road that runs parallel to the river.

She's quiet though when I pull up to the small cabin, and for a minute I worry I missed the mark with this one. Then she gets off the bike, takes her helmet off, and does a full spin before zooming in on me, a wide grin on her face.

"This is absolute perfection!"

I have to say; I'm feeling pretty good about myself when I let us into the place.

It's basic, open concept living with a small kitchen, a rickety dining table with a couple of folding chairs, and an oversized couch facing the river. The sliding doors open onto a patio with a couple of chairs and a firepit.

I drop Sophia's bag in the room with the queen-sized bed, while I claim the bottom bunk in the other room. We'll have to share the bathroom. I can't believe I'll be sleeping under the same roof but in a different bed. I don't think I've ever tried wooing a woman before, and if my brothers knew, I'd never hear the last of it, but I'm determined not to rush Sophia into something she's not ready for.

Let's hope I can scrounge up enough self-discipline to stick to that plan.

ARROW'S EDGE MC

SOPHIA

IT'S RIDICULOUS HOW excited I am.

My ass is still sore from the ride here and has had less than an hour to recover, but when I slip that cool helmet on my head and climb on behind Tse, I feel like I'm about to go on an adventure.

"Hold on to me, Fee," he rumbles over his shoulder.

I wrap my arms around him, and this time I don't hesitate to press myself against his back.

The ride is short—too short—and when we pull into the visitors' center at the Arches National Park, I see we're far from the first ones. A virtual sea of shiny bikes is lined up in tight rows taking up half of the parking lot. The other half is fenced off, holding six or seven pavilion-like tents, a mass of bodies, and eighties rock music streaming from a couple of speaker towers positioned around the perimeter.

As Tse cruises around to find a spot to park I scan the crowd, suddenly eager to see a familiar face.

"You okay?" Tse asks when I hand him my helmet to store in the seat.

"It's a bit overwhelming," I admit, checking out a couple of rough-looking guys appearing to admire a bike a few rows over.

"Hey," he draws my attention before cupping my face in his hands. "This is all good fun, Fee. As rough as we look on the outside, most of us are here just to have a good time."

"Most?"

I watch as his mouth stretches into a smile.

"Yeah. No different than any other crowd, there's always gonna be a few assholes who like stirring up shit, just for the hell of it, but that rarely gets out of hand."

"Rarely?"

I can't help it, it's like I've suddenly developed cold feet, feeling completely out of my depth. My earlier excitement has been replaced by anxiety now that I'm about to enter a world I don't quite understand.

Without warning Tse's mouth covers mine.

Not like the gentle, tentative kiss we shared in my office this past week, but one that empties my mind and steals my breath as his tongue slips past my lips and sweeps inside. My hands find purchase, fingers curling around the edges of his vest, as he crowds everything else from my awareness. The scent of man and sun-warmed leather, combined with the taste of hunger and Tse, overwhelms my senses until every cell in my body is consumed by him.

"Yo! Benny!"

I'm not prepared when Tse breaks the kiss abruptly, lifting his head to whoever called out. I have to remind myself to breathe and rest my forehead against his chest.

"Catch you later," he yells back, the vibrations of his voice against my skin. Then softer, "Fee, baby, look at me."

"Mmmm."

I don't want to leave this little bubble that includes only him and me.

"Time to mingle."

Reluctantly I lift my head and tilt it back, looking up at him. His eyes are warm and smiling, deepening the lines on his face.

"Who's Benny?"

I watch a shadow pass over his expression.

"Ben. That's me, but I'm gonna need a quiet night, a beer, and you in my arms before I tell you about him."

I note he talks about himself both in first and third person in the same sentence and I get the sense the separation is on purpose. As interested as I am to discover more, I recognize this may not be the place or time.

"Let's go mingle," I concede, slipping my hand in one of his as we start walking toward the crowd.

When we finally find Brick and Lisa, I've already been introduced to about two dozen people. I only vaguely remember a few names, but I do recall none of those people called Tse by his real name.

"You made it!" Lisa exclaims, wrapping me in a fierce hug that feels a little desperate.

"Are you okay?" I ask her softly while the men greet each other.

"Yeah. Nothing I ain't used to or can't handle."

I set her back by the shoulders and dip my head to look in her eyes.

"What does that mean?" I have a sneaky suspicion I already know.

"A few rotten apples in an otherwise friendly bunch. Nothing to worry about. I'm just glad you're here."

I nod and turn to the guys, as I wrap an arm around her shoulders and give her a squeeze.

"Where are you guys staying?" Tse asks.

"Red Rock Motel," Brick responds. "It ain't the Ritz, but it's got a king-sized bed so you're not gonna hear me complain."

"Oh, you'll be complaining tonight, Brick Paver," Lisa hisses at him, and it's all I can do to keep from laughing.

Tse, however, doesn't hold back, barking out a laugh as he claps Brick on the shoulder.

"Burn, brother."

"Nah," Brick says with a warm smile for his wife. "Plenty of time to turn her around."

"Good luck with that." Tse grins and turns to me. "Drink, Fee? Lisa?"

He tilts his head in the direction of the beer tent. I'm pretty sure that's the extent of what they serve as well.

"Sure, I'll have a beer," I tell him.

When Brick ends up walking to the bar with Tse to give him a hand, I ask Lisa, "Where are the restrooms?"

"I'll come with you."

She leads the way through the crowd, keeping a firm hold on my hand. Around the side of the visitors' center is a row of portable toilets and I'm almost tempted to turn right back around, but the pressure on my bladder is already uncomfortable. There are only three people waiting before me but something tells me as the afternoon progresses and the beer flows, that will change.

Lisa is waiting for me when I step out, grateful for the bottle of disinfectant gel left on the small ledge inside. A line has started to form behind her already.

"Figured I'd be smart to go now. This'll only get worse."

I nod my understanding and point at a spot a few feet away from the line.

"I'll wait over there."

I notice the stares and do my best to ignore them. I guess Lisa and I make an odd pair, both of us looking a little out of place. Pulling my phone from my pocket I shoot off a quick text to Mack, who is covering for me.

"Hola, Mamacita."

I lower my phone and look up at a handsome, dark-haired man with a smile blinding enough to star in a Colgate commercial, but I note the smile doesn't reach his dark eyes. They appear to assess me. I'd guess him to be around my age, and by the leather cut sporting a patch saying 'president' on his chest, I conclude he's used to getting his way.

Not with this girl.

I straighten my back and turn fully toward him, raising an eyebrow, something he appears to find funny.

"My brother and I always had the same taste in women. Tits, ass, legs, a sweet pussy, and plenty of attitude. I see he hit the jackpot with you, but I'm here to tell you, you could do a whole lot better."

I know instinctively it was him calling out to Tse in the parking lot.

It's difficult not to laugh when he slightly puffs out his chest. His arrogance is ridiculous, but I also realize men with big egos can be dangerous when provoked.

"I appreciate your input, but I think it all depends on your point of view," I tell him sweetly, "and the way I see it, I already broke the bank."

With relief, I see Lisa coming this way and shoot a saccharine smile in the man's direction. When I start moving toward her, a strong hand around my upper arm holds me back.

"Give my brother my regards," the asshole says before letting me go.

"Who the hell was that?" Lisa asks when I reach her, and I glance over my shoulder to see him walking in the opposite direction.

"Nobody I want to know."

TSE

SOPHIA HAS BEEN quiet most of the afternoon, and by

the time we get ready to go out on a late afternoon ride through the park, I wonder if I made a mistake bringing her here.

I asked her a few times if she was okay, was having fun, and she'd smile at me and assure me she was, but I didn't miss the furtive glances she cast around all afternoon.

It was good to catch up with some of the guys I haven't seen in a while, but I'm eager to get back on my bike, with only Sophia for company. Other than that quick glimpse earlier in the parking lot, I haven't seen Manny around. I fully expected him to make his presence known but I wasn't about to go seek him out. A former brother, he tends to bring out the worst in me and that's not something I want to expose Sophia to.

We have quite a history, he and I, going back decades. For part of that history I was Ben, a fact he likes to remind me of. He's always been Manny, while I embraced the name the club awarded me. For me it was a way to leave the rocky start I had in life behind. Manny's hadn't been much better, but he seemed to use those darker days as justification for who he is now, which is why our relationship has been strained since he left the club.

I catch sight of Brick and Lisa getting ready to get on his bike and turn to Sophia, who is already fastening her helmet.

"Are you up for this? We can go back to the cabin, or home, if you prefer."

She seems genuinely shocked.

"Are you kidding? I'm looking forward to this."

I'm relieved to hear her say that and bend down to brush her lips with mine.

"Good."

The ride is north along Arches Scenic Drive to where it loops around Devil's Garden. Then we take smaller side roads to take us back to Highway 191 and south to Moab. The entire loop takes about two hours including a stop or two, and the vastness of the scenery is perfect to take in from a bike. It's one of my favorite rides, especially when the sun is starting to set in the sky.

Sophia snaps a few pictures on our stop at Devil's Garden, including one of Brick and Lisa with their arms wrapped around each other as they take in the rock formations.

"Now you two," Lisa says, reaching for the phone and taking a few steps back from us.

Sophia lifts her face to me, smiling without reservation this time, as she places her hands on my chest. Even with my shades on, I note the waning beams of sunlight give her skin a golden glow and set her eyes alight. I've never seen something so beautiful in my life.

Slipping my fingers in the short hair on the side of her face, I use my thumbs to lift her chin, and touch my nose to hers.

"Perfect!" Lisa calls out, interrupting the words threatening to spill from my lips.

Instead, I kiss Sophia's upturned face.

Brick and his wife opt out of a late dinner in Moab and instead turn off at their motel when we pass it on the way back. I don't particularly feel like eating out, but I drive into town anyway and stop in front of a Mexican restaurant I've been at before.

"You good with Mexican?"

"Absolutely. I'm starving," she announces, but then she looks at me hesitantly. "Would you mind very much if we did takeout? I'd love to enjoy the view at the cabin before the sun is completely gone."

"Wouldn't mind at all. Let's go place our order and then we'll pick up a few beers at the liquor store down the block while they get it ready."

Half an hour later I'm outside on the patio, building a fire from the wood stack at the side of the cabin, while Sophia is inside putting the food on some plates. The only noise you hear out here comes from the river. It's quiet and peaceful, a welcome change from the decibels that were ringing my ears all afternoon.

I glance up when she steps outside, carrying two plates with one hand, two beers in the other, and a smile on her face.

"Waiting tables pays off," she jokes when I rush to relieve her of her load.

Then she sits down balancing her plate on the armrest and turns her attention to the view.

"This is perfect," she mumbles.

I couldn't agree more.

I wish we were staying for a week and not just tonight.

9

SOPHIA

"ANOTHER BEER?"

I twist my head back to see Tse standing in the door opening.

He'd taken the dirty dishes inside earlier—I could hear the water running in the sink—while I put my feet up on the edge of the firepit, leaned back in my chair, and watched the stars slowly appearing in the sky.

Tse in just a white T-shirt stretched over his chest and a pair of well-worn jeans low on his hips, casually leaning against the door, makes for an equally excellent view.

"Sure."

I'll admit, my response is not as much about the beer as it is about the opportunity to watch Tse turn and walk his tight ass back inside.

A full belly and the beer with dinner have done a lot to relax me, but I could use another to fortify me. So far I've avoided telling him about the earlier encounter I had today. There's no doubt in my mind the guy intended his message to Tse to be a taunt, but I didn't want to get him riled up when we'd just arrived.

He still needs to know, though. There is a lot left for me to learn about this, but one thing I know for a fact, he won't like what I have to tell him. I just hope I don't set something off.

I hear him close the sliding door and walk up, handing me a bottle. Then he tosses another log on the fire, sits down beside me, and taps my beer with his.

"Thanks."

"You're welcome."

I turn my torso toward him.

"I mean for everything," I persist, needing him to understand what this trip meant to me before I piss him off. "For pushing me to come, for forcing me out of my comfort zone, for the amazing experience of stunning views and feeling free. Hands down the best day I've had in a long time."

A faintly sardonic smile forms on his lips.

"You're still welcome."

"I had a really good time."

Now the smile stretches wide.

"I'm getting that. Glad you enjoyed."

He takes a sip of his beer and I do the same, straightening to face the fire and wondering how to broach the subject.

Turns out I don't have to.

"Now are you ready to tell me what you've been mulling on all afternoon?"

I look at him, surprised. Guess I wasn't as good at hiding it as I thought.

"I was waiting for Lisa at the portable toilets. This guy approached me and told me to give you his regards."

I can feel the air go static, even though he doesn't show any reaction.

"What did he say? Exactly," he adds with deadly calm.

"Don't know who—"

"I know who it is. What did he say?"

"He called you his brother, said you always had the same taste in…" I hesitate a moment, wondering how much detail I want to give him, and finally deciding on, "…a certain type of woman."

That draws a reaction, one of narrowed eyes and flaring nostrils.

"I need the exact words, Sophia."

The fact he uses my full name is a little disconcerting and I'm not so sure I want to repeat those words. They made me feel dirty and cheap at the time and I'm sure they won't feel any better coming from my own mouth. Still, I brought it up, now I need to see it through.

"Tits, ass, legs…" I look away from him as I recite the words verbatim. They've been bouncing around my head all afternoon. "…a sweet pussy, and attitude."

It's silent for a beat and I sneak a glance at him, noting

a muscle working in his jaw. Then he suddenly gets to his feet, his chair scraping the patio tiles, and stalks to the door.

I catch up with him just as he's shrugging into his vest, and put a restraining hand on his arm, which he shakes off like a pesky fly.

"Please, Tse. Don't do this. Don't make me regret I was honest with you," I plead with him, as he reaches for the front door.

I hold my breath when I see him pause, leaning his forehead against the doorpost.

"What else?" I finally hear him say softly.

"He said you hit the jackpot with me, but that I could do better."

He snorts derisively as he turns around and moves toward me.

"I just bet he did."

"Well, I may have disavowed him of that thought."

He stops in front of me, his head low. Then he slowly lifts it and I'm surprised to see a glimmer of humor in his eyes. He reaches out a hand and cups my chin.

"Did you now?"

The annoying blush, which has been a torment my entire life is back.

"Told him I already broke the bank with you," I confess.

TSE

DAMN IF THAT doesn't make me feel good.

When I look down in her flushed face, my anger at Manny disappears as fast as it surfaced.

I'd been ready to track him down and let him know exactly what I thought of him approaching a woman he knows damn well is mine, but that would've played right into his hands. It had been a taunt, which is nothing new, needling me is something Manny likes to do every chance he gets. Making sure I know he's still around to remind me of a past I've tried to leave behind.

The only difference this time is the woman standing in front of me. The way she instinctively knew what to say to break through my rage. In the past I would've gladly duked it out with Manny, getting my punches in where I could before brothers would pull us apart until the next time he got under my skin.

This time Sophia makes me want to be the better man. The kicker of it is, I realize not reacting will likely drive him crazy. He thinks he knows me so well, but as it turns out, Sophia knows me better.

"Thank you."

I brush my thumb over her bottom lip before following it with my mouth. I keep the kiss light, despite the immediate need coursing through me.

Regardless of my intent to keep this weekend casual, Manny's stunt puts me in a position where I either shut her out or let her in. It's against my nature to share, but I owe her more than what I gave her this morning at breakfast.

She grabs the front of my shirt as I try to pull away.

"Hold that thought," I mumble against her lips. "Let's

sit down a bit."

I shrug out of my cut, and drop it on the couch, before grabbing her hand and pulling her back outside where the fire is still going.

"My legal name is Ben De León, probably not my birth name if I had one to begin with, but that's the one I was given."

I glance away from the flames and notice I have her full attention. Good, because I sure as fuck don't want to repeat anything.

"I already told you I grew up in the system. I spent most of the time in and out of foster homes. Some were okay, some sucked, but none of them were in for the long haul. I wasn't exactly an easy kid, but when I was about twelve, I was taken in by a couple who liked the regular checks and found ways to keep me in line."

I glance over when I hear her shift in her chair. She's pulled up her knees, wrapped her arms around them, and is observing me closely.

"They weren't nice people," she concludes.

"No. They took Manny in a few years later." I can tell that surprises her. "He was a bit younger, but we looked out for each other the best we could. Even after we ran and were picked up by the club, we stuck together. The club going legit changed that. Manny was drawn to the darker side—drugs, money, violence, power—while I was ready to shed that life. He wasn't happy when I chose the club over him and tries to get under my skin at every opportunity."

"I see," she mumbles.

"Yeah." I reach for one of her hands and tug her to her feet before pulling her onto my lap, locking my arms around her, despite the tension in her body. "He saw you on the back of my bike, guessed you mean something to me, and decided to poke the bear."

She turns her head, her face inches from mine.

"Just because I was on the back of your bike?"

I grin. "Fee, it may have escaped your notice, but bikers tend to be particular about who they invite on the back of their bikes. It means something."

"Oh."

I smile when I see that blush is back.

"Yeah, oh." I slide a hand to the back of her head and pull her closer. "Now…where were we?"

All it takes is a brush of my lips for her to relax in my arms. Her hand comes up, fingers tangling in the longish hair brushing my collar, and her mouth opens in invitation.

Fuck.

Clear night, smell of wood fire, beautiful woman on my lap, her taste in my mouth—it doesn't get better than that.

I slide a hand from her hip to the back of her knee and groan when she shifts her weight on my lap. My cock is painfully hard, but fuck if it isn't a beautiful pain. Running my hand up the back of her leg, I rub the tips of my fingers along the seam of her jeans until I can feel the damp heat of her through the material.

She makes a small sound in the back of her throat I can feel down to my bones, and my resolve shatters.

Suddenly this chair is not big enough for everything I want to do to her.

"Hang on to me," I growl, hooking an arm under her knees while keeping the other firmly wrapped around her waist.

She lets out a little squeal, grabbing on to my shoulders when I get to my feet and lift her in my arms. She giggles softly when I try to open the sliding door, cursing under my breath. Letting go with one arm she reaches down and takes care of the door.

Her mouth is back on mine as I try to balance her in my arms and head for the bedroom. The moment we step inside, I let go of her legs. With my free hand I cup the back of her head, while I slide the other into the waistband of her jeans, palming the smooth skin of her ass.

I'm lost to her, giving in to the restless hunger of her mouth and wandering hands. She tugs the back of my shirt free and scrapes her nails over the skin she exposed. I tilt her head, slanting mine so I can taste her deeper. I want to devour her, claim every part of her body while imprinting myself on her skin.

She drives me mad when her small hands start pulling at the buttons of my fly. In one last flash of sanity as she frees me from my jeans and sinks down in front of me; I pull a condom from my pocket. The next moment my brain empties of everything but the feel of her hot mouth closing over my engorged cock, and my back hits the door.

Bracing with one hand on my thigh, she cups my balls

in the other, stroking the tight skin behind them with a finger. I almost blow on the spot, which is not how I saw this night going.

With Herculean effort I pull my hips back, reach down, and hook her under the arms, lifting her off the ground.

"But I—"

"Too many clothes," I cut her off brusquely, ripping my own shirt over my head.

She looks gorgeous, eyes shining with heat, lips swollen and slick, and that blush deepening all the way from her chest to her cheeks. Without hesitation she strips off her shirt and while she tugs down her jeans, I roll on the condom. There's much I want to explore, but I'm afraid even the slightest touch or taste will set me off.

I don't even have time to really look at her before her arms are around my neck, her tits pressed against my chest, and her mouth is on mine. Running my hand down over her ass and down the back of her leg, I hook her behind the knee as she hops up, wrapping her long legs around my hips.

Instead of dropping her on the bed, I turn and press her back against the door, spread my stance, and position myself at her warm, wet entrance.

"Fee, baby…look at me."

Her honey-brown eyes focus on mine, and as I slide inside, her mouth falls open.

Fucking incredible.

Sophia

I LISTEN TO his breathing deepen as he gives in to sleep.

Tse's body is curved around me, his knee cocked between my legs, his face in my neck, and his hand cups my breast possessively. The same hand explored and exposed every inch of my body in the past however many hours.

All I know is my body feels like a limp noodle, devoid of any tension. Tse took care of that. With his fingers, his talented mouth, and his highly satisfying cock.

I feel a smile spread on my lips. It took me six years to get back on that horse after my last relationship crashed and burned, and now I wonder what the hell I'd been waiting for.

Maybe it was the beer, the sense of freedom, or the fact Tse shared of himself, but for once I let go, took what I wanted, and it was spectacular.

Sure, tomorrow's ride back to Durango will probably cause a bit of discomfort, but I already know it was well worth it.

I guess one shouldn't compare, but my best experience so far was pleasant, polite, and enjoyable. What Tse gave me was an out-of-body experience. There was nothing pleasant or polite about it, and enjoyable doesn't even begin to describe the bone-deep satisfaction I feel.

I sure as hell better not have been a one-off for him; he's already spoiled me for anyone else.

Covering his hand on my breast with my own, I close my eyes and drift off.

10

Sophia

"Where are we?"

I take off my helmet and look around.

Tse mentioned he wanted to make a stop before taking me home. To my surprise he took the road up to my new place, but pulled off on a driveway about halfway up the road.

I'm looking at a nice plot of land that isn't visible from the road and at some point had a building on it. Nothing but the foundation is visible now, as well as a massive pile of dirt about a hundred feet out. It smells a little funky.

I must've made a face.

"Sorry, forgot about the smell," Tse apologizes. "We dug up the old septic tank before the weekend. A new one should go in this week."

"This is yours?"

What a crazy coincidence that would be.

"No, it's Paco's. He's building a house and I'm helping out where I can." He suddenly seems a little uncomfortable, rubbing his hand through his hair. "I... uh...shit. I don't even know why I dragged you up here. I guess I wanted show you where I'll be working for the foreseeable future."

I take a step closer and nudge him with my shoulder.

"Thank you. I like the idea of knowing where you're hanging out."

"Yeah?"

His eyes smile down on me, fine lines framing them.

"Only seems fair. You've already seen where I work." A light breeze carries another whiff of what I now know is eau-de-septic and I pull my shirt up to cover my nose. "Although my workplace smells a hell of a lot better."

"You're not lyin'," he says, putting on his helmet again. "Let's get out of here."

"Actually, I have something to show you as well. Mind if we go up the road a little?"

"Where are we going?" he asks, swinging a leg over his bike.

I climb on behind him.

"I'll show you when we get there."

I fit my arms around his middle as he turns the bike up the mountain.

It's only a minute to what will soon be my driveway and I tap Tse on the shoulder.

"Slow down into the bend, there's a driveway just on the other side on the right. Pull in there."

I'm guessing Meredith will be at work, but either way, I'm sure she won't mind me stopping by to show my new place.

Tse stops the bike in the driveway and stays when I climb off.

"What is this place?"

"My new house as of this coming weekend. I get the key on Friday and the moving truck will be here on Saturday afternoon."

He looks at me with eyebrows raised.

"No shit? This is yours?"

"Well," I rush to correct him. "I'm renting. It belongs to Meredith Carter; she's the county coroner. She's moving in with her man."

"Jay VanDyken," Tse surprises me by saying. "I heard they were an item."

I don't think I'll ever get used to the fact everyone seems to know everyone here.

"Yes. She's not ready to sell yet, and I was looking for a slightly more permanent place than Sandra's garage apartment."

He swings one leg over the handlebars but keeps his butt on the seat. Then he reaches for me and pulls me closer, his hands on my hips.

"This is going to be convenient," he says, smirking.

I grin back. "Oh yeah?"

"You'll have to get a dog, though." He nudges his head to the A-frame. "Great place, but it's a little remote for a girl by herself, and I can't be here all the time."

My smile disappears and I try to take a step back, but his hands hold tight. I manage to twist free anyway.

"I don't even know where to start, there are so many flags going off at the same time right now."

"I don't get it."

He looks genuinely perplexed. He doesn't even recognize the misogynistic crap he just spouted, but I don't mind enlightening him.

"I've made this mistake once before, let myself get swept off my feet only to turn around and find every aspect of my life controlled. Took me six months to be rid of him. Took me six years to work up the guts to try once more. I'm not going down that rabbit hole again."

He pushes off his bike, removes his helmet, and closes the distance between us. He doesn't touch me though, just stands really close but I hold my ground.

"I'm glad you told me about the asshole or I'd be seriously pissed right now. We'll get to the asshole and the six years later, but for now let me clear something up."

Last thing I want is to discuss Dave, but I let that genie out of the bottle myself. Still, I lift my chin in a touch in defiance.

"What?"

It doesn't deter Tse.

"What I said comes from a place of concern. Some of it ingrained reflex, I'll admit, but let me remind you about the attack on your employee, the drug deals taking place behind your restaurant, the fact the cops are still actively investigating both, and you are smack in the middle of all of that."

Shit.

It says a lot about the weekend, and the company I kept, it was so easy to let those facts slip my mind.

"And, Fee? This is who I am. I'll always be protective, but don't mistake that for control, and if you can't deal with that maybe I'm the wrong guy for you."

Wow. Talk about putting it out there. Yesterday at this time we were still dancing around each other and had separate bedrooms we fully intended to use. This morning I woke up to this man worshiping my body, washing my hair in the shower we shared, and already I may have brought this budding relationship to a screeching halt.

A dog is not that far-fetched, and neither is the assumption he'll spend time here for whatever his reasons may be. Although, I guess that entirely depends on the response he gets from me. Judging from the scowl on his face, I'd better not make him wait too long.

"I can deal."

"You sure?"

I nod. "If you can deal when I get defensive, I can deal when you get protective.

He pulls my body flush to his and wraps me tightly in his arms.

"Good fucking answer, Fee," he mutters right before he kisses me.

TSE

"How was the ride?"

Ouray is leaning against the side of the clubhouse, smoking. It's where he hides from Luna, who's been hounding him to quit.

"Good. Nice couple of days for it." I shove my helmet in the seat and take the strap of my bag. "Red was asking where you were."

"I'm sure he was, never mind I told him last week I wasn't gonna be there. He just doesn't like my reasons."

I'm sure he doesn't since he called Ouray pussy-whipped, but I'm not about to share that remark.

Luna, who is an FBI agent, had to work and Ouray won't go to rallies without his wife anymore. As far as I'm concerned that's their business, although there was a time I might've agreed with Red's assessment.

"Everything quiet here?"

He stubs out his cigarette in the sand-filled bucket and looks up at me.

"Had a little scuffle in the boy's dorm overnight. Ravi got into it with Maska. Hit him over the head with a crowbar."

"What?" I'm shocked, Ravi is a quiet kid but he's not violent. He'll avoid conflict if he can. "How's Maska?"

"He'll have a scar he can brag about. Fourteen stitches above his ear. Damn proud of them too." He chuckles.

"Ravi?"

"Looks like he's about to bolt. Trunk's been trying to talk to him, but he's not saying much. Kid was sleeping with a crowbar in his bed. Remind you of someone?"

Damn.

We didn't know much of Ravi's history when he came to us, and he hasn't shared, but I'm starting to get a better picture.

"Where is he?"

"Yuma's old room in the back."

Swinging my bag over my shoulder, I start toward the door, my step a little heavier than normal.

Lisa's already back in the kitchen getting dinner ready, and the clubhouse is crowded with brothers grouped around the bar, a few of the kids working on homework at the big harvest table, and the rest of them crowded around the big-screen TV.

I get called over by Paco, who tells me the tank and a load of lumber are being delivered to the building site tomorrow. I spend a few minutes talking, but refuse the beer I'm offered. I want to have a clear head when I talk to the kid.

Tossing my bag on my bed to take care of later, I walk across the hallway. The door to Yuma's old room is closed and I notice the key in the lock.

"Like I said, he was ready to bolt."

I look up to where Ouray is standing in the doorway to his office down the hall. I nod my understanding and turn the key.

At first glance I don't see him. The TV is on and someone's clearly been sitting on the bed. It's not until I take a few steps into the room that I see him sitting on the floor underneath the window.

"Hey, kid," I say as casually as I can, keeping my eyes on the TV when I take a seat on the edge of the bed.

"Just talked to Paco, he says lumber will be dropped off tomorrow and I was wondering if you'd wanna help out getting the framing for his house up?" I notice movement from the corner of my eye, but continue talking, "It'll have to be after school, of course, and you'd have to get to your homework after dinner, but I could sure use a hand."

He puts a dent in my patience, making me wait a long time for an answer, but when it comes I breathe a sigh of relief.

"Okay." The mattress dips a little when he sits down beside me. "But am I not in trouble?"

I glance over, recognizing the look in the kid's eyes. Part defiance, part hope, and part fear.

"Oh, you're in trouble. Can't whack a brother over the head with a piece of iron and not expect there to be some consequences. Unless of course there was a good reason why you decided to use Maska's melon as a piñata."

I don't miss the flash of a grin before his face turns surly again.

"He was the one sneaking around in the middle of the night, I was in bed," he says defensively, but at least he's talking.

"Right. With a crowbar you stole from the shop under your blankets?"

"Gotta protect myself." He shrugs.

I can almost hear the vault locking in place. Not much more I'll be able to get out of him tonight, but I sure as hell am gonna have a chat with Maska.

"Come on," I tell him as I push to my feet. "Lisa's

about to serve dinner."

"I can come out?" he asks hesitantly behind me.

"If you're ready to apologize to Maska you can. Provided you're not gonna take off, because boy, I'll find you if you try."

I don't look back when I open the door and walk out, but when I'm halfway down the corridor I hear his shuffling footsteps behind me. I head straight for the bar, signaling to Shilah for a beer. Only then do I look behind me to see Ravi had walked over to the group of kids watching TV. He's standing in front of Maska, who is lounging on the couch, his fists clenched by his side.

"Get him to talk?" Paco asks, sidling up to me at the bar.

"Claims he was protecting himself, but from what is unclear."

I take a swig of my beer and keep a close eye on the interaction between the boys, in case they can't keep it civil. Ravi nods sharply and turns away. He looks a little lost as he wanders toward the kitchen, where Lisa just pokes her head out the door.

"Boy, you've got nothin' better to do? May as well give me a hand settin' that table, yeah?"

Over dinner things look to have returned to normal, with Ravi quiet—as expected—and the other kids rowdy as usual. I stay for a few beers at the bar with my brothers until Shilah starts herding the kids to the dorm, Ravi with them.

In my room I take a quick shower, turn on the news, and lay down on my bed, my phone in hand.

Me: Get everything done you wanted to?

I have to wait a few minutes before I get an answer.

Fee: Just got back from Sandra's with my last load of laundry and heading for bed.

Me: I'm already there, although I'd rather be in yours.

When she doesn't respond through the next commercial break, I type out a less loaded message.

Me: Work tomorrow?

Fee: Heading in for eleven. You?

Me: I'll be up at the build first thing. An issue with a couple of our kids here, so I'll probably stick around the club for dinner tomorrow, but will try to pop in after.

I watch the dots bouncing for a long time, stopping and starting again, indicating she's typing a response. I'm expecting a lengthy one and am surprised when it's only one word long.

Fee: Night.

Huh.

11

SOPHIA

I WAKE UP when something brushes my cheek, only to shoot straight up when I find Tse sitting on the edge of my bed.

"Morning."

His smile is relaxed, looking like he has every right to be here.

"How'd you get in here?"

He looks over his shoulder at the front door.

"Wasn't that hard. Your lock is pretty basic."

"You broke my lock?"

The shock of waking up to him in my bedroom is slowly replaced with anger. The fact he's grinning and doesn't seem at all repentant only makes it worse.

"Didn't have to. It was easy enough to pick."

Pulling the sheet with me, I swing my legs out of the opposite side of the bed, wrapping myself up.

"I can't believe you broke in. Ever think of knocking?"

Tse gets to his feet as well, and I hate that I notice he looks good in a white T-shirt and a pair of old work pants covered with paint stains.

"Oh, I thought of it, but had a feeling you might not answer, so I let myself in."

What do you say to that?

Especially since he's right, I probably wouldn't have opened the door.

Yesterday after he dropped me off, I started thinking about our earlier disagreement.

I like him—a lot—but I'm not so sure someone with a personality as big as his would be good for me. Hell, I left home young because there was no room for me to be my own person. Then I met Dave, who was charismatic and charming, and he completely overwhelmed me. I've been able to be my own person for the past six or so years and I like who I am now.

Someone like Tse, who already has issues with boundaries, could easily force me back into the shadows without intending to. The text exchange last night seemed to underscore that.

So no, I wouldn't have opened the door, and yet here he is, in my bedroom, breaking down my boundaries.

I turn on my heel and without a word dart into the bathroom, locking the door behind me.

Fifteen minutes later when I walk out, he's no longer in my bedroom, but I can smell fresh coffee brewing.

Even though it's only eight in the morning, I get dressed for work, taking my time, and secretly hoping he'll have to leave before I'm done.

No such luck, when I walk into the small living room, he's standing by the window, drinking coffee.

"You made coffee."

He turns and sets down his cup before walking right up to me and folding me in his arms. I'm instantly enveloped in his earthy scent, his strong hold, and his calming energy. Without thinking I slip my arms around his waist and burrow in.

"There she is," he mumbles, resting his chin on the top of my head.

He makes it hard for me to remember all the reasons why this thing between us isn't a good idea.

"I'm scared."

His arms squeeze a little tighter.

"I'm gettin' that."

We stand like that for a bit, arms around each other, when he speaks again.

"Asked you yesterday to take me as I am. Shoulda clarified that goes both ways."

I rub my cheek against his chest.

"We're so different."

"Yeah, we are, in a lot of ways. I'm sure there'll be times we butt heads, but that doesn't mean I wanna give up before we've even tried."

It's my turn to squeeze him back.

"I'm a coward," I say by way of apology.

He leans back, forcing me to look up at him.

"Nah. Wasn't that long ago I had my own doubts."

"What changed?" I ask, my heart thudding in my chest.

"Nothing, other than realizing my doubts had little to do with you and everything with me."

For a man who at first impression seemed a player—shallow—he sure puts me to shame. He shows a lot more insight and depth of character than I would've given him credit for. Thus proving how true his words ring for me as well.

This isn't about him; it's about me. About fear of my own weakness, instead of trusting my strength.

I unwrap my arms and lift my hands to his face, pulling him down so I can reach his lips. Then I rise on my toes and apologize with a kiss.

IT'S NOT EVEN nine when I park in my slot behind the restaurant.

My car is the only one there.

Mandy, who's taken over the early shift for Bernie, won't likely be here before ten since most deliveries are scheduled later in the morning.

I glance to the edge of the parking lot but there's no one there. Maybe that extra police presence Detective Ramirez promised is proving to be a deterrent.

I get out of my Jeep and head for the back door, my key at the ready. Before I step inside, I turn and wave at Tse, who followed me in a beat-up pickup truck filled with tools. He insisted on following and didn't seem to care he'd have people waiting for him at the building site. Since I knew there'd likely be no one in this early, I didn't argue.

Nor did I object when he said someone would be there at the end of business every day. The club owns the restaurant, they can do whatever they feel is necessary, and truthfully, I'm relieved. I wasn't looking forward to walking out at night to a dim parking lot by myself.

The first thing I do in my office is turn on the monitor with the camera feed. Then I spend the next half hour or so going over Sunday night's print-offs and the deposit slip Mack prepared, entering all the numbers into my online software and my ledger. Call me paranoid, but even with the entire accounting system computerized, I still like to keep a paper file as a backup.

I focus my attention on the monitor when I notice movement and watch the Clover Produce truck pull into the parking lot. A little early, it's not even quarter to ten. I watch as the driver backs up to the rolling delivery door at the other side of the bin, the back of the truck no longer visible to the camera. Guess I should go let him in since Mandy's not here yet.

Heading through the kitchen to the storage room beside the walk-in cooler, I hit the button to lift the door. The driver is already rolling up the loading door at the back of the truck.

"Morning."

He turns around at the sound of my voice, eyebrows raised.

"Where's Mandy?"

"She's not here yet. I can give you a hand."

"I've got it," he grumbles, turning his back.

Friendly guy, obviously not much of a morning person.

Instead of unloading our supplies, he appears to be rearranging the rear of his rig, every so often glancing my way. Maybe he forgot to load our order?

"Everything all right?" I ask, taking a step closer.

There is no answer as he keeps his back turned and I'm about to repeat my question when I hear running footsteps outside.

Mandy comes charging around the side of the truck, her face flushed.

"I'm so sorry. Traffic accident blocked the road and I was—"

I stop her with a raised hand and a smile.

"No worries, I happened to be in early." I indicate the driver in the back of the truck. "I think he's still looking for our order anyway."

"I've got it right here," the driver says, putting a hand on the stack of boxes near the door.

What an ass.

The order was right there the whole time.

Tse

"GRAB ME ANOTHER coil of nails from that box, will ya?"

Ravi, who's been here since I picked him up from summer school again, rushes to the back of my truck.

Paco is the only other guy left here, working on the opposite end to help me brace the framed front wall until the beams go in. That work is supposed to happen next week, along with a start on the roof trusses.

If working on the Habitat for Humanity project taught me anything it was that many hands truly do make light work, as long as everyone works together well. Jed was here with a crew of three for most of the week, along with Paco and myself, and some of the other brothers popped in for a couple of hours here and there to lend a hand. It's the only reason we were able to get the exterior walls framed and up in five days.

"Thanks, kid." I reach down and grab the coil from Ravi. "Last one, then we'll head back to the clubhouse. I bet you're hungry."

"Starving," he grumbles, and I bite off a grin.

Not much later I'm lifting the compressor and nail gun into the back of the pickup, while Ravi hauls over the ladder. Until the structure is up and sealed in, we'll have to contend with lugging tools back and forth.

Paco looks to be done on his side as well and is loading up his truck.

"Why don't you get in?" I tell Ravi, taking the ladder from him. "I'll be right there."

I secure everything in the back of the pickup with a couple of straps and walk over to Paco.

"Plan on being back here tomorrow?"

"Yeah. Yuma said he'd bring the Bobcat from the compound and I'm hoping to get the foundation for the garage dug up. Nothin' but sun in the forecast the next couple of days, so with a little luck the concrete can be poured."

"I've got plans tomorrow, but I can help out on Sunday. At least part of the day."

"That's fine. You sticking around tonight?"

This weekend is the big rally in Pueblo and traditionally some of the local clubs stop in Friday night for a cookout at the clubhouse and head out in convoy in the morning. The Arrow's Edge has passed on that rally for a few years now, but has continued the traditional cookout.

I won't be there. I'll stop in for a shower and head out again.

"Nah, I've got shit to do."

Paco chuckles and shakes his head.

"Lemme guess, at the Backyard?"

I don't bother denying anymore. Every-*fucking*-one in the clubhouse seems to know where I am when I'm not there, which has been every night this week. I swear these guys spend more time gossiping than the local sewing circle.

"Damn right," I confirm. "And if you were smart, you wouldn't waste every night at the clubhouse either." I walk away and toss a casual, "Later," over my shoulder.

"Can I come all day next week?" Ravi asks when I get behind the wheel.

"What about summer school?"

"Today was the last day."

"No shit?" I twist in my seat and catch the grin he tries to hide by tipping his head down. "So how'd you do? Did you pass?"

"Yeah."

I flick the bill of his ball cap.

"Nice work, kid."

I start the truck and do my best to avoid the potholes in the drive down to the road.

"So can I?"

"Weren't you supposed to be working on a car with the other boys this summer?"

He's suddenly quiet and when I glance over, his face is turned to the side window.

"Hey, Ravi." I nudge his shoulder, but he shrugs off my touch.

"I wanna work with you."

"Is this about that thing with Maska? Didn't we already clear that up?"

I'd talked to the kid myself this week to find out what happened. He said he sometimes sleepwalks— something both Shilah and Wapi have seen him do in the past—and doesn't remember what happened. Ravi hasn't mentioned the incident at all.

"I'm better with a hammer."

I slow down for a stop sign and turn my head to look at the boy. He's facing me, a plea in his eyes that tugs at my heartstrings. If only he would open up, even a little, but I know only too well how slim those chances are.

Fuck.

"Tell you what; let me talk to the brothers this weekend. See what we can come up with."

"Sure."

I can tell he doesn't believe me.

"You're here."

Sophia gets up and comes around her desk toward me.

"I am."

I tug her close and drop a kiss on her lips.

"I thought you said there was something going on at the club tonight?"

"There is."

In fact, the cookout was already in full swing by the time I left. Trunk and Jaimie were at the clubhouse with the little ones when I got back with Ravi. Lisa took one look at the boy and sent him to the dorm to have a shower before dinner. I figured it was as good a time as any to have that talk with Trunk, but unfortunately, with the crowd around the clubhouse growing by the minute, we didn't really get a chance.

It took another hour and a half before I finally managed to walk back out of there.

"You know Mack could've walked me to my car, right?"

"Not the only reason I came, Fee."

She tilts her head back and smiles up at me.

"Is that right?"

"Mmm."

I slide a hand down the back of her pants over the swell of her ass and give it a playful squeeze.

"Tse...I'm working," she reminds me, peering over

my shoulder to see if anyone's coming.

"Wasn't Mack supposed to close?"

That's the reason no one could've convinced me to stay at the clubhouse tonight. The few times I followed her home this week, we didn't get much further than a little petting before she'd start yawning. But tonight she was going to take off early and tomorrow I'm helping her move her shit to the new place. I have a few ideas how I want to spend the time between.

"He is, but I still have some work to do."

"How much longer?"

"I'm off tomorrow so I have to finish payroll tonight or no one will get paid."

"How long?" I push.

She shakes her head and grins, giving my chest a little pat before she steps out of my hold and returns to her seat behind the desk.

"Longer if you stand here distracting me." She waves a dismissive hand at me as she drops her gaze to the computer screen. "Go have a drink at the bar, and get Mack to order you something from the kitchen." A little tease of a smile appears on her lips. "You're gonna need the extra fuel."

I can still hear her soft laugh when I take a seat at the bar.

"What can I get you?"

"Beer and brisket."

12

Sophia

"Get there, baby."

His fingers dig into my ass as he surges up.

I hold myself up with my hands planted flat on his chest, while I grind down on him. His cock fills me completely and I roll my hips to create a delicious friction. He shifts one of his hands, reaches down where our bodies are joined, and puts firm pressure on my clit.

That's all it takes for me to fly apart with my head thrown back and my mouth open, gasping for air. The next moment I find myself on my back, Tse pistoning inside me while I'm still riding the convulsions of my climax.

His, "Fuck, yeah," is followed by a long, deep groan, as he burrows his face in my neck and his body bucks with his release.

I'm not sure how long we lie like that, skin slick with our early morning exertions, trying to catch our breath. I welcome the weight of his body on mine as my fingers drift up and down his back and firm ass. At some point I wonder if he's fallen back asleep when he mumbles against my skin.

"Never thought I'd say this, but I think you wore me out. I can't move."

His soft chuckle vibrates through my body and a satisfied smile forms on my lips.

We hadn't wasted any time last night. The instant the door to my apartment closed behind us, he had my shirt off and was working my pants down.

I had my first orgasm of the night still in the hallway, with my back pressed against the front door, a leg hooked over his shoulder, and his mouth creating magic. From there we hit the couch, the shower, and finally rolled exhausted into bed, where I was the first one to wake up this morning.

I'd fallen asleep like I had last weekend at the cabin, with Tse's big body curved around mine, but when I woke up, he was on his stomach beside me. His arm was tucked under his pillow and the covers were riding low on his hips. The full expanse of the impressive tattoo on his back was on display and I couldn't resist examining it closer.

At the center was a Native depiction of the thunderbird reaching from shoulder to shoulder. Underneath its wings were a compass, a feather, an arrow, and a broken chain, all blended together into one large intricate piece.

I swung my leg over his hips to straddle him and traced every outline with the tips of my fingers. His body had gone rigid under my touch and I pressed my lips between his shoulder blades. That's when he'd suddenly rolled over, his sleepy eyes dark with heat as he lifted me on his growing erection.

Sucking in a sharp breath I try to move Tse off me.

"I have to get up."

He must hear the urgency in my voice because he immediately rolls off, his expression questioning.

"What's wrong?" he asks, but I'm already out of bed, rushing for the bathroom.

I'm sure he'll clue in when he sees the wet spot on the sheets.

Sinking down on the toilet I slap my hands over my face. How could I have been so stupid?

I relieve myself quickly, flush, and reach for the shower, turning the water on. Battling back the panic constricting my chest, I pull open the medicine cabinet, grabbing the round container of contraceptive pills. I just had my prescription renewed last weekend after letting it lapse a few months ago. So much had been going on in my life I hadn't been too careful. Then with the move to Durango, and the busy weeks after, it hadn't been at the top of my list until I was faced with a weekend away on the back of Tse's bike. Even though I hadn't planned on having sex with him then, I figured the time would come sooner than later and aside from expecting to use a condom, I also wanted the extra protection.

Six pills are gone from the pack.

"Fee?" I hear his voice outside the door, followed by a soft knock.

Ignoring it, I get under the shower, cursing the fact the bathroom door doesn't have a lock when it opens and Tse stands there in all his naked glory.

He glances at the pill container I left on the vanity before his eyes come to me. Not sure what to say, I turn my back and grab the bottle of shampoo.

Behind me the shower curtain opens and he steps in, his large body taking up a lot of space in the moderately sized shower. Reaching around me he takes the bottle from my hands and the next thing I know his fingers are massaging the shampoo in my short hair.

"Haven't been that careless since my much younger years," he murmurs, his mouth close to my ear. "Never without a condom in the past twenty-odd years. Last physical was a year ago but I'll happily get tested to put your mind at ease."

Jesus. He's talking about STDs.

I'm thirty-five years old, never been one to sleep around, a sexually transmitted disease hadn't even occurred to me yet. I was too preoccupied with the possibility of a pregnancy.

"What about pregnancy?" I broach, turning to face him.

He looks shocked before glancing over his shoulder at the sink.

"Aren't you on the pill?"

"Wasn't for a while and just started up again last

Saturday," I admit. "I'm not sure that's long enough for it to be effective."

His face blanks as he runs an agitated hand through his wet hair.

"*Fuck!*"

His voice echoes off the tile in the confined space.

I immediately turn my back and slip out of the tub at the other end, dripping water and soap all over the floor. He doesn't try to stop me and surprisingly, that upsets me more than anything else.

The shower is still running when I pass the bathroom door a few minutes later on my way to a much-needed cup of coffee. I'm dressed in jeans and a shirt that can handle a bit of dirt for the move. I'll pack up my sparse belongings from the bedroom and bathroom when he is gone.

I'm just pouring a cup when he comes walking out, shirtless and barefoot, with his jeans hanging off his hips.

"Coffee?" I ask, turning my back as I reach for another cup.

I'm trying to be gracious when I really want to scream.

"Fee…"

"Black, right?"

"Please look at me, babe."

I set the coffee pot back, steel myself, and turn around.

I can handle this. I'm thirty-five, I can handle anything, and I don't need anyone.

The words run like a mantra through my head as I try to look him in the eye without flinching, bracing myself for what's to come.

Because despite the fact we are fresh out of the gate, are still getting to know each other, and this would be horrible timing, part of me hopes.

When Kelsey was expecting Finn, I started hearing the occasional faint ticking of my own biological clock. Pregnancy was nowhere in my immediate plans, but if I turn out to be I'd consider it a welcome—albeit untimely—surprise, and nothing Tse may have to say is going to change that.

"We'll deal."

It takes me a second to process what he's saying.

"We'll…what?"

His hands land heavy on my shoulders.

"Whatever happens, we'll deal with it."

"I'm not getting rid of it," I snap, shaking my head.

"Wouldn't ask you to," he responds instantly. "I'm not gonna lie though, never saw that in my future. But then again, it's not the first time my life's taken an unexpected turn." He cups my face in his hands. "And so far I'm not complaining." He brushes his thumbs under my eyes, clearing tears I wasn't aware I was crying. "So, my beautiful Fee, whatever happens, we'll deal. Yeah?"

I nod, my voice stuck behind the lump in my throat.

"Yeah," I finally manage, sounding as raw as I feel.

TSE

I THINK I'M still in a state of shock.

Christ.

When you come with a background like mine, the

possibility of becoming a parent is not exactly at the forefront of your mind. If anything, my kind of childhood is an automatic deterrent for procreation.

I'm probably the least equipped for parenting. Oh, I've seen my brothers take to it like fish to water—most of them no younger than I am—but now the possibility exists, I just can't see myself in that role.

Still, I meant what I said to Sophia: we'll deal. That's one thing I *do* know, if she ends up pregnant, there is no way I will abandon her or our child. By God, I'll do everything I can to be a better parent than the ones I had.

"I think the truck is here," Sophia calls from the sliding door.

We got here a few hours ago. I ended up grabbing one of the club's trucks—mine still has all my tools in the back—and easily hauled her stuff here in two loads. In addition to her things from the apartment, she also had some boxes stored in Sandra's garage. Including a new bed, which we put together earlier.

I left her to unpack her stuff and went outside to split some of the wood I saw stacked against the side of the house. It's summer and not likely she'll need the wood-burning stove this time of year, but I'm thinking there's a good spot to build a nice firepit right off the deck.

It's a nice place, exposed beams, big windows, great views, new deck, but it's missing a grill, which I'm planning to pick up tomorrow when she's back at work.

Instead of going through the house, I head around the side just as the large truck is backing down the driveway.

Two guys climb down; the one with the clipboard

coming straight for me while the other opens the swing doors.

"Mr. Vieira?"

I look over at Sophia, who folds her arms over her chest, and I can almost hear her foot tapping.

"Not me. But Ms. Vieira is standing right there."

I point at Sophia, whose eyes are shooting darts by now, and the guy moves a little hesitantly in her direction. I have a hard time not laughing at his expense. The burly mover has the good sense to apologize right off the bat. Always a good idea.

When it looks like they've made their peace and the guy with the clipboard—his name turns out to be Bert— joins his partner at the back of the truck, I walk up to Sophia.

"Where do you want me?"

"I thought as the stuff comes off the truck, I'd tell them where it goes, if you could point them in the right direction inside?"

"Sure thing."

I start moving to the front door when she calls out.

"Hey, Tse? Thanks."

"Any time, Fee."

It doesn't take long for the guys to unload the truck before we're alone again. This time with furniture and moving boxes all over the place. What takes a lot longer is arranging the furniture to Sophia's liking. Not that she has a lot, but she's apparently very particular about the placement. She says the room needs to have a good 'flow,' whatever that means.

I swear I've lugged this massive couch all over the large open space until she finally decrees the first spot we had it in was best. The pattern is repeated for every piece of furniture I put my hands on, and by the time she's settled on the right spot for the dining table, my muscles are burning. I need a break.

"Beer?"

I had the foresight to grab a few six-packs, while Sophia picked up some groceries, and I could really use one now.

"I think I'll have a water, please."

I grab both from the fridge and hand Sophia her bottle. Then I take her free hand and lead her to the sliding doors.

"I was just gonna finish—"

"Let's take a break, we've been at it all day. Your bed is made, your food is in the fridge, there's nothing that can't wait for another day. Besides, we need to take in that beautiful view out there before the sun is completely gone."

"All right."

We sit down in the Adirondack chairs that came with the house.

The first thing I notice is the fresh mountain air and the absolute quiet. No fumes from Brick's shop, no noise from the busy clubhouse. Nothing but a fucking great mountain view and a sense of peace.

Reaching for Sophia's hand, I link my fingers with hers.

"It's so pretty," she whispers.

"It is." I point at the spot off the deck. "I think that's

where the firepit should go. You could light a fire after the sun is down and the night chill sets in."

"Yeah, I'd like that."

She sounds a little melancholy and I glance over. Lifting her hand, I press a kiss to her knuckles.

"What's on your mind?"

She shakes her head, keeping her eyes focused on the view.

"Kelsey loved the mountains. She would've loved this house; she talked about raising Finn somewhere away from the city. I wish she…"

Her voice trails off and I watch her swallow.

"Hey." I give her fingers a squeeze. "I'm sure she'd be happy to know Finn is loved and will have a chance to experience the kind of life she wanted for him, both with Brick and Lisa, and here with you."

"Yeah. I miss her, you know? So many times today I wished I could call her, talk to her, get her advice. A few times I even reached for my phone."

Pretty sure we're talking about more than the new house now, and I get the need for a friend right now.

"What about your sister?" I suggest carefully.

"She's busy with her family. I'll talk to her tomorrow morning."

She yawns deeply, covering her mouth with her free hand.

"Tired?"

"A little," she admits with a weak little smile.

"Maybe I should—"

Her fingers curl around mine, holding tight.

"Please stay."

I lean over the armrest and curve my hand around the back of her neck, pulling her within kissing distance.

"I meant to say; maybe I should run out and pick us up a pizza. I fully plan to stay the night."

Then I kiss her softly.

What I don't tell her is I'd already thrown a change of clothes in the truck when I picked it up at the clubhouse. I'd feel much better leaving her here alone if she had a dog. Actually, that's a lie, I'd feel much better sleeping in her bed every night, but I recognize that may not always be possible—or welcome for that matter—so a dog will have to do.

I have all of tomorrow morning to convince her.

13

SOPHIA

"I FUCKIN' LOVE your new bed."

I roll over to find Tse awake, head resting in his hand, and his sleepy eyes on me.

"Yeah?"

The smile is automatic, despite spending the past ten minutes since I woke up worrying. Somehow one look at the sleep creases in his face, and the beard and hair going in every direction, blows the worries right out of my head.

He's been awesome. Yesterday I probably wasn't the most fun person to be around, but you wouldn't have been able to tell from the way he treated me.

I don't like the feeling of not having a handle on my life and frankly, yesterday morning I felt like the rug got pulled out from under me. My knee-jerk response to that was to behave like a dictator, keeping a tight hold on everything around me. The poor guy spent the whole afternoon moving furniture from one spot to the next until I deemed it perfect. To my surprise he didn't complain once, although I'm sure it cost him.

"Scores better than the rickety old double I have in my room at the club."

He rolls on his back and scoots up so he's leaning his head and shoulders against the simple wooden headboard.

"That's why I got rid of my old bed in Denver. My parents bought it for me when I went to college, and I hung on to it all those years. Never even replaced the mattress. I figured moving to a new place was as good a time as any to invest in a new bed."

"Was a good buy. I slept like a log. How about you?"

He reaches for me and I willingly snuggle up to him, my head on his chest.

"I actually did too. More than I thought I would anyway."

His fingers play with the short hair behind my ear and I snuggle in deeper, enjoying the rise and fall of his chest. He feels like an anchor, solid and strong enough to keep me afloat should I need it.

"When will we know?"

The question is matter-of-fact and requires no clarification.

"Maybe two weeks." I never thought I'd be discussing my periods with a tattooed, rough-looking biker, but then I never thought I'd end up in a relationship with one either, and here I am. "That's when I'm supposed to get my next period."

"Okay, two weeks," he repeats, cool as a cucumber.

Then he suddenly rolls me on my back and lands on top, hands planted on either side of me.

"Ever hear the expression: don't borrow trouble?"

"Yes," I respond a little breathless.

"We're gonna deal with whatever the outcome is, but until we know, no amount of fretting or worrying is going to change anything."

"Easy for you to say," I grumble.

"No, it isn't. I told you, I'm in this with you. If you need to talk, talk to me, but don't spend the next two weeks tied in knots. It's not healthy."

He's right, it isn't healthy, but it's not so easy to shut down a mind used to working nonstop. I appreciate the offer to talk things through with him, but he's a big part of what's been on my mind.

I need to talk to my sister.

"I'll try." Knowing myself well, that's as much of a promise I'm able to make.

A corner of his mouth lifts in a lopsided smile before he lowers it to mine. His kiss is gentle, and like last night when he kissed me goodnight and simply held me, I don't feel any pressure. It's like he knows I need some time. Surprising, since I'm pretty sure his testosterone levels far outmeasure most other men's.

"I'm gonna grab a quick shower. Get some coffee going. Why don't you try and catch a few more winks?"

Another brush of his lips and he rolls off me, swinging his legs over the side and giving me a perfect view of the artwork on his back.

"Tse?" I reach out and trace the broken chain. "Do these have a special meaning?"

I know he had a troubled childhood and I wonder if the question is too personal when he stays silent. I withdraw my hand and am about to apologize for intruding when he speaks up.

"Which one?"

Encouraged, I touch his back and run them over the tattoo, feeling a ridge under my fingers.

"This one. The chain."

"Freedom," he answers right away. "First tattoo I got. Ouray took me to a friend of his, a tattoo artist in Cortez. I'd just turned seventeen."

I sit up and lean closer, now able to see the long scar the ink conceals. I press my lips against his skin.

"They hurt you. Your last family."

He doesn't answer, which in itself is answer enough.

I move on to the next one.

"And the compass?"

"For guidance, direction. That's what the club gave me." There's no hesitation this time. "The arrow stands for a path to follow. I got that one when I was officially made a club prospect."

"What about the feather?"

"It represents courage. My brothers got that for me when I patched in."

I notice now that the four smaller items appear a little

more faded than the large bird that spans his back. I use the fingers on both hands to measure its full width.

"I thought this would've been there first, but you got this last, didn't you?"

He looks over his shoulder at me, his eyes smiling.

"Yeah. I'd started covering my arms and chest with shit I liked the look of, but my back was reserved for things that had meaning, that I was proud of. Then twelve years ago, when the club had changed its direction, I had the Thunderbird added."

"And it means?"

"Power, protection, and strength. The power to make a difference, the protection of innocence, and the strength to stay the course."

I close in behind him, wrapping my arms around his waist as I press my cheek between his shoulder blades.

"The older ones are your journey, but this last one is your destination."

What appeared at first a haphazard collection of ink; now makes all kinds of sense. His past and present connected on his back.

The protection of innocence.

However this man presents himself to the world, what he stands for—what his club stands for—runs deeper than his skin.

He covers my locked hands on his abs with his own.

"Yeah," he simply confirms.

Then he loosens my grip, gets to his feet, and I watch his naked ass walk into the bathroom. Instead of lying back down, I hop out of bed, pull on some clothes, and snag my phone from the nightstand before heading downstairs.

"What's wrong?"

It's the first thing my sister says when she answers.

I'm curled up in a chair on the deck, watching the morning fog lift from the trees in the warmth of the morning sun.

"Nothing. We always talk on Sunday morning."

"Baloney. I call you, not the other way around, and this is the second Sunday in a row you beat me to it. So I'll ask again, what's wrong?"

My sister...I don't know whether that sixth sense is something she always had or whether it developed with motherhood, but I can tell from her tone she means business. Good, because I really need to unload.

I tell her about Tse, about the trip to Moab, about the things he says, and the way he makes me feel.

When I'm sure she's already halfway in love with him from what I've described, I hit her with the rest of it.

"Pregnant?"

By the time I hear the sliding door open behind me and Tse steps out, all that's left of the long-distance tears I shared with my sister are a few wet stains on my shirt, but my heart already feels lighter.

Tse

IT WAS CLEAR she'd been crying.

I figured she was talking with her sister when I came down the stairs and saw her on the phone outside. Giving her some space, I turned to the kitchen where I was able to find the makings of a pot of coffee, and checked the fridge for breakfast food.

The coffee was passable but the eggs were rubber and I'd burned the bacon, but she'd eaten everything I piled on her plate without complaint.

I didn't ask, and she didn't volunteer, but it's safe to guess she talked about what happened yesterday. I try not to let it bother me she didn't talk to me, but I get it. If I had a sibling I might've called them too.

Instead I'm on my way to the clubhouse, where I'm hoping to catch Trunk.

I park the truck next to the shop and stick my head in when I see Brick working on a car.

"Morning."

He looks up from under the hood.

"Morning's almost over." I grin at his grumbling response. It's like he needs to get his licks in everywhere else since Lisa and the kids all have him wrapped around their little fingers. "Bedroom door's been open the past couple'a days too," he adds with a pointed look. "That girl is like a daughter to me. I find you're fuckin' around on her—"

I cut him off, my grin instantly gone.

"Hold onto your suspenders, gramps. First of all, I was with her—not that it's any of your goddamn business—and second of all, fuck you. If you'd been paying any attention last weekend you'd've seen it's not like that with her."

He turns his attention back to the engine he's working

on and I'm about to turn my back when I hear him say, "Don't want her gettin' hurt. Just lookin' out for the girl."

"My job now," I bite off. "And don't call her a girl, she's all woman."

I start walking toward the clubhouse and throw back a last glance, catching him watching after me, a grin on his face.

Asshole. I let him get under my skin.

I spend a few minutes chatting with Nosh and he directs me to Ouray's office, where I find him and Trunk in conversation.

"Come in." Ouray waves me inside. "We're talking about Ravi."

"Why? Something else happen?"

"Close the door and take a seat."

I kick the door shut but instead of sitting, I perch my ass on the edge of the large conference table.

"The boys are talking," Trunk volunteers.

"What do you mean? Talking about what?"

"Turns out for the past year Ravi has managed to get up before anyone else to take his shower."

The showers in the dorm are set up like a locker room. A bunch of showerheads and nothing but a pony wall to separate them from the lockers where the kids keep their shit.

My mind immediately goes back to the campground and Ravi's reaction when he saw there were separate shower stalls. He'd even commented on the locks. That should've been a clue and I missed it.

What was a suspicion before turns into a certainty.

"And?" I ask sharply, almost defensively.

"The other kids noticed. It apparently became something they teased him with. You know how kids are."

Yes, I can imagine. I heard most of those myself twenty-six years ago, when I first came to Arrow's Edge.

I avoid looking at Ouray because he'd remember. It was the reason he'd taken me to get a tattoo. Said we'd give my dorm mates something to look at. That's when I got my chain.

"The night Maska got hurt he wasn't sleepwalking. He and Elan got up when Ravi snuck into the shower. Followed him, wanting to give him a hard time, but then they saw scars all down his backside."

I hiss sharply, still not prepared, despite already knowing the truth. Trunk's eyes snap to Ouray, who calmly nods, even as his eyes stay focused on me.

"Ravi flew past them straight for his bed. When Maska tried to apologize, putting a hand on the kid's back, Ravi swung around with the crowbar he'd pulled from under the covers."

I lean forward, my hands on my knees, as I focus breathing in through my nose and out through my mouth. I hear Ouray continue.

"The older boys decided to pretend Maska had been sleepwalking when it happened."

"Did you have a word with them?" I direct at Ouray.

"Or two," he confirms. "Problem is, what they did is no more than boys do in a group setting. They tease, they rib each other, they initiate newbies, none of it good, but all of it fairly innocent."

"Tell that to Ravi," I snap.

"Brother," he says calmly. "There was no way for the boys to know. Heck, I was thinking back on the times I've seen him without a shirt and realized I never have."

"Me neither." This from Trunk.

That should've been another clue, even when we swam or fished while camping, the other boys would whip off their shirts, flexing their baby muscles, but never Ravi. At the time I figured it was because he's so scrawny.

"Or me," I admit.

"The moment they saw the state of his back, they could guess and they regretted it immediately," Ouray continues. "And after I talked to them, trust me, they regret it even more."

"The problem is Ravi. He won't talk. He's closing off even more than he already was, and according to Shilah, he's not sleeping," Trunk explains. "Not sure what to do if he won't talk, brother."

"First of all, get him out of the dorm. He needs to feel safe, and unless he has control he won't sleep. I bet he hasn't had a shower in the dorm since. Give him my room; he'll have his own bathroom. I'll get my shit out."

"Tse, man, we can't do that. It sets a precedent. The boys go in the dorm, that's the way it's always been," Ouray says pointedly.

He's right. That is the way it's always been. I stayed in the dorm but I wasn't alone, I had Manny—who had my back—and I had his. Besides, I was one of the oldest kids at the time.

"You know this isn't the same. Unlike me, Ravi has no one to stand up for him. No one he trusts enough."

I feel the energy in the room change and look at Trunk, who suddenly narrows his eyes on me.

"I'll be fuckin' damned," he swears. "That's why the boy's drawn to you. He senses a kindred spirit. Shee-it, brother. It all makes a fuckload more sense now."

"Don't waste your psychoanalysis on me, focus on the kid." I turn back to Ouray. "Fuck precedent. We've had kids sick stay in the clubhouse before. Ravi's no less in need of special care."

I start pacing the room while Trunk, who appears to be siding with me, convinces Ouray to let Ravi have my room.

"Where the fuck are you gonna stay?"

"I'll be fine." It'll be a good excuse for me to stay with Sophia, but my brothers don't need to know that.

"Not gonna help him form any bonds with the other kids, though," Ouray mentions. "If anything, it'll set him apart."

I don't disagree with that, but I've already thought of that.

"Ravi asked if he could work with me on Paco's house, instead of the project Brick had in mind for the kids. Let me see if I can't win his trust first."

"Are you gonna tell him about you?" Ouray asks.

"I might, if I feel it helps any. Once he's comfortable enough with me, we can ask the older two kids to come help out a day here or there. One at a time."

"That's actually not a bad idea," Trunk admits.

"Good, I'll tell Paco to bring him along in the morning."

I walk out of the office and cross the hallway to my room. The only bag I have is still at Sophia's, but I peel off the pillowcase to use for my clothes, and can get a garbage bag for whatever else I need in the short term. This'll just be temporary, at least that's the way I'll sell it to Sophia.

"You okay?"

I turn to find Trunk in the doorway.

"I'm fine. I'm good. Don't need anything."

He raises an eyebrow, which causes wrinkles all over his bald scalp.

"Actually," I change my mind. "I could do with some advice."

"Anything."

He crosses his massive arms over his chest and leans against the doorpost.

"Pregnancy. How much do you know?"

14

Tse

"Shee-it."

I'm still grinning at Trunk's reaction a couple of hours later.

He'd kicked the door to my room shut and sank down on my bed, spending the next half hour asking questions and giving me a chance to unload all my insecurities. Because as much as I'm keeping a confident front around Sophia; I'm scared shitless.

Turns out that was all I needed, the reassurances from a brother who had his own insecurities about fatherhood, as it turns out. Trunk and Jaimie have two kids now, three-year-old River from Jaimie's first marriage, and Eden, who is a year and a half and her father's daughter. Trunk was forty-six when they had her.

If Sophia turns out to be pregnant, I'll be forty-three when I become a father. The thought doesn't nearly make me as lightheaded as it did before my talk with Trunk.

I spent some time with Nosh, feeling guilty because I haven't been around much lately for our nightly chats. He said he was fine with it, more time to watch the old westerns he's become partial to in his old age. It doesn't seem that long ago he would go on runs with us, and for the longest time he ran the club's shooting range, but he handed that over to Honon.

He's become an old man since Momma died last year and that hurts to see. Where he once was the driving force of the club, now he simply hangs out there, like he's biding his time. It's sad; he deserves more but doesn't want it. I won't say Nosh was always a good man, but he certainly had a good heart.

I managed to corner Paco, explained Ravi would be taking my room at the clubhouse for now, and asked him to bring the kid to the build tomorrow. On my way out I popped into to the kitchen, drawn by the smell of good food, where I got slapped on the hand by Lisa when I tried to steal a taste of the stew she had simmering for dinner.

By the time I get to The Backyard it already has a decent dinner crowd. I don't see Sophia when I walk in, but Mack cocks his thumb over his shoulder, indicating the hallway. I find her in her office, and as usual, she's so engrossed in what she's doing it takes a minute for her to clue in I'm standing in her doorway.

"Hi."

"How are things?" I ask her, walking over to drop a quick kiss on her lips.

"Busy. I'm trying to finish up my orders for Tuesday's delivery before I get out there."

I grin down at her.

"Is that your way of telling me to get lost?"

She raises both eyebrows, bulging her eyes, and I bark out a laugh.

"Okay. I may be thick but I know when I'm not wanted. Have you eaten?"

"Mandy brought me something earlier."

She points at the empty plate on the corner of her desk and I pick it up.

"You finish up. I'll be keeping Mack company," I tell her with a wink before walking back to the bar.

"Kaga mentioned I might see quite a bit of you around here."

Lea, Kaga's wife, is by the bar waiting for a drink order.

"I swear, the older the brothers get, the more they turn into a bunch of old maids with their gossiping," I grumble to Lea's amusement.

She elbows me. "You know you're aging right along with them, right?"

"Don't remind me," I groan, picking up the beer Mack slides in front of me. A good barkeep knows what you'll have to drink before you do. "How are you enjoying working here?"

"Love it." She grins. "Especially the tips."

"Order's up."

Lea walks over to where Mack sets a few more drinks on a full tray. She easily swings it up on one hand like she's an old pro.

"Try the pulled pork tonight," she directs at me. "Almost just as good as Lisa's."

I'm about to tell Mack to put an order in for me when Ramirez comes in with his wife, who's an EMT for the fire department. He spots me and they walk over.

"Smelled the food from this kitchen but haven't had a chance to taste it yet. Figured it was time we give it a try."

"You'll be pleasantly surprised." I get up to give his wife a hug. "Looking good, as always, Blue. Still don't get what you're doing with this guy though. You could do so much better."

She shakes her head and grins.

"Let me guess; you?"

"Isn't that obvious?"

Ramirez puts his arm around Blue, pulling her to his side.

"Quit flirting with my wife. Don't you have your own woman to bother?"

Not long after, Sophia appears and shows them to a table, while I order my dinner from Mack. Lea was right, the pulled pork is good and I tell her so when she checks in with me.

From my vantage point at the bar I have a good view of the dining room, where Sophia has taken over serving drinks. Mack comes to hang out with me in between orders. He may look like he came straight from prep school, but he surprises me when he tells me about the old bike he's working on with a buddy.

I'm about to order another beer when Ramirez passes me on his way to the men's room, giving me a pointed look. I motion to Mack to get me another draft. Then get up and make my way down the hall. Ramirez is leaning against the sink, arms folded over his chest.

"It's date night. Blue would have my balls if she knew I was talking shop, but I wanted to give you a heads-up."

"About?"

"Shit's gonna go down tomorrow. Finally gathered enough intel to convince a judge to sign off on a search warrant for the house on the other side of the parking lot back there. We've been observing for a week now, noted a number of drug transactions in the area, and have been able to identify a number of key players. The one thing they have in common is that house. We suspect it's used as a distribution hub. Like a goddamn Sam's for dealers."

It's not making me feel good this is going down a hundred yards from where Sophia parks her fucking Jeep.

"No shit?"

The door opens and an older man walks in, eyeing us with suspicion before ducking into a stall.

"Dead serious," Ramirez says in a low voice. "Hope we get some answers."

We hear the toilet flush and step aside so the guy can wash his hands. I wait for the door to close behind him before I speak.

"Restaurant is closed tomorrow."

He nods. "That's why I suggested holding off until then."

"What about the attack on the cook? Has he talked to you?"

"Bernie's recuperating at his sister's place in New Mexico, but he says he doesn't remember anything. I don't believe him, though. I have a gut feeling it's linked to what's going on across the parking lot, but at this point it's nothing more than a hunch and that investigation is dead in the water."

"What about the delivery guy?" I suggest, but Ramirez shakes his head.

"Doesn't know anything, didn't see anything." He turns to the sink and washes his hands. "Better get back to Blue before she comes looking for me." He dries with a couple of hand towels and tosses them in the trash. He turns to me with his hand on the door. "Do me a favor? Wait until after we're gone to tell Sophia? I don't want this conversation to get back to my wife. That would ruin the plans I have for tonight."

"More than I needed to know," I grumble, as he opens the door and slips out.

I give him a few beats before I walk out as well, but as I make my way to my barstool, I find Blue's eyes narrowed on me from across the restaurant.

I'm grinning as I sit at the bar, my draft waiting for me.

It would appear Ramirez is busted.

SOPHIA

I WATCH TSE walk over to the bar.

Five minutes ago I saw him slip into the men's room, moments after the detective disappeared inside. I'm not an idiot, I'm sure they were discussing something they don't want me to know, but I'll be damned if I let either of them leave me out of the loop. This restaurant is my responsibility and I'm not a wilting flower. If there is new information, I should be the first one to know.

Unfortunately, we are at the peak of the dinner rush and I'm stuck at the cash register, doing tallies for the tables getting ready to check out. When we have half the tables cleared off—including Ramirez and his wife's—and I'm about to have a word with Tse, a group of twelve walks in, keeping both Lea and me busy for the next hour and a half. By the time they leave it's close to nine, time for the kitchen to close. Other than a few drinking stragglers Lea and Mack can handle, the dining room is empty. Except of course for Tse, who is still on his perch at the bar.

"I have to check with the kitchen and I need to run my reports, but don't think you're off the hook," I warn him.

I walk past when his arm shoots out and he grabs my wrist, pulling me back toward him. His other hand comes up to my face, and he surprises me with a hard kiss that robs me of some of the steam I've been building up.

"I like it when you get feisty on me," he mumbles, his eyes full of humor. "Go do your thing. I'll fess up after."

"You'd better."

When I stick my head in the kitchen, Chris is just on his way out.

"Busy night."

"Yes. I'm running low on these." He hands me a list with nonperishables. "If this volume is the new normal, we're going to need to adjust the standing orders as well."

He's talking about our fresh deliveries.

"Fair enough. Let's talk next week."

He nods and darts out without a goodbye for Lauren and Mandy, both of whom are left to scrub the kitchen. Despite his arrogant personality, I like Chris. From a professional perspective at least. I wouldn't invite the man to a social gathering but I sure like working with him. He's on the ball, organized, reliable, and a damn fine chef. If he didn't have such a tight rein on the kitchen, my job would be a lot more challenging.

I sit down at my desk and pull our bookkeeping software up on my computer. Most of our transactions are debit or credit card, but there are still some who pay cash. Since I wasn't here yesterday—I normally do the week's deposit Saturdays—I'll be making a bank deposit as well tonight. I grab the cash we keep in the safe in my office and sort the bills before stuffing them in a pouch along with the deposit slip. Next are the reports, which take a while to print off.

I'm just filing the print copies in the filing cabinet when Lauren and Mandy walk past, giving me a wave.

"Night!"

"See you next week," I call after them.

Lea is the next one to leave, and when I walk into the restaurant Mack is locking the front door.

"We ready?"

Tse gets up from his seat, rubbing his ass with both hands.

"Jesus, my ass is sore."

"Right now I can't find it in me to sympathize."

The snark is more to remind myself I still have a bone to pick with him than anything else, but it has Mack throw up his hands defensively.

"Leave me out of it, please. I just work here," he says, flicking off the lights before he heads for the back door.

Tse is grinning as he drapes an arm around my shoulders.

"No offers to make it better?" he teases.

"Don't answer that!" Mack yells from in front of us, right before he darts outside.

I stop outside my office. "I need to grab my purse."

"I've got it."

Tse walks in, finds my bag on top of the credenza behind my desk, flicks off the desk lamp, and pulls the door shut behind him, before following me outside.

"So…" he drawls. "Are you? Gonna make it better?"

I roll my eyes at him and turn the deadbolt on the back door.

"Why don't you tell me first what you and Ramirez were discussing in the men's room?"

"Let's get home first. There are a few things I need to tell you about."

I try not to let the fact he calls my place home affect me; I don't want to admit I like the sound of it.

"Fine."

I look around the parking lot, but all I see is my Jeep

and Mack's taillights.

"Where's the bike?"

"I've got the truck, it's parked out front. Parking lot was pretty full when I got here."

He walks me to the Jeep, waits until I'm behind the wheel, tells me he'll catch up, and then jogs around the building to the front.

I start the Jeep and pull out of my spot. It's not until I turn onto Main Avenue I remember the deposit pouch on my desk. *Shit.* I can see Tse's truck, with him behind the wheel so I drive by and hold up one finger, indicating for him to wait a minute. Then I turn into the narrow alley on the other side of the restaurant, leading to the rear parking lot, and notice a car parked halfway down, the front of the car pointing in my direction.

The sky-blue Honda is Mandy's car and I can see the trunk is open but I don't see her.

I pull up, get out of the vehicle, and walk to the rear of the Civic just as Mandy appears from behind, the large tote she always carries with her in her hands. She stops in her tracks when she spots me.

"What's going on?"

She covers her shock with a smile but it doesn't reach her eyes, and I'm suddenly uncomfortable.

"My car is acting up. I was hoping someone would still be here."

I don't believe it for a second. Her eyes dart over my shoulder, just as I hear the crunch of a footstep right behind me. Before I can look behind me, something hits the back of my head and I yelp, toppling forward and landing facedown in the gravel.

I have the presence of mind to keep my eyes closed and stay perfectly still.

"Gimme the bag," I hear a man's voice. Then I hear rustling and the car trunk close. "Now get the fuck out of here."

The door slams shut; the engine starts, and gravel sprays up from the tires as the car backs out of the alley. I almost cry out when the guy kicks me in the back but manage to stay as still as possible. Then I hear Tse's voice.

"Hey, you fucking son of a bitch!"

15

Tse

"I'M FINE."

My fucking heart stopped when I saw her Jeep halfway down the alley, door open. I noticed a man haul back and kick at something on the ground, realizing too late it was a person.

The guy took off through the trees and I probably should've gone after him but I was more concerned with Sophia, who was pushing herself up into a sitting position by the time I got to her.

"Like hell you are," I growl, as I probe her head with my fingers, looking for injury. "You have a bump on your head and look at your hands, they're bleeding."

"Trust me." She brushes my hands aside. "I'm fine. Go after him."

I only half trust her at her word, but I scramble to my feet.

"Wait," she calls out when I start to move. "I need your phone. Mine's in the car."

I toss her my phone and haul off in the direction I saw the guy run. I dart through the trees where I saw him disappear and end up in an alley between two houses. These aren't in much better shape than the one Ramirez has had his eye on.

When I hit the road on the other side I look in both directions, hoping to catch a glimpse of the guy. There's no movement on either end, but when I look toward the river, I see movement on the far side of the railroad tracks. I immediately take off across the road and through the brush. When I get to the other side of the tracks I stop, looking and listening for any signs of movement, but all I hear is sirens in the distance.

By the time I get back to the alley behind the restaurant, the cops are already on scene.

"So much for date night."

Ramirez shakes his head and grins at my comment.

"You don't even wanna know."

Probably not.

Flashlight beams bounce through the trees and between the houses bordering the parking lot, where officers are looking for evidence and knocking on doors.

Detective Jay VanDyken got here first and took

Sophia's statement. He's already gone again, trying to track down the employee Sophia mentioned. From what I overheard, the woman must've known the guy who knocked Sophia down.

I look up and see her sitting on the gurney in the back of the ambulance, getting treated for the cuts and scrapes on her hands where she tried to brace her fall. She catches my glance and smiles reassuringly.

"We're likely going to execute our search warrant as soon as we're done here," Ramirez offers. "The police presence will spook whoever is dealing from there, and I don't wanna give them a chance to clear out. I've got someone keeping an eye on the place."

"Gonna be a long night then."

"Sure is, because after that I'd like to get into the restaurant as well."

"The restaurant?"

He shrugs. "Kitchen specifically. Two violent incidents involving kitchen staff within weeks of each other, drug deals going on in the restaurant's backyard, hard to ignore the coincidence, my friend."

I hate to admit he's got a point and it has me even more pissed. It was just a few years ago Arrow's Edge properties were targeted in an effort to force the club back into the weapons trade. It depleted most of the club's reserves to keep our businesses up and running. It's taken a lot to build both the funds as well as the public's confidence back up, and the Backyard Edge was supposed to put us ahead.

"It ain't us."

"Not saying it is," Ramirez replies immediately. "Otherwise, I wouldn't have alerted you, but I have to get in there, and I'd like to do that with club permission. Don't want to wait around for a warrant and end up having to do a search during daylight or operating hours."

It's not exactly a threat, but I glare at him anyway.

"Gonna have to call Ouray."

"Do it. Because as soon as we're done that place," he jerks his head in the direction of the house, "I wanna tackle the Backyard Edge. The sooner we're in and out of the place the better it is."

I give him a curt nod, glance over at Sophia—who is now sitting on the step at the rear of the rig sipping from a bottle of water—and pull out my phone.

"Fuck."

I hear Luna's voice in the background calming her husband down. Probably the only person who can when Ouray is pissed, and he is *pissed*.

"I'm on my way," he barks.

"It's fine. I'll stay."

"You've gotta take Sophia home."

I let out a humorless laugh. "Not so sure she'll wanna leave."

"Then don't make it a goddamn option."

I hear some rustling and then Luna's voice comes on.

"Tse? What my husband is attempting to convey—and is clearly failing at—is it's safer for Sophia not to be around. If this turns out to be some kind of setup like we've dealt with before, we don't want it to touch her."

"Gotcha. I'll see if I can get her out of here."

"That'd be good, we're on our way. And, Tse? Keep your eyes open, because if it turns out the club is a target, then so are each of its members."

"I hear you."

I hang up and turn back to Ramirez when I catch sight of a security camera, it's pointed away from the alley toward the parking lot.

"Ouray and Luna are incoming. Want me to get Sophia out of here."

He nods in understanding. "Probably best."

I point at the camera.

"Those are on a forty-eight-hour loop, but Paco has it set up so it downloads the feed on a server before it overwrites. You need access, Ouray can give him a call."

"Will do. Go, get her home, I'll be in touch."

I give him a mock salute and walk over to the ambulance.

According to the EMT, Sophia is good to go home, but if she develops a headache, blurry vision, or any other symptoms of a possible concussion, he wants her to call her doctor.

"He already told me that," Sophia snips when we walk to her Jeep. "You could've just asked me."

I open the passenger side door and lift her in, ignoring her grumbles. Then I lean in the door.

"I asked him, because I suspect even if things turned out more serious, you'd still be telling me you're fine."

She opens her mouth to protest but snaps it shut again, averting her eyes. I chuckle softly as I clip in her seat belt and close the door.

"Wait," she says when I climb behind the wheel. "What about your truck?"

"Wouldn't start. That's why it took me a while to come after you on foot. I'll get Brick to tow it up to the shop first thing tomorrow. Was waiting for that to happen. I've had that truck for near twenty years and even then it was old. Hanging together with duct tape and twist ties by now."

Probably time to go looking for a new truck. Never felt the need before. I figured as long as it got me from A to B it was fine. But now I feel I need to maybe invest in something a bit more solid. More reliable.

I glance over at Sophia, who covers a yawn. I put a hand on her knee.

"Tired, baby?"

She nods and turns those pretty eyes my way.

"Take me home."

I can do that.

SOPHIA

"WEREN'T YOU SUPPOSED to work?"

Tse looks up from the dishes he volunteered for after breakfast.

I had a quick shower before I rolled into bed last night and didn't even notice when Tse joined me at some point. I was awake first, feeling a little banged up, but that got better when I started moving around. I let him sleep a little longer while I went down to get coffee and breakfast going.

"Talked to Paco after you went to bed. He knows I'm starting a little later." He dries his hands and hangs up the towel before turning, leaning a hip against the counter. "A few things we didn't get a chance to discuss last night," he clarifies.

Something in the way he said that instantly has me on the defensive.

"Like?"

"Where do I start," he mocks. "Like the fact you took off down an alley where you *know* there's been drug traffic, and without backup. But that's not even the worst part of it: you got out of your vehicle. There's a car parked in an alley where drug deals take place that are under investigation by the police, after one of your employees was attacked *inside* your restaurant, and what do you do?"

"It was Mandy's car, and I thought something was wrong with it!" I argue loudly, but it's like I never spoke.

"You get out of your goddamned vehicle. That's what you do. No protection, not even your fucking phone on you, but you get out of the Jeep and walk right on over."

The sarcasm is thick and I'm pissed he's talking to me like a three-year-old, but then I hear what he's saying and it's embarrassing. I'm embarrassed. Because he's right, it was a stupid move and I wasn't thinking.

"Scared the fuck out of me, Fee. Seeing you lying there, that fucker kicking you and you not moving, 'bout stopped my heart. You were on my watch, if something had happened to you…"

His words drift off and I'm already on my feet, rushing

up to him. Clearly this has been simmering under the surface since it happened.

"I'm fine."

"You were fucking knocked to the ground, Fee" he persists, his jaw clenched and his eyes angry on me.

I put my hands on his chest where his heart beats a staccato. He's worked up all right.

"I was stupid. I wasn't thinking, you're right. But I'm okay."

His lungs expand under my palms as he takes a deep breath in before blowing it out audibly. Then he covers my hands with his own.

"Almost gave me heart attack."

"I know and I'm sorry."

"Good. Remember that, 'cause you're probably gonna get pissed again when I tell you what's on the agenda this morning."

"What?"

"Animal shelter. We're gonna get you a dog. Today."

"Wait a minute."

I try to pull my hands back but he has a firm hold on them.

"No. Not waiting. Not after last night. You're getting a dog, and you're getting a good security system."

"Now hold on."

I shake my head. Things are moving too fast and I'm not getting a chance to process. Tse takes my face in his hands and the intensity in his eyes has the hair stand up on my arms.

"The cops planned a raid on the empty house behind

the parking lot for today. That's what Ramirez told me in the men's room. But given what happened last night, they moved that search up. He was also gonna search the restaurant."

I grab onto his wrists, my eyes wide with shock.

"Why?"

"Because he'd be a shit detective if he brushed this off as just a coincidence, babe. When we left last night, Ouray was on his way with Luna. Cops are looking for Mandy. I don't know what the fuck is going on, but with this many unknowns, we're not taking any chances."

"Okay."

I'm stubborn but I'm not stupid. I can see the concern in his eyes and I'm sure by now there's fear in mine.

In a softer tone he continues.

"Paco's on his way here. He's gonna install a security system and you and me are going to the pound. Otherwise, I'll be forced to shackle myself to you, but I'm afraid that would sour our relationship."

His lips brush lightly over my partially opened ones.

"And I'd really hate for that to happen…"

He kisses me again, this time a little deeper, and I lift my arms up and around his neck. One of his hands fists in my hair, while the other grabs a handful of my ass. Suddenly my blood is pumping for a different reason altogether.

I moan into his throat, rubbing my breasts against him, ready to climb him like a tree.

"Truck," he mumbles against my mouth as I try to slip a hand under his shirt. "Fee, baby, truck coming."

I'm not sure if it's embarrassment or lust that has my cheeks burn, but I know I'm probably beet red when Tse opens the door to Paco.

"Morning," I mumble when he steps into the kitchen.

Paco just grins and does that chin lifting thing these guys all seem to have in their repertoire. I tried it once in front of the mirror and I look like I'm having a seizure, so I just stick to words or waves.

"Ravi, you remember Sophia?"

I look beyond Paco, where Tse is standing with his hand on the shoulder of a lanky teenager. I remember seeing the kid around the clubhouse. He's a quiet one.

"Hey, Ravi," I greet him and get a barely audible, "Hey," in return.

But when moments later Tse announces we're heading to the animal shelter to look at dogs, I see the kid's eyes light up.

"Ravi, wanna come? Help me pick out a dog?"

He tries to look aloof but the way his shoulders straighten and his teeth bite into his lips, I can tell he wants to.

"He's supposed to be helping Paco," Tse points out, and I shoot him bug eyes.

"Helping Paco or helping me, what's the difference?"

Tse stares at me hard before turning to the boy.

"Would you mind?"

"Sure," Ravi says with a shrug, making it sound like it's all the same to him.

But it isn't, and I know it isn't, because half an hour later when I see him crouch down in front of the ugliest dog I've ever seen—talking softly as he scratches the creature under his chin—the expression on his face is one of pure happiness.

"Good call, baby," Tse whispers in my ear, as he drapes an arm over my shoulder.

"So what do you think?" I ask Ravi, as I step closer and let the mastiff mix sniff my hand.

In all honesty, whenever I thought about getting a dog, I envision something cute and fluffy, not the big brown scarred face in front of me. Half of one of his ears is missing, the jowl on the same side of his face looks like it was patched together, and a thick rope of scar tissue runs from his flank down his back leg.

"What's his name?" I ask the woman who is showing us around.

"He didn't have one when he was brought in, but we've been calling him Van, for Van Gogh."

She points at his missing ear. Makes sense.

The dog leisurely licks my hand as the woman continues.

"He listens to it well enough. Seems to be well-trained and is good with the other animals, even though we suspect he may have been used in dog fights. The vet guesses him to be about five years old and other than the obvious scars, he appears to be in good health."

"I like him."

I look down at Ravi in surprise. It's the first thing he's said since he got in the back of my Jeep earlier.

"What do you think, Fee?"

I glance over at Tse and then back at the dog. He's watching me with woeful brown eyes.

"I like him too."

16

SOPHIA

I DON'T RECOGNIZE the SUV parked beside Paco's truck in the driveway when we pull in.

"That's Ouray," Tse announces.

While we get out of my Jeep—Ravi holds on to Van's leash—I wonder what he's doing here. We've been gone a couple of hours, stopping in at Walmart to grab all I would need for the dog and a few groceries, before returning to the animal shelter to pick up Van. He reacted as if he'd already adopted us, with full-body wagging in lieu of a nonexistent tail and enthusiastic licks.

He hopped right onto the back seat, sitting up straight with his nose pressed through the small crack I rolled the window down to. He looked almost happy, insofar as a dog can look happy. Ravi sat beside him, putting his hand on the dog's back, and kept it there for the trip back to my place.

I have a feeling I'll be seeing more of the boy.

"Ravi, keep a hold of him for now, okay?"

I'm not sure how Van is going to react to the two men somewhere in my house.

"Sure."

Tse walks ahead, opens the door, and I follow him in with Ravi and the dog on my heels.

"Whoa, what is that?"

Paco is standing underneath the stairs by the open electrical panel. I can see Ouray outside on the deck, his phone by his ear.

It's weird having these guys appearing to be at ease in my house. My guess is that's what life would be like if Tse lived here too, his brothers automatically feeling at home. Come to think of it, he's spent as much time here as I have this weekend. Stranger yet is the fact I haven't even tried to claim this place as my own.

"A dog," Ravi answers innocently, and something about that twists in my heart.

"His name is Van Gogh," I provide.

"He friendly?" Paco wants to know, approaching slowly.

"Seems to be."

Proving me right, Van sticks out his nose and his butt starts wagging when Paco scratches his head.

"Damn, but he's ugly."

"He's not ugly, he's different, that's all," Ravi blurts out angrily, and I watch Paco's expression soften.

"Yeah, bud, you're right."

I'm about to tell Ravi to take off his leash when the dog's head snaps around, and he growls deep in his throat as the sliding door opens and Ouray steps inside.

"It's all good, boy," Tse rumbles, and the dog's single ear twitches at the sound of his deep voice. "Give me the leash, Ravi."

Ouray stopped inside the door and waits for Tse to walk toward him; Van's head low between his shoulders as he tentatively follows.

"He's a friend. Friend," he repeats as the dog approaches, sniffing Ouray's hands he keeps by his side.

Ouray doesn't move until Van nudges a hand with his nose, asking for a scratch.

"Good choice," Ouray comments, his eyes on me. "No one's gonna walk in here uninvited."

Tse asks Ravi to take Van outside, but keep him on the leash for now. After he closes the door behind the boy, he walks up and pulls me close, wrapping an arm around me before turning to Ouray, suddenly all business.

"What's going on?"

Instead of looking at Tse, Ouray looks at me.

"Cops found thirty-five thousand in cash in the storage room."

"What?"

I about launch myself forward, but Tse tightens his hold on me.

"Hidden in large denomination bills under false bottoms in the empty produce boxes. And that's not all," he adds. "They also found a bag containing fentanyl and meth in the house backing up to our property. It looked like the one you told Ramirez Mandy was carrying. The house also wasn't as empty as it looked from the outside. They surprised a couple of young guys crashed there with loaded weapons. Took 'em into custody. Luna ended up calling in her crew. She's still on the scene, the FBI is stepping in."

I sink down on the couch and drop my head in my hands. All that money in my kitchen? Holy shit.

"I don't get it," I mumble.

"I do," Tse responds. "Wouldn't be the first time produce was used as a cover to transport illegal drugs, and it's not a surprise the FBI is taking over. Drugs are likely shipped in with the produce. They used the Backyard as cover for the distribution. Next delivery they pick up the empty boxes," he emphasizes his words with air quotes, "and the money hidden inside."

"Looks like it," Ouray agrees with Tse before turning his attention to me. "What do you know about Mandy Roberts?"

I can feel the blood drain from my face. I hired her. I gave her the keys to the restaurant when she took over for Bernie. I was so relieved at the time I didn't think twice.

"She's a friend of Bernie's. I needed a replacement for a waitress, and he said he knew someone with experience he'd worked with at his previous restaurant. She worked out great. Then when Bernie got injured, she offered to help out in the kitchen. She did a good job there too. I didn't know—" I'm rambling but I can't seem to stop myself when Tse does it for me.

"Nobody's blaming you for anything, Fee," he says, and I notice him exchanging a meaningful look with Ouray.

I shake my head. I can't quite believe it, but then I remember that weird incident last week with the delivery guy. I sit up straight.

"That's why the guy was an asshole." Ouray and Tse both throw me confused looks. "Last week," I continue. "Uh, Tuesday morning. I went in early and was alone at the restaurant when the truck showed up maybe ten or fifteen minutes early. They're supposed to be there after ten, but I remember it was earlier because Mandy wasn't in yet. The guy was weird when he saw me. Asked where Mandy was." I pause, recollecting the incident and my eyes drift out the sliding doors where Ravi is running around, the dog bounding at his heels. "He wouldn't unload," I remember, looking up at Ouray. "He was moving around stuff in the back of his truck to kill time, but he wouldn't unload until Mandy got there a few minutes later."

"You figure Mandy took over more than just kitchen duties from Bernie?" Tse asks Ouray, who shrugs.

"Could well be. Maybe he got caught with his hand in the cookie jar and the attack on him was punishment?"

"Bernie?" I can't wrap my head around the jovial sous-chef being involved in anything as sinister as drug dealing. I don't get a chance to say more because Ravi walks in with Van.

The dog instantly moves to my side, sits down at

my feet, and tilts his head back for scratches. I readily comply, the dog's presence making me feel a little more composed.

Tse looks down at me, his forehead furrowed, and his lips set in a hard line, before turning to Paco.

"How's that alarm system coming along?"

Okay. No.

I'm still freaked way the hell out.

TSE

I WATCH PACO drive off with a reluctant Ravi in the passenger seat.

The kid really took to the dog and, almost by association, to Sophia, and wasn't ready to leave. Luna just called Ouray though, giving him a heads-up that she and Ramirez and Luna's boss, Damian Gomez, are on their way here.

I had a quiet word with Paco and he agreed to take Ravi with him to the build, but first quickly showed me how to set the alarm. He said he could come back for a couple of hours tomorrow to add a few features, including a camera aimed at the driveway.

I'm about to push the door shut when a dark SUV turns into the driveway. I'm on alert until it's halfway to the house and I recognize Gomez behind the wheel and Luna beside him in the passenger seat.

Waiting for them, I step aside and wave them in. The smell of the fresh coffee Sophia was putting on permeates the air. I have a feeling it'll be a long fucking day.

"ABSOLUTELY FUCKING NOT."

I glare at Gomez, who calmly stares back.

"It's perfectly safe."

"Like hell it is. You're putting a target on the restaurant, and on Sophia."

Gomez and Luna just finished outlining a plan of action and it doesn't sit well with me.

Mandy Roberts was picked up and is singing like a canary. Sounds like she's not necessarily a hardened criminal but participated in the scheme under pressure. The setup was simple, but ensured the actual supplier never interacted with the dealers. That was first Bernie and then Mandy's job, leaving only the two of them exposed. Something goes wrong, there's only one person to take care of.

Gomez suggested that's what probably happened to Bernie. He may have ripped off one of the dealers, who decided to punish him and take what was owed to him from that morning's delivery. It wouldn't have been the supplier; they would've taken care of business away from their distribution location.

The other guys they picked up—the ones in house behind the restaurant—only represent one dealer. According to Mandy there are more and she doesn't know who is supplying the drugs. All she claims to know is that they come in on the Clover Produce truck and she's supposed to hide the money in the empty boxes.

"It's the only way to identify the other dealers,

but more importantly, who is bringing in the drugs," Luna offers. "Bernie's sister approached Mandy in the hospital parking lot when she went to visit Bernie. Showed her pictures of her younger sister at her campus at the University of New Mexico, where she studies engineering. Told her, the sister would be safe as long as Mandy played along. She's terrified, the sister is the only family she has left."

"Bernie must have set her up." Sophia speaks for the first time since Gomez and Luna got here. She's been quietly listening, processing, and apparently thinking. "He's the one who knew her, suggested I hire her."

"That's what we figure," Gomez answers, turning his eyes on me. "And that's another reason why it's important we keep the restaurant functioning as normal. We need time to ensure her sister is safe before we make a move."

I need some air and walk to the sliding doors where Van is lying on the floor, with his front paws crossed and his chin resting on top, looking outside. The moment I open the door he darts outside but stops at some brush where he relieves himself. Then he saunters back and sits down on the deck at my feet.

"Good boy." I drop my hand to scratch his head.

I don't like this plan. I understand it, get the reasoning behind it, but I don't like it. It could be dangerous. Then again, so could disrupting the restaurant's daily operations. It's a fucking Catch-22 and either way Sophia could be hurt.

A-fucking-gain.

Behind me I hear the door open and Van twists his head to see who it is, but I already know. I can feel her. A small hand is pressed to my back.

"It'll be okay," she says in a soft voice. "Luna says they'll have nonstop surveillance on the place and an agent inside posing as waitstaff."

"I still don't like it," I grumble, turning toward her.

She puts her hands on my chest when I slide an arm around her waist. Van shoves his nose between us, whining softly.

"He's jealous." She smiles down at the dog's ugly mug. "Aren't you, boy?"

"He's sleeping downstairs."

Her brows snap together when she looks up at me.

"Says who? This is my dog, my place, my bed. If I want him—"

I tug her a little closer.

"Yes, but I'll be spending every fucking night here until this mess is over." And I may not stop then, but I don't tell her that. "He can watch over the house while I watch over you."

Immediately her eyes soften.

"I'm gonna be okay."

"Yeah, you will. I'll fucking make sure of it."

She shakes her head, steps out of my hold, and grabs my hand, pulling me to the door.

"Come on, let's hear the plans so they can get back to it. We can discuss the dog later."

"Nothing to discuss," I grumble stubbornly.

She wisely ignores me.

WE STAND IN the doorway—my arm draped loosely over her shoulders—watching Ouray's SUV pull onto the road. The only vehicle left in front of the house is Sophia's Jeep, and I realize I don't have my bike here.

It's fucking summer and I've barely looked at my bike in the past week. That's not like me. Normally I'd take it out every chance I get but since the ride to Moab, I've mostly driven around in the pickup—which is now in Brick's shop—or in Sophia's Jeep.

"Wanna go for a walk?"

"Sure."

I wait for her to grab her keys and the dog's leash, and I set the alarm.

"Ravi mentioned there's a trail back there." I point to the tree line behind the house. "Seeing as Paco's property is a mile or so down the road on the other side of the curve, I figure maybe it'll take us there. If you wanna see the progress we made?"

She grabs my hand, lacing our fingers, and starts walking.

"Absolutely. Show me the way."

I'm not sure where that came from, I don't go for walks; I go for rides. Who the fuck am I turning into? I've barely been to the clubhouse, haven't hung out at the bar, having a beer and shooting the shit with my brothers, or playing cards with the old man. Instead, I've been following Sophia around.

Me.

Nice and easy, then love 'em and leave 'em has always been my MO. My life is supposed to be all about the club, the brotherhood, with women only a very temporary distraction. Definitely no complicated entanglements but I sure am entangled now, and this one has complication written all over it.

Seems I've hooked my wagon to a woman and the fuck of it is…I like it. I like waking up in the morning and the first thing I see are those honey-brown eyes of hers. I like the smell of her lingering on my skin all day. Hell, I even like going for a damn stroll, holding hands while her dog leads the way.

I'm turning into someone I may not recognize, but I'm not complaining.

17

Sophia

IT'S BEEN STRESSFUL, the past three days.

Going into work, pretending nothing is going on, even though I feel like I'm sitting on a powder keg that could go off at any minute.

On Tuesday after the lunch rush, Mandy walked into my office, closed the door, and promptly burst into tears, rambling how sorry she was. I ensured her I understood, that if someone threatened my family, I'd do anything to keep them safe. It took me ten minutes to calm her down.

Then Wednesday afternoon our new 'employee' started. Krystal, the agent's name, is supposed to relieve me of my dining room duties for the dinner run, mostly greeting and seating. I still do lunch, which isn't nearly as busy, but this leaves me free to focus more of my time on the actual management of the restaurant. At least that's the story we're going with and no one questioned it.

Yesterday Luna called to give us an update. She said they'd managed to intercept another dealer the night before, after Mandy handed off the drugs. They were able to do it quietly, without flashing lights or public scrutiny. That was the plan, for the Bureau to slowly whittle away at the network while they tried to trace the money back to the supplier.

That was the more complicated part of the investigation. The moment they make a move against any of the players on that side of the trafficking—the driver, or Clover Produce—chances are whoever is behind this setup would find out and disappear before they can bring him down. They put surveillance on Bernie and his sister, as well as on the warehouse in Farmington. Luna explained the key now is to gather as much intel as they can, see how all the pieces fit together, and then coordinate arrests, so all of the players are taken in at the same time.

On top of all of that swirling through my head, Tse has been weird this week. I can't quite put my finger on it but he's pensive. Still attentive to me with touches and smiles, but just now I woke up again with the outline of his erection pressing against my ass, like I have for days, only to have him roll away the second I moved.

It's been almost a week since Tse touched me in any sexual way. I'm starting to wonder if he'd still be here if he didn't feel some kind of compulsion to keep me safe. I know he feels a sense of responsibility I suspect may stem from the time I got shot. Or maybe it's because I might be pregnant with his child. Maybe that's what is keeping him around.

"I can hear you thinking," he mumbles sleepily.

I can feel him rolling over on his side and I turn to face him.

"Just woolgathering."

He runs the pad of his index finger from my forehead, down the slope of my nose, and stops at my bottom lip, pulling it down a little. His eyes followed its path and are now fixated on my mouth.

"Why do I get the impression it's more than that?"

As much as I don't want to hear the answer, I ask him the question anyway.

"Tell me honestly; is this not working for you?"

He props himself up on an elbow, a frown on his forehead.

"Is what not working for me?"

"This thing between us."

The frown deepens, making him scowl, and given he's hanging over me I'm feeling a little disadvantaged. I pull myself up into a sitting position, pulling the sheet up under my chin. Van, who's taken to sleeping just inside the door to my bedroom, lifts his head.

"Explain," he growls.

"I mean, I understand. I seem to be walking under a dark cloud or something—a magnet for trouble—it would turn anyone off. I'm sure you've got—"

My ramble is cut off when I'm suddenly pulled down, Tse's weight covering me, and his eyes burning in mine.

"Be quiet."

"But—"

Then his mouth is on mine, robbing me of the ability to talk. To think.

His hands tug up on the nightshirt I'm wearing, a rough palm finding my breast, and I arch my back, chasing the connection. This is what I missed. This hunger I feel coming from him. An insatiable need to touch, no, *claim* every part of me and make it his. It's the most profound compliment I've ever been paid. Honest, raw, and so empowering. I've never felt more beautiful or desired as I do now.

His leg slips between mine and I'm not in the least embarrassed to rock my hips, rubbing myself against him shamelessly.

Our kiss is wet and wild, teeth clashing and tongues battling for domination.

My hands slide in the back of the boxer briefs he's been wearing to bed, pushing them down and digging my fingers in his muscular ass. The responding groan from deep in his chest reverberates through my body.

Then he rips his lips from mine with a second groan; this one pained, and buries his face in the crook of my neck.

"Please, Tse…" I beg, for what I'm not entirely sure, but I'm aching with need.

"Fee, baby. We've gotta stop."

It works like a bucket of ice water.

Planting my heel in the mattress, I heave him off me and escape the bed, ignoring Van who lets out a startled woof.

"Fee, dammit!"

I dive into the bathroom, locking the door before I sit down on the toilet and relieve myself. I will myself not to cry. I'm not wasting tears.

The click is faint and I don't have time to register what is happening before the door flies open, and Tse's large frame suddenly fills the small bathroom.

Suddenly I'm furious.

"Hello? I'm on the toilet!" I yell at him. "Can you not leave me with a small shred of dignity?"

"I don't give a flying fuck, and no!" he yells back.

His booming voice bounces off the tiles in the tiny space as he shoves the door shut, locking a suddenly alert Van outside. Then he folds his arms and glares at me. I glare right back until I realize I'm in a rather precarious position with my bare ass hanging over the toilet bowl.

With as much poise as I can muster given the situation, I grab a handful of toilet paper, wipe, and tug my nightshirt down as I lift off the seat and flush. Then I turn my back and run my hands under the faucet. When I turn it off and lift my eyes, I catch his reflection in the mirror. His hands are rubbing at his face, hair standing on end, and his shoulders slump forward.

He looks like a man on the edge.

"Even if I wanted to, I couldn't stay away, Fee," he says so softly it's hard to make out. "And believe me, I don't want to. Do you know how hard it's been to leave you at the restaurant in the morning and drive away, when every bone in my body wants to stay close enough to you I can hear you breathe?"

He looks up and all anger is gone from his eyes, replaced with something I can't describe any other way than desperation.

A fist squeezes all the air from my chest and a deep pressure remains right under my breastbone.

"Then why?"

TSE

WHY?

Oh, I know what she's asking. I'm just not sure I have an easy answer to give her.

The only saving grace to this whole week was coming home with Sophia at night. With the house locked up, the dog close by, and the alarm set, I could finally breathe.

Danger doesn't normally faze me—heck, I have two bullet wounds attesting to that—but it's been a very long time since I've experienced fear so acutely. Especially for someone else, or in this case, perhaps two someone elses. This constant tingle up my spine, like something dark is out there, looming.

I put my hands on her shoulders and coax her to turn around. Then I slide them to the base of her neck, the pads of my thumbs touching her rapid heartbeat.

"You have the ability to make the world around us disappear, Fee. I lose myself when I'm inside you and I can't let that happen. Not while there's a threat out there."

Her expression softens a bit but there's still a stubborn

set to her mouth.

"The doors are locked, we have an alarm, and Van, I think I'll be okay."

That right there is the fundamental difference between us. She believes she can control her safety, and I know such a thing doesn't exist. Safety is an illusion, a trap, because the moment you believe in it you become vulnerable.

I don't tell her that. She grew up in a family where her welfare was never in question. She sees evil as an anomaly, while I've learned the hard way it exists everywhere, but I'm not willing to take that sense of security from her. I prefer to shield her from that reality.

"This is the protector in me, Fee. There could be an army guarding you and I wouldn't be any different."

She snorts, averting her eyes.

"You said you could deal," I remind her gently. "It's who I am, as much as the guy addicted to your pussy is. I'm him too."

An internal struggle is visible on her face, but I simply wait her out until she finally settles on, "Okay."

I press my lips to her forehead.

"I'll get coffee on and let the dog out. You do what you need to in here."

She leans back and looks at me incredulously.

"Really? 'Cause that's what I was trying to do before you—"

My mouth swallows the rest of her words in a hard kiss before I reach for the door, grinning.

Van, who was clearly poised right outside, pushes his

way into the bathroom, checking to make sure everyone is all right.

"Come on, boy. Let's go."

Van bounds down the stairs in front of me and is already waiting by the back door while I disarm the alarm. He's a good dog; someone trained him well, although I better never bump into whomever that was because I'll shoot them on fucking sight. It's a miracle the animal is as friendly and well-behaved as he is after the start in life he's had.

He seems to have instinctively focused on Sophia and on Ravi to protect. He sits in the back seat and softly whines when we drop Sophia off at work. Then when we get to Paco's place and he spots Ravi, he takes a flying leap from the Jeep and sticks to the boy like glue.

That's been the routine this week; drop Sophia off at work, get to the build and work until about six. Take the dog home, have a shower, and by seven I'm having dinner at the Backyard, either with Sophia in her office if she's not busy, or at the bar where Mack or Emme—whoever is on that night—keeps me company.

Last Tuesday Paco hauled my tools to the work site and I transferred them to the back of Sophia's Jeep, where they have remained. Brick is on the lookout for something new for me. Or, as good as new. A truck with a crew cab and a shorter bed, still functional but also safe for transporting people, which I seem to do a lot more of these days. There's no rush, for the time being one vehicle is all we need.

By the time I pour my first cup of coffee, Van is

wolfing down his food, and I just hear the shower turn off upstairs. Since that first time I made breakfast, Sophia made me promise to let her take care of the cooking. Apparently, I make a mess and I don't need to be told my talents don't extend to the kitchen.

So she cooks and I take care of the dog and the dishes. Quite the domestic picture we paint. To my surprise, I'm more than comfortable with it.

I'm about to check my phone, which is plugged in the charger on the counter beside Sophia's, when hers starts to ring. The name Blossom appears on the screen. Not one I recognize. As far as I know her sister's name is Bianca and she has a younger brother, whose name I don't know, but I doubt it's Blossom.

I swipe the screen.

"Hello?"

It's silent on the other end until I hear a woman's muffled voice.

"Duff! A man answered her phone!"

"Who is this?"

"Well, I'll be…last time our Sophia had a man answer her phone was too long ago. It's about time. *Woohoo*!" She lets out some kind of battle cry that has me move the phone a few inches from my ear. "Good voice too. Deep, solid. I'm getting good vibes. *He's got a good voice, Duff!*"

Enough of the yelling.

"Still haven't told me who I'm talking to," I prompt gruffly, but that doesn't appear to have any impact on Blossom, or whatever the hell her name is, because she giggles.

"Ooh. Forceful. I like. It's Blossom and Sophia is the fruit of my loins," she clarifies. "Thirty-seven hours of killer labor but what a prize she was. She had a set of lungs on her, though, yelled the—"

"Uh, Blossom?" I quickly interrupt, afraid I'm going to get a detailed description of Sophia's formative years. "Let me get her for you."

I'm already heading to the stairs when she appears at the top.

"Are you kidding? I'd rather talk to you for a bit first," Blossom announces, as I watch Sophia's eyebrows lift questioningly. "What's your name? What do you do? I bet you're large. You sound large. *Duff! Sounds like our Soph snagged herself a big guy!"*

I lift the phone up at Sophia, who is halfway down the stairs, her eyes growing big when she hears her mother's voice. She runs the rest of the way and snatches the phone from my hand. Not that it makes a difference, she could put the phone on the coffee table and you could still hear Blossom through the entire house. No need to put it on speakerphone.

Leaving Sophia to deal with her mother, I grab my coffee and head outside, sitting on the steps of the deck. Van, who was sniffing around a tree in the back, spots me and comes to keep me company.

Wow.

That may well go down as the weirdest telephone conversation I've ever had. Her mother is really out there. Blossom and Duff, definitely not what I'd expected for

Sophia's parents. Weird, and clearly without boundaries, but loving all the same.

Ten minutes later Sophia comes outside, a coffee in her hand, and sits down on the step beside me. I turn my head to catch her letting out a deep sigh before putting the mug to her mouth and taking a deep swallow of the dark brew.

"So…" I prompt her when she abandons the coffee and uses both hands to give Van his good-morning rub.

Her eyes slowly find mine.

"That was my mother."

I grin at her. "Gathered as much, babe."

"She's…my parents are…oh, hell. I don't even know how to explain them," she wails, covering her face with her hands.

I lift an arm around her shoulders and tuck her close, her face burrowing in my chest. I do my best to hold back my chuckle, but I know I'm failing when her head snaps up and her eyes narrow on me.

"Are you laughing at me?"

"You've gotta admit, it is kinda funny," I point out.

"Yeah, well, you won't be laughing when they show up here on Sunday and park their new RV in the driveway."

Shit.

18

SOPHIA

"HE DIDN'T SHOW."

Mandy sticks her head around the door of my office.

I just sat down at my desk after Tse dropped me off.

"What do you mean?"

The back door opens and Mack walks by, calling out a greeting.

"Get in here," I tell Mandy, and motion for her to close the door. "We didn't get our delivery?"

"We got our delivery, but it was a different driver. Never seen this one before." She leans over the desk and whispers, "I think there's something wrong. The drugs weren't there, but he took the boxes. I'm scared."

"Sit down."

I pull my cell from my purse and dial Luna.

"I'm around the corner," Luna says as soon as she answers, without waiting for an explanation for my call. "I'll be right there."

"Okay."

She knocks a few minutes later, closes the door, and takes the free seat.

"We saw on the camera feed. Different driver. This one wasn't wearing a ball cap like the other guy; he made sure we couldn't make out his face. We actually managed to get a good look at this man. He's also shorter and stockier."

"They didn't send any drugs. Does that mean they found out?" Mandy wants to know. "He took the boxes."

"*Shit*. I need to make a call," Luna says and pulls her phone from her pocket. "Barnes, it's Roosberg. Are you on the truck? ... Good. See if you can get close on his next delivery. It's a different guy today. ... Yeah. I know. ... He's got the empties with the money; we need to know where it goes. ... Not yet. Let me know when he's back at the warehouse. ... I'll talk to Gomez but I think it's time to bring him in. ... Yeah, later."

"What now?"

"Nothing changes." Luna leans over and puts a hand on Mandy's arm. "Is it possible they suspect something? Yeah, but by the same token the regular driver could be sick or have had some kind of emergency. We don't know what's going on, but I promise we have eyes on you at all times."

"But what do I do without the drugs? I'm supposed to do an exchange tonight."

"We can come up with what you need from what is currently in the evidence room. That's not a problem. You just need to sit tight a little longer," Luna coaxes her.

There's a knock at the door and Chris sticks his head in.

"Everything okay here?"

"It's fine, Chris," I reassure him.

He looks at Mandy. "Well, in that case, are you gonna sit here fucking chitchatting all day or were you planning on doing anything productive?"

The poor girl shoots to her feet and hurries out of my office, Chris looming behind her.

"Charmer," Luna comments sourly.

"Yeah, he may be lacking in personality, but he makes the best brisket."

"Can't argue that." Luna gets up. "Look, I've gotta run. I need to talk to the boss and see if he wants to bring the driver in for questioning. One way or another, I have a feeling this is coming to a head soon, so stay vigilant."

"I will."

It takes me a few minutes after she leaves to get my head back on my job. What a way to start my workday.

Lunch is a little busier than usual, especially with the group of women who picked the Backyard Edge to celebrate one of their birthdays. I sigh a breath of relief when Krystal and Lea show up. They take over cleaning up and prepping the dining room for the dinner crowd, which promises to be substantial as well. Reservations have come in all day, and at this point, two-thirds of the restaurant is booked for tonight and about fifty percent for tomorrow.

I pop into the kitchen to see how things are there and warn them it'll be a heavy crowd tonight.

Mandy is at the prep table cutting vegetables, looking gaunt, while Lauren is stirring what smells like the restaurant's signature barbecue sauce in a large pot on the stove. The two large smokers on the far side of the kitchen are sending off mouthwatering smells, despite the large exhaust fan mounted above them.

That's where Chris makes all the magic happen. When orders start coming in, he will take whatever cut of the smoked meat he needs, slather it with the sauce Lauren is prepping, and give it a delicious crisp on the huge, hot grill beside the smokers.

But Chris isn't there.

"Where's Chris?" I ask Lauren.

"Not sure. He said he was stepping out for a minute." She cocks her thumb at the door to the storage room. "Did you need him?"

"I was just going to give you guys a heads-up, it looks like it might be a full house tonight. I have three waitstaff and the bussers, but I might call Emme in for backup so we have an extra pair of hands we can apply where needed."

"May not be a bad idea," Lauren agrees.

Because the menu is fairly straightforward—simple fare done to perfection—and because we're still building our clientele, we've been able to manage with three in the kitchen not counting the bussers. I suspect, if tonight's expected crowd becomes the norm, we'll have to look into some extra kitchen and front-end staff for the weekends.

I walk past Mandy and put a hand on her shoulder and keep my voice low.

"Hang in there."

She nods and gives me a watered-down smile. Then I poke my head into the storage room, my eyes catching on the stack of boxes I know are empty. For now. No Chris to be seen.

Heading to my office, I spot a garbage bag left by the back door. I take the opportunity to peek outside if I can see Chris.

I hear his voice coming from behind the dumpster when I open the back door, as I'm sure he hears me when I toss the bag in the bin.

"I've gotta go," he says when I walk around the dumpster and slips his phone in his pocket. "Did you need me?"

"Didn't mean to interrupt."

"I was done."

He's abrupt, which is nothing new, but his eyes look worried.

"All right, well, I just wanted to let you know we've got a lot of reservations tonight so I'm calling Emme, but if this is the new normal, we need to talk about hiring a few more bodies. Depending on how your kitchen manages of course."

He nods and starts walking around me.

"I'll let you know," he says right before he disappears inside.

A chill runs down my spine and I cast a furtive glance around the parking lot. It's late afternoon with plenty of daylight left and I don't see anything out of place, but then again, it's early yet.

I duck in my office and give Emme a call. She agrees to come in, says she has nothing better to do anyway. With that out of the way, I do a quick check of our order coming in from the butcher tomorrow morning. It might be a little light. I manage to catch my sales rep on his way out the door, and he ensures me he can up the order in time for our delivery.

I should probably put something in my stomach before the dinner rush; I've been ignoring those hunger pangs all afternoon. Or maybe it's my bladder. I haven't been since I got here this morning. I better take care of that first.

The bathroom is empty and I duck into one of the stalls. I'm just grabbing a wad of toilet paper when I hear someone come in and get into the stall beside me. I've always hated public bathrooms for that reason alone, lack of privacy. Although as of this morning, I officially don't even get privacy in my own bathroom at home.

I stand, start pulling up my pants, and turn to flush when I notice the smear of blood left on the paper I just tossed in the bowl. Immediately I check the crotch of my panties and my stomach drops.

Shit.

The word must've escaped me because I hear Lea from the stall beside mine.

"Everything okay?"

"Yes," I answer automatically before changing my mind. "No. You wouldn't happen to have a pad, would you?"

"Actually, I do in my purse. Give me a sec, I'll get it for you."

I sit back down as the lump of disappointment in my throat grows. Most women in my situation would be ecstatic to have dodged a bullet. I'm not one of them. I allowed my fantasies to run away with me and already imagined myself pregnant.

I tell myself firmly this is for the best and when Lea hands me a pair of pads underneath the door, I feel almost in control.

Except, when I open the door a few moments later and walk to the sink, I catch a glimpse of my wet face in the small mirror.

"Oh no, honey. What's wrong?" Lea asks and I let out a sob.

Tse

"VAN! COME HERE boy."

The dog lifts his head from the pile of scrap wood where he's been sniffing all afternoon—probably rodents or something—and trots toward me.

I look over at Ravi, who is helping Paco tidy up the site. We're supposed to have a few more hands tomorrow to help put down the roof decking. The exterior of the house is already sheathed, we finished that today, and it's ready for wrapping next week. After that's done, we'll have Jed's crew back to work on electrical and plumbing.

It's moving much faster than I thought it would, but the weather has been good and so far we've had no delays. I'm sure those will come once we have different contractors working on different aspects. There's a certain order in which things need to be done, and all it takes is one thing to go wrong and the entire schedule is fucked. I'm glad Jed's in charge of that; I wouldn't have the patience.

The boy seems to enjoy working with us, although it took him a while to get comfortable around Paco. He's getting pretty good with his measurements and already handles the nail gun like a pro. He wanted to use the saw as well, but I won't let him do that without Paco or me standing right there.

From what I hear, he's still avoiding the older boys, and either hangs with the young kids, or with Nosh or Lisa in the kitchen when he's at the clubhouse. A few times I tried to get him to talk, but he quickly shut down.

Then yesterday I took off my shirt on purpose and he asked me about the tattoos, so I told him the same I told Sophia. He seemed interested in their meaning and actually stared at me for a few minutes when I mentioned I got my first one to cover up my scars. I almost fell off the log I'd been sitting on when he wondered out loud what age he'd need to be to get tattooed. He didn't wait around for an answer and walked off. I didn't want to push the issue and scare him off, so I left it, hoping he'd come back to it on his own.

"Hop up, Van."

I pat the passenger seat of the Jeep, wait for him to get in, and close the door. The window is halfway down and he immediately sticks his face out when I walk over to Paco.

"What time do you start tomorrow?"

"Nine?" he suggests with a shrug. "It's the weekend, I don't think we'll get those guys outta bed any earlier.

"Fair enough," I agree. "I'll be there but I'm gonna have to run out to drive Sophia to work around eleven. I think I might leave Van at home though. Too many people around and if I'm going up on the roof…"

"I can keep an eye on him," Ravi offers, his voice cracking halfway through the sentence.

Guess he's that age. Paco and I grin at each other over the boy's head.

"You sure? Might get boring."

He nods eagerly. "I'm sure."

"All right then, I'll bring him after I drop off Sophia."

I ruffle his ink black hair, throw a wink at Paco, and head to the Jeep.

My phone rings as I pull up in front of the house. It's her.

"Hey."

"Are you home yet?"

Her voice sounds a little funny.

"Just drove up, why? Something wrong?"

I get out, let Van jump down and walk to the front door.

"I have a favor to ask. It's…uh…"

Definitely sounds off.

"Spit it out, babe."

Inside I punch the code into the keypad for the alarm.

"I need some clean clothes. Any pair of jeans is fine, they're in the bottom drawer of my dresser, and I also need some underwear. Top drawer for those."

I chuckle as I bend down to pick up the dog's bowl. "Jesus. What happened? Did you spill something? What about a shirt?" She's not laughing with me and it's suddenly very quiet on the other end. Then I hear a sniffle. "Fee? What happened?" I repeat in a serious tone this time.

"My shirt's fine. *Shit*," I hear her mumble. "Hate to do this, but I'll need some sanitary pads from the bathroom as well. I'll tell you when you get here."

I can tell she's crying when she hangs up the phone. *Fuck.*

After throwing a scoop of kibble into Van's bowl, I take the fastest shower I've ever had, and quickly collect what she asked for, stuffing it in a plastic bag I find in the kitchen.

"Be a good boy," I call out to the dog as I rush out the door.

I avoid as many traffic lights as I can—not an easy feat in Durango—and pull into Sophia's parking spot behind the restaurant, barely twenty minutes after she called.

She's in her office and the moment I walk in her face crumples. Damn.

I'm around the desk and have her in my arms in a few strides.

"Ah, babe."

"I should be happy," she sobs in my shirt. "Relieved. So why am I so upset? I can't stop crying and I hardly ever cry."

She tilts her head back and it strikes me she's even beautiful like this, eyes red-rimmed from crying, her face a blotchy mess, and her mouth wobbling as she tries to get hold of herself.

"You're probably pumping your inner fist right now," she says with a hint of bitterness.

For some reason that offends me, and I let go of her waist to grab on to her upper arms.

"I'm not."

She snorts and tries to look away so I give her a little shake.

"Fee, look at me." I wait until I have her eyes. "I'm disappointed too. *Fuck*, I was starting to imagine you, beautiful and round with my baby, so don't accuse me of celebrating this. Because I'm not."

She quietly observes me for a moment.

"You mean that?"

"Yeah. Why would I lie about that?"

The next instant she does a faceplant in my chest.

19

SOPHIA

LAST NIGHT WAS chaos.

A profitable chaos, because it was our best night so far, in terms of sales, but chaos nonetheless.

Thank God Emme ran interference everywhere. Covering the bar with Mack, serving drinks when the servers were running behind, and lending a hand in the kitchen, loading the dishwasher and helping plate orders.

I didn't have much time to think about anything; I was too busy trying to keep up with the steady flow of diners. Tse stayed at the bar the entire night, a steady presence, and would occasionally shove a bottle of water in my hand and tell me to drink. When we got home my feet and back were sore, and Tse suggested I have a bath while he took care of Van. I was too tired for that so opted for a quick shower instead and ended up rolling into bed right after.

No time to think last night, but this morning I woke up with a head that was already churning. I always feel a bit off during my period, which tends to be light—achy, grumpy, touchy—but I'm really out of sorts this time.

I'm sitting out on the deck with Van romping around in the yard, sipping a coffee. I snuck out of bed at six, leaving Tse to sleep. He mentioned they're working at Paco's place today—something about the roof—but that he'd be back to drop me off for work at eleven.

It's a gorgeous morning; the air fresh and alive with the peaceful sounds of nature waking up, and my coffee is hot and strong. Still, I feel a weight on my chest. I guess that's the way it goes when dreams disappear into thin air. Even one I never fully considered until a short week ago.

I've never been prone to fantasies—instead opting to stay firmly rooted in reality, grounded in the familiar— but since taking the leap and moving to Durango I've changed. Become more open to possibilities.

The job itself has been a huge leap, new and different in many ways from the mostly solitary work I'd been doing before, but one I love. Then I found myself getting involved with a man I thought wouldn't be good for me, until I jumped into a relationship with him to discover it isn't just good, it is outstanding.

Turns out that once you take that first chance—make that first big jump—the ones to follow become easier. Not that the risk is less, but you find out the rewards are worth it. It's like graduating from a merry-go-round to a roller coaster. Less safe and predictable, with extreme highs and significant lows, but the view from up high is amazing, even if the dips are tough.

"I can hear you thinking from inside," Tse says, as he steps out on the deck.

Van, who eventually came to lie down beside my chair, gets up and does his cute little butt-wag. The dog, another leap that is paying off in spades. It's amazing how fast we can become attached. To animals *and* to people.

He leans over my chair and I tilt my head back to share a sweet good morning kiss that tastes of coffee.

"Woolgathering," I mumble, and he grins down at me before taking the other chair.

"You do that quite a bit," he observes.

I glance over and see from the look in his eyes it's not an accusation, it's curiosity.

"Guess it's what happens when you're used to being alone. You learn to process on the inside."

He turns and lets his gaze roam the view.

"I can appreciate that, but sometimes it's helpful just to talk things through."

I smile to myself.

"Like you do?" I tease and watch his lips twitch into a grin.

"What can I say; I'm a work in progress." Those warm eyes swing to me and some of that weight lifts off when I see the sparkle. "I'm even learning to listen, should you want to try me out."

I hesitate only for a moment.

"I was thinking how much I've changed in the few months I've been here. How much my life has changed from what I was used to."

"In a good way, I hope?"

"A little scary, a little sad, but yeah, for the most part."

He reaches and grabs my free hand in his. I love the feel of his callused palm against my soft one.

"Are you talking about the baby that never was?" he asks gently.

My smile for him is a little wobbly but determined.

"Mmm. But I was mostly thinking about the way I've thrown caution to the wind at every opportunity, when I've always been so careful. So responsible." I snort. "My parents will be thrilled."

Gah…my parents.

They're supposed to be here tomorrow, but weren't sure when. When I mentioned I might be working, they told me not to worry, that they had everything they needed in their RV and would wait until I got home.

I have no idea how long they intend to stay. They visited me in Denver all of two times in the years I'd been there. They hated the city and stayed for only two days each time. This place is much more up their alley. Durango is more relaxed, quaint, and they'd definitely love it up here where they can be one with nature.

"What time are Blossom and Duff gonna get here?"

"They didn't say. Also, my parents' names are really Maria and Gustavo Vieira," I explain. "They got caught up in the seventies. Moved into a commune on the edge of the Tonto National Forest, about two hours east of Phoenix, when they were barely of legal age, and changed their names. They still live there, like some of the other die-hards, although things have evolved some since the seventies. They don't call them communes anymore, but eco-villages."

"You were born in a commune?"

He seems stumped and I can't help laugh.

"We all were, and let me tell you, it's a miracle there aren't ten of us. They were already thirty by the time they had my sister, and my brother was a surprise baby at forty-two. He's twenty-five and lives in Vegas."

"So, I'm surprised they gave you such a classic name."

"Dad says I was named for Sophia Loren, his lifelong crush. Bianca was for Mick Jagger's wife—big Rolling Stone fans, my parents—and Arlo was for—"

"Arlo Guthrie," Tse guesses, interrupting me. "I'm starting to see the pattern."

"Right. The irony is, despite our somewhat eccentric upbringing, all three of us lived up to our more conventional names. Although, I'm arguably the most straightlaced of the bunch. At least I used to be. Hence my earlier point that my parents will be over the moon to see I've wandered off the beaten path."

He brings my hand to his lips and kisses my knuckles.

"You mean living here. Out in the boonies."

I glance over at him, taking in his messy hair, unkempt beard, and tattoos peeking out of his shirt and covering his hands. I'm expecting over the moon may not sufficiently describe my parents' reaction when they meet Tse. Heck, even his name will go over well.

"That, plus the fact one look at you will have my mother convinced, after years of being a devout atheist, there is a God after all."

Tse

"MAKE SURE TO KEEP an eye on him. Don't want him taking off."

"He won't."

I hand over the pop and the small box of donut holes I picked up for him and watch as the dog follows Ravi to the wheelbarrow in the driveway. Paco had a load of gravel hauled in this morning to take care of the worst of the potholes and ruts left behind from all the recent traffic. He eventually wants it asphalted or something, but for now is content to keep it as level as possible. Ravi was given that task.

I just got back from dropping Sophia at the restaurant. I've only been gone maybe half an hour but already I can see progress. Yuma and Honon are perched on the ridge—the beam bridging the roof rafters, hammering down sheathing—while Paco and Ouray measure and cut the next piece.

Ouray must've arrived while I was gone. He looks up when I approach with the tray of coffees and box of donuts I picked up in town. I whistle to the guys on the roof and hold it up before setting it on the stack of lumber beside the saw.

"You can grab mine. Didn't know you were coming."

I offer Ouray my coffee, but he shakes his head.

"I'm not staying long. Was just checking the progress."

I open the box of donuts and grab one, shoving half of it in my mouth.

"All quiet at the restaurant?" he asks.

"As far as I know. Why?"

"Luna just called. Feds picked up another dealer last night and not too long ago they intercepted the truck driver and took him in for questioning. Not much to report on the supplier side yet, but they're shutting down the setup. There weren't any drugs on the truck again this morning. Luna says they figure somehow the supplier got wind of the operation and pulled the plug. Maybe setting up shop elsewhere."

I take a drink of my coffee and consider what this means.

"I'd have felt better if they got those guys as well," I confess. "No sign of that Bernie guy?"

"Gone to ground from what I hear. The sister too."

"So what happens with the girl? The one in the kitchen, Mandy?"

"That's actually what Luna was calling about. They're recommending she stay away from the Backyard Edge and are looking into getting her set up near her sister."

"That's gonna leave Sophia short a server as well as a cook. Again," I grumble, because the FBI agent who'd been working every night this week was hustling as hard as everyone else was yesterday.

"I'm aware, brother, so is Luna. I've got one of the part-time line cooks from the Brewer's Pub coming in tomorrow, and we can shuffle the shifts there and at the Backyard to make sure both businesses are covered. At least temporarily, giving us time to find replacements."

I glance over at Ravi who is dropping a shovel of gravel into a rut, stomping it down with his feet. Van is lying in a patch of grass off to the side, his snout resting on his crossed front paws, watching the boy.

"Timing sucks," I point out. "Sophia's parents are coming to visit. Arriving tomorrow."

"So get her to take some time," he says matter-of-factly.

"Gonna be a tough sell now. She'd never go for it."

Ouray claps me on the shoulder and grins.

"Then you've gotta get creative in finding a way to convince her."

Easier said than done.

It's still on my mind when I sidle up to the bar that night.

Emme walks over and sets a draft in front of me. I don't even have to ask anymore.

The place is busy again. Not quite like last night, but two tables and all the booths are taken, so staff is hustling.

"Food?" Emme asks.

"Got any left?"

"I can check with the kitchen," she says and darts out from behind the bar, leaving just Mack behind it, who lifts his chin in greeting.

Sophia, who was chatting with a couple on the far side of the dining room when I walked in, cozies up to me, lifting her face for a kiss.

"How are things?"

"A little crazy. Luna was here earlier to pick up Mandy and brought a temporary replacement for her. Luckily Emme was willing to jump in again, even though she wasn't on the schedule for today. She says she can do with the extra pay." She shakes her head. "I can't keep up."

"Talked to Ouray earlier," I volunteer. "He filled me in. I'm sure we'll be able to fill those spots before next weekend."

"I sure hope so."

A group of four comes in and Sophia rushes over to greet and seat them.

"How does half a rack of beef ribs sound?" Emme wants to know as she slides back behind the bar.

"Sounds good to me."

I watch as she grabs empties off the bar and rinses them in the sink.

"Emme?"

She looks over. "Yeah?"

"Sophia's saying you're looking to make a few extra bucks?"

"Always," she answers with a grimace.

I'm sure there's a story there, but it's not my place to pry.

"I wanna run something by you."

20

TSE

"I CAN'T BELIEVE you did that behind my back."

Sophia isn't taking too well to the fact I've arranged for Emme to work overtime so Fee can take some extra time off. All she has to do is go in for a few hours to do the paperwork but her dining room responsibilities Emme will take care of.

"Been a tough couple of weeks, Fee. On top of that, your parents are showing up today. You need some downtime."

She pulls her feet from my lap and gets up, waking Van who'd been snoozing on the deck beside us. We'd been enjoying an early morning coffee on the deck, as we've taken to doing this past week, when I mentioned the arrangement I worked out with Emme last night.

"And you think this is a good time? The restaurant is crazy busy and I have new staff to hire because we're shorthanded. There are a million and one things I need to take care of, Tse," she says, clearly agitated as her hands gesture wildly. "Yes, I know my parents will be here, but I haven't even put a full three months in. I can't start taking vacation, because they suddenly decide, out of the blue, they need to come see me."

Clearly she's not happy. Tough.

I grab at one of her flailing hands and give it a small tug, tumbling her onto my lap. She immediately struggles to get back to her feet but can't because my arms are holding her in place.

"You can't just call the shots for me," she sputters, giving up her struggle. "I'm a grown woman."

"No mistaking that, Fee."

Even my body recognizes that fact, having risen to the occasion with her ass wiggling on my lap. It's been a frustratingly long week and I have a serious case of blue balls by now.

"I'm perfectly capable of making my own decisions," she continues.

"Aware of that too,"

"Are you? Because this is starting to feel familiar, I've been there, done that, and am pretty sure I don't wanna go down that road again."

Now *I'm* pissed.

I release my hold and she scrambles off my lap. I get to my feet as well and poor Van, sensing trouble brewing, is looking from one to the other as we face each other.

"You comparing me to that asshole ex of yours?" I challenge her.

She cocks a perfectly shaped eyebrow. "If the shoe fits."

I close the distance between us and bend my neck so I'm almost nose to nose with her. Those eyes are shooting fire.

"Not interested in controlling you, Sophia."

"Could'a fooled me," she scoffs, refusing to back down.

Despite the urge to shake some sense into her, I appreciate her moxie. She's standing up for herself and I admire her for it. She may have a temper, but then so do I.

Suddenly the anger drains from me and I step away. I grab my mug from the floor and head for the house. Sliding the back door open, I stop and turn to where she's still standing, Van now sitting at her feet, still confused about the energy he must sense.

"Not cool comparing me to that bastard," I say in a calmer tone. "Not fair either. There's a world of difference between being controlling and trying to look after someone you care about."

Without waiting for a response, I head inside and grab a refill, taking my fresh cup upstairs to hit the shower. It's that, or hop on my bike I collected earlier this week, and take off. Can't do that and leave her alone, so a shower it is.

By the time I step out, my coffee is only lukewarm, my balls are a little lighter, and my head is a lot cooler.

I've also come to the realization I could've handled that better, especially given the history she entrusted me with. The accusation I'm anything like her ex still burns, though.

I pull some jeans and a clean shirt from my duffel on the floor of her closet, pick up the dirty clothes I've been tossing beside it and add it to her laundry basket. Then I carry the whole thing downstairs, noticing she's still outside, back in her chair, with the dog on the deck beside her.

Her laundry room is more like a closet, and located under the stairs. It takes me a minute to sort out the light colors first and I make sure to check the labels. Back at the clubhouse I'd shove everything in at the same time, but I have a feeling Sophia wouldn't appreciate her pretty white lace underwear getting mixed in with my work jeans and dirty socks.

The machine takes a little figuring out, but a few minutes later I have it going. I back out of the small space at the same time Sophia walks in the back door. Her face is blotchy and red.

Fuck.

I hate when she cries.

Taking a few steps toward her, she lifts her hands defensively, stopping me in my tracks.

"I'm a mess," she says, and promptly tears start rolling down her face. "I'm sorry, I'm PMSing hard. I usually get cranky but I've never turned into a bitch before. I'm not this person."

"Fee, baby…"

That's all it takes for her to walk right into my arms, wrapping hers tightly around my waist.

SHIT. THAT FIGURES.

An old, ugly motor home is parked in front of the house when I turn onto the driveway.

When her parents hadn't showed up by midday, and her mother wasn't answering her phone, Sophia suggested she head into the restaurant for a couple of hours to prepare orders and do payroll for the week. She wanted me to stay home in case her parents showed up, and I didn't want her to go alone. We compromised. I dropped her off at the Backyard and headed right back up the mountain.

Looks like they arrived shortly after we left.

I pull in beside their vehicle and get out, hearing Van's furious barking from inside, but before I can take a step a woman comes flying around the side of the house.

"I thought I heard a car!"

She's short. Shorter even than Luna, who may be tough as nails but barely makes it up to my chin. This woman is all soft, though. Smiling round face, comfortably plump body, and covered literally head to toe in yards of colorful, flowing fabric. A few stray graying curls escape the shawl wrapped artfully around her head. She looks like a benign fortune-teller.

"Blossom?"

She stops right in front of me, tilting her head way

back.

"That's right, and I recognize your voice. I was right; you're a big one. Sophia never told me your name, though."

"Tse, ma'am."

I stick out my hand but instead of grabbing it, she wags her index finger at me.

"Good name, but you dare ma'am me again and we're gonna have issues," she scolds me, and it's all I can do to keep from laughing.

Sophia may not have inherited her mother's looks, but I'd recognize that attitude anywhere.

"So noted," I mutter, trying to keep a straight face.

"Good. Now, Tse…please tell me that's Navajo?"

"Name is, but I'm not. At least not that I know of."

"Means rock, did you know that?"

"I did, ma…Blossom," I quickly correct myself when her eyes narrow.

"Good name for you. Fitting. Sophia at work?" She jumps from one subject to the next without taking a breath.

"Just for a few hours."

She smiles big.

"Excellent, that'll give Duff and me a chance to get to know you. He's in the back checking out the yard." With that she turns and starts walking to the rear, calling over her shoulder, "Well, come on then. You can introduce us to that sweet puppy."

Forgot about Van, although sweet puppy isn't quite the description I'd have picked for him. I tell her I'll go in the front and she raises her hand in acknowledgement.

This has to be the weirdest fucking encounter I've had. I feel like I just got run over by a bulldozer.

The two hours until I'm supposed to pick up Sophia suddenly feel like an eternity.

SOPHIA

"You were looking for me?"

Chris is standing in the doorway.

"Yes, have a seat. Oh, and close the door."

I'd gone looking for him earlier, but Lauren mentioned he'd stepped outside again.

He hesitates for a fraction before he walks in, shuts the door, and sits down across from me.

"What's up?" His tone is almost defensive. "I've got to get back to my kitchen."

"Won't be long," I placate him. "I understand Agent Gomez spoke to you this morning as well?"

Gomez was around when I got here earlier, talking to some of the staff. I'd been pissed at first he'd go ahead without me there, but he calmly told me Ouray had been informed.

"Yes," is his curt answer. "Drugs in *my* kitchen. Still don't see how something like that could've been kept from me."

I shrug. "That wasn't my call to make, Chris. It does leave us with staffing issues now business is picking up."

He harrumphs, looking at me impatiently.

"I was hoping to get your input. At least for kitchen

staff. Know any good line cooks? Maybe even two. Have any ideas?"

His expression mellows a fraction.

"Not off the top of my head, no, but I've got some connections. I can ask around."

"That would be great. Let me know."

"Sure." He stares at me for a few beats. "Was that all?"

It had been all, but now I have him here…

"Actually, is everything all right with you?"

I can almost see his hackles go up.

"Why? Someone complain?"

"No complaints, just my observation. You seem…a bit sharper than your usual self."

His eyes drift over my shoulder to the small window over my credenza. It's too high to get any kind of view, but at least it lets in some daylight, otherwise this office would be a dark dungeon.

"It's Rick."

I wait. I have no idea who Rick is, since Chris doesn't talk about anything other than pertaining to the restaurant. When it looks like nothing more is forthcoming—he seems lost in thought—I finally prompt him.

"Rick?"

His gaze drops to me and I'm shocked to find a deep well of emotion visible in his eyes.

"My partner. He was diagnosed with Amyotrophic Lateral Sclerosis last week."

I suck in a sharp breath. I didn't know he had a partner to begin with, and that is a devastating diagnosis.

"ALS, Lou Gehrig's disease," he explains.

"I know. I'm so sorry."

He shrugs. "It is what it is. We'll deal."

"Look, if there's anything I can do. Do you need time off?"

I don't know how the hell I'm going to make that work but I'll think of something.

"Hell no," he says, getting to his feet. "Rick doesn't want me underfoot and I need to stay busy."

"If that changes, let me know?"

He nods but doesn't say anything when he disappears into the hall.

The moment he's gone I burst into tears.

Jesus.

What on earth is the matter with me?

"I'M SO SORRY."

Tse looks over at me and grins.

"Don't apologize. It was fine."

It's clear he's lying. Hell, I don't have to look at him to know the last few hours have been a chore. Especially for a man like him. I know my parents. My mother, to be more specific. Duff just lets everything roll off his back—the embodiment of chill—while Blossom is a lot. Of everything. All well-intentioned and coming from a huge heart, but despite her small stature she can be like a tidal wave.

It's not for nothing all us kids had to escape to become

our own person.

"You get done what needed doing?" he wants to know, taking my hand and weaving our fingers, as he not so subtly changes the topic.

"And then some." I sigh deeply. "Turns out Chris's partner is very sick. ALS."

"Shit. That's not good."

"No."

"Does that mean more scheduling problems for you?"

I glance over at him and see warm concern in his eyes. Despite this morning's spat, I'm starting to think I've struck gold with this man.

"He says he needs to stay busy."

He nods. "Understandable."

My mother is already waiting beside the ugliest motor home I've ever laid eyes on. Not the picture she painted when she mentioned they'd bought an RV. I wouldn't have trusted it to drive to town, let alone all the way from Arizona here.

"My beautiful Sophia!" she exclaims when I get out of the passenger side, and immediately folds me into a tight hug.

"Blossom," I mumble, letting the familiar feel and smell of her envelop me.

Despite our differences she still feels like home, even though she won't let me call her Mom. I tried for years, as did my siblings, but she insisted it was a label. She doesn't believe in them, feels it minimizes who she is, and only wants to be known as Blossom.

"Let me have a look at you," she says, pushing me

back by the shoulders and squinting her eyes.

She does this a lot. Claims to be able to read people's auras. "Hmmmm," she hums thoughtfully, but to my surprise she says nothing else.

It's not often she doesn't share her 'findings' and is usually eager to impart her wisdom, but this time she stays mum, which is a little disconcerting.

We find Duff in the back, holding a one-sided conversation with Van, who appears fascinated, even though he can't possibly understand a word being said.

"There's my baby," he calls out when he spots me.

Another big hug, one in which I'm forcefully swayed from side to side. Signature Duff.

"Do you like the new wheels?" he asks when he finally lets me go.

"Is it safe?" immediately comes to mind and out of my mouth.

He looks a little hurt. "Baby-girl, I've fixed it up myself."

It's on my lips to say that doesn't make me feel any better, but I hold myself in.

"It sure is handy," I opt for.

"That it is," he beams at me. "Our new house on wheels. We plan to roam the country in it. Stopped here first, then we're heading in the direction of Montana. Then Washington state, Oregon—of course we'll stop in at Bianca's—south to California, and from there we're hitting up Arlo in Vegas. Do a little gambling. After that the plans are open."

"That's…ambitious."

Not quite the word I'm thinking—*insanity*—but I manage to hold it back.

"Been picking Tse's brain on good places to go. He's a biker." Duff lowers his voice on that, leaning in as if he's sharing a secret I didn't already know. I can tell he's pleased with my choice of man. Not that I doubted that for a minute.

"I need a drink. Anyone else?" Blossom pipes up and turns to me. "Give me a hand, Sophia."

I know when I'm being summoned so I look at Tse, who is wearing a bemused, perhaps slightly exasperated look on his face. I did warn him.

"Beer, honey?"

"You bet."

I give his arm a reassuring squeeze and follow my mother into the kitchen, where I can see she's already made herself at home. I have to dig through wax-paper-wrapped produce I'm sure they brought from home to find a couple of beers. When I close the fridge and turn around, she's a foot away, her hands on her hips.

"You're not drinking that, are you?" she says, pointing at the beers.

"Uhh, I was planning to."

She reaches out and snatches it from my hand.

"You're not supposed to drink when you're pregnant."

You could've knocked me over with a feather and it takes me a minute to gather my words.

"I'm not pregnant."

She raises an eyebrow in a way that tells you she knows something you don't know.

"I had my period."

The eyebrow goes higher.

"It was a light one, barely lasted the day, but you know mine have always been a couple of days at most. I can't be."

"When did you have sex?"

I close my eyes and do some deep breathing. This is what I mean when I say no boundaries. Everything is subject to discussion in my family. At least, with my parents.

"Mom…"

"Don't Mom me, you know how I hate labels. When?" she insists.

"Couple of weeks."

Her stern face suddenly breaks into a huge smile.

"I knew it!"

"Knew what?" Duff calls from the back door.

"Our baby's having a baby!"

I turn to find Tse has come in after my father, his face a mask of shock.

21

SOPHIA

"HOW THE FUCK was I supposed to know there's something called implantation bleeding?"

I'm standing in the doorway to the bedroom, Tse is still in bed, an arm tucked behind his head as he calmly observes me have my second major freak-out since yesterday. He seems to be taking this much better than I am.

Last night's freak-out—while my parents were giving each other high fives and loudly declaring they'd never thought they'd see the day—was snuffed out by Tse getting in my tear-streaked face and declaring we weren't gonna borrow trouble until we had cause. His calm voice and strong presence drowned out my parents' boisterous celebration, helping me to get a grip.

I ended up in the kitchen with Blossom to start working on dinner, while Tse lured Duff back outside with a beer. My mother was a bit more subdued, and I hyperventilated only a little when she told me there were early tests I could take and she'd pick me up one in the morning.

At some point Tse offered to go into town to pick up some tamarind sauce I didn't stock but Blossom absolutely needed, and I begged him to bring back a vat of vanilla ice cream. I had a feeling I'd need it—my go-to comfort food—before the night was done.

That turned out to be a good call because while my parents and Tse anesthetized with beer and my mother's homemade elderberry wine, ice cream was my only option. Over dinner Blossom explained at length, and in great detail, how the best time to take a pregnancy test was in the morning because of the higher concentration of urine. I wanted to dive under the table but Tse just grinned.

I noticed he'd been doing a lot of that.

By the time my folks retreated to their motor home and Tse took Van out for a last pee, I went upstairs in a bloated food coma and fell asleep the moment my head hit the pillow.

"Fee, baby, just take the test. We'll know, and we'll deal."

The test he's referring to is the one I just found on the counter in the bathroom. Turns out tamarind sauce and ice cream had not been all he picked up in town last night. Nothing like the sight of a pregnancy test to make me forget the urgent need to relieve myself I woke up with. Not even the mental picture of Tse going into a drugstore checking out the family-planning aisle makes a dent in the wave of panic.

"Why are you so calm?" I snap.

He scoots up in bed, resting his back against the headboard, and patting the mattress beside him.

"Sit with me."

I'm stubborn for only a moment before my feet move me to the bed. He tugs me to his side and my head automatically comes to rest on his chest. His heart beats steady and strong, just like he is. If you had told me last year that annoyingly cocky, womanizing, and persistent flirt was hiding the man I've gotten to know, I wouldn't have believed it.

Whoever gave Tse his name picked wisely. He's a rock. My rock.

"I'm calm because I'm starting to believe the best things in life are unexpected. I mean, look at us. It wasn't that long ago you could barely stand to be in the same space as me, and I fully expected to grow old in the clubhouse. Now I get to wake up with you every day. Look at us, Fee."

I put my hand on his chest beside my face and close my eyes.

"But it's all still so new. So...uncharted," I mumble softly against his skin, and his arm tightens around me.

"I know. If we're lucky it'll stay that way. An adventure at every turn of the road I hope never has to end." I feel his lips brush my forehead. "Toss out your itinerary, my Fee, you don't need it. Just feel the wind in your face, look at the beauty already around you. It's never about the destination, it's about the ride."

Turning my head, I press my face to his skin, smiling. How is it possible I have fallen for a man who is in many ways so like the free-loving parents I ran from?

I always thought I wanted stability and figured it was synonymous with predictability.

I was wrong. This man is both rock and adventure.

All I have to do is hold on.

I struggle to find words to express what I'm feeling, but in the end I say nothing and simply press a kiss over his heart. Then I lift my head and find his warm eyes on me.

"I should go pee on a stick," I whisper, and those crinkles I've grown to love appear at the corners of his eyes.

"Yeah."

Not long after he walks out of the bathroom, the stick I left on the counter in his hand. He managed to distract me with some kissing and light petting while we waited, but now the butterflies are back. I don't even know what I want it to say.

"Tell me," I prompt him.

Too nervous to look myself.

"WE'RE HAVING DINNER at Arrow's Edge," Tse announces.

He's about to leave to go to Paco's place.

We've just finished breakfast and Blossom announced she wanted to go into town and stop in at Nature's Oasis to grab some groceries for dinner tonight.

This is after Tse and I filled in my parents over waffles, something I felt we couldn't avoid. Surprisingly they took the news in stride and agreed to keep it to themselves until I was much further along.

I'm going to be a mother.

When Tse told me we would need more space, it took me a moment to clue in. Then I burst out in tears I now know are the result of raging hormones. No wonder I'd not been feeling myself and seemed weepy all the damn time.

I'm pregnant.

I'm having a baby and I'm terrified, but also excited.

Tse's words from earlier keep coming back to me; *It's never about the destination, it's about the ride.* I'm trying, but still my mind is already attempting to anticipate and problem-solve any roadblocks up ahead. Tse and my parents seem almost too casual about this.

I haven't been paying much attention to the conversation but I did hear what Tse just said.

"At Arrow's Edge? Since when?"

"Finn's birthday," he answers dryly.

Oh no. With everything happening this last little while, I'd almost forgotten about it. In fact, I just now realize I haven't seen him in over a month.

"I can't believe I forgot."

Tse's hand finds the back of my neck and he gives me a little squeeze.

"We've had a lot going on, babe."

"What about my parents?"

"They'll come," he says matter-of-factly, as if that wasn't even in question.

I make a mental note to call Lisa at some point this morning anyway; to give her a heads-up there'd be two more mouths to feed. I can't bring myself to think about my parents in a motorcycle clubhouse, it's too much to wrap my head around, so I just let it go.

"I don't even have a gift for him."

"Good thing we're heading into town, then," Blossom pipes up. "Tse can go to work, Duff will take care of the dishes and the dog. Right, Duff?"

My father nods. He doesn't care as long as he doesn't have to go shopping.

Ten minutes later, we've dropped Tse off with his tools from the back of the Jeep and are heading down the mountain.

"It'll be good for him," Blossom mumbles, as usual starting somewhere in the middle of her thought process. It can be hard to follow.

"What'll be good for whom?"

"The baby, for Tse."

I stop at the stop sign at the bottom of the road and turn to her.

"What makes you say that?"

"Oh, my Sophia, you've found yourself a good man, but it won't be smooth sailing. His aura is full of dark shadows. Tse carries a lot of pain."

My mind instantly goes to the scars on his back.

Over the past weeks I've discovered the thick rope of tissue under his chain tattoo isn't the only one. There are others, not quite as visible, but definitely there. The pretty ink only skin-deep, barely covering the story underneath.

I haven't asked him how he came by them. I already know he had a very difficult childhood and concluded he'd been abused. He never talked, and I never questioned. Now I wonder if I should have.

"Good thing my baby girl is strong," Blossom says, patting my knee. "You'll need to be."

TSE

"FUCK. I KEEP thinking the woman is talking to me, the way she's waving her hands."

I'm sitting beside Nosh at the bar in the clubhouse and follow his line of sight into the kitchen, where Blossom is wildly gesturing while talking to Lisa.

"Strange bird," he signs, shaking his head.

I grin. She does look like some kind of exotic bird with all her flowing scarves in bright colors. Duff isn't much better in his tie-dyed shirt and socks in sandals, sitting on the large sectional with some of the kids who are trying to explain their game to him. They look entirely out of place in the clubhouse, but oddly enough seem perfectly comfortable here. I bet they'd be comfortable anywhere.

Sophia, on the other hand, is tense. She's walking through the clubhouse with Finn's little hand in hers—he just started walking—but every so often darts looks in the direction of her parents. My eyes are constantly drawn to her. Watching her with Finn has a whole new meaning now.

I watch as Wapi stops by her, exchanging a few words. The bright hot jealousy I used to feel at seeing him with her is now no more than an alert awareness; no different from any other man who'd stop to talk with her.

A split second later she looks over at me, a smile teasing her lips. That feeling I sometimes have, when my heart feels too damn big for my chest, washes over me. It's moments like this—when we're physically apart, but still somehow connected—I wonder if this is what love feels like.

I jump at the sharp elbow in my ribs, and look over at Nosh.

"Goner," he rasps in his monotonous voice. Then he signs, *"Didn't think I'd live to see the day, brother. Wish Momma was here. She'd be happy to see another one of her boys finding his rightful place beside a good woman."*

Jesus.

Shit's getting way too emotional here. What's fucking next? Holding hands and singing "Kumbaya"?

I glare at Nosh, but he doesn't give a shit. He's grinning his crooked grin; one we rarely ever saw in the clubhouse until recently. I'm not sure if that means the man is getting mellower, or whether he's slowly losing his marbles. Both are possible at his age, I guess.

The door to the clubhouse opens and Luna walks in with her son, Ahiga. The kid just turned seventeen and makes a beeline for the group playing games on the big-screen TV. I'm surprised when his mother walks over to me.

"Gonna say hello and then I'd like a quick word in Ouray's office."

"Sophia?"

"Yeah."

A few minutes later I walk to the back, Sophia's hand in mine. Ouray and Luna are both in his office.

"Nothing bad, just an update," Luna is quick to say when she catches the worried look on Sophia's face. "First of all, Mandy is safe with her sister in New Mexico. Classes don't start up until the end of August, hopefully we'll have this case wrapped up by then, but for now they're in a secure location."

"That's good," Sophia mumbles beside me, and I wrap an arm around her, tucking her close.

"We also picked up the driver, but he wasn't much help. Turns out he always did the Durango run but was recently changed to another route, round about the time the restaurant opened. The guy who took over was new and he doesn't know much about him. We checked with the warehouse manager, who couldn't tell us much more, other than there'd been pressure from higher up to put Jim Marquez, the new guy, on the Durango route."

"That's gotta raise some flags," I comment.

"Sure does. Especially since Jim Marquez doesn't exist. At least not anymore. The social security number belongs to someone who died in 2019 in a car crash outside Shiprock. Apparently, Clover Produce doesn't look too closely at their new hires. The Farmington Field Office is looking into the company. Talking to staff and management, shaking a few trees to see what'll fall out, but other than that we don't have a whole lot to go on. The lab is doing analysis of the drugs we have to see if they can match them up with other contraband from recent busts. Maybe we can retrace the steps that way, see where it came from, but that takes time too."

"So what now?"

Luna turns to Sophia with a sympathetic smile. "Now we pick away at loose threads. It's what we're good at. It may take some time, but sooner or later we'll find something."

"In the meantime," Ouray jumps in, his eyes also on my girl. "We're gonna stay vigilant. We'll keep eyes on the Backyard, but it'll be business as usual. You don't have to worry about a thing, we'll take care of it."

I can feel Sophia tighten up under my hand.

"Spoken like a true caveman." Luna, who is very observant, gives her husband a sharp look before she turns back to Sophia. "Ignore everything he said after *business as usual,* and replace it with we've got your back. I'll make sure you're kept up-to-date."

A soft knock has me turn around to find Ravi in the doorway.

"Lisa says dinner's ready."

"Perfect. Let's eat."

Ouray gets up and walks out of the room, Luna right behind him, but Ravi is lingering by the door.

"Not hungry, kiddo?" Sophia asks him.

"Yeah, but I was just gonna ask…" He flashes a glance my way. "Can Tse bring Van tomorrow?"

When I got to the site this morning, he'd looked disappointed when I was the only one getting out of the Jeep. He'd asked me when I left if I'd be bringing the dog and I told him to check with Sophia. I would've said no if her parents weren't planning to be around for a couple of days. I'd rather she not be alone.

She grins at the kid.

"Fine by me, as long as he doesn't get in the way."

His normally solemn face lights up. Not quite a full smile, but a start.

22

SOPHIA

BLOSSOM AND DUFF are starting to get on my nerves.

A few days have turned into more than a week and I've gone back to my normal hours for the past few days, but they don't seem in a hurry to continue on that trip they started.

Tse doesn't seem to mind, which is almost more annoying. I'll complain about having absolutely no privacy in my own home, and he'll brush it off.

I've been feeling a little off in the morning the past couple of days, a little sick to my stomach. Nothing that has me heaving over the toilet, just enough I don't want to eat when I get up. Blossom has been forcing ginger tea and crackers on me as soon as I get downstairs, when I just want to be left alone for a few minutes.

This morning I snapped.

Tse just left for Paco's place and my mother was trying to get me to chew on some fennel seeds when I blew. I wasn't so nice to my mother, then Duff mumbled something about hormones, and I lost it. Ran upstairs with Van on my heels and flung myself on my bed like a teenager, not a woman in her thirties. Not unlike the many times I did the same thing during my teenage years.

I know I'm being ridiculous, but I can't stop the waterworks. I just feel so…out of control.

Everything is new and unfamiliar: new place, new job, new relationship, new dog, and now an unplanned pregnancy all within the span of a few months. Oh, and don't let me forget a drug ring operating from my restaurant and my parents virtually moving in.

Each time I think I'm starting to feel some solid ground under my feet, it turns out to be quicksand. The landscape keeps changing on me before I have a chance to adjust to it.

All I want is…

God, I don't even know what I want anymore.

Van, who jumped on the bed with me, shoves his nose under my arm, whimpering. I'm even driving the dog crazy.

"It's okay," I mumble, as he tries to get to my wet face.

Suddenly his head snaps up and his tail starts thumping on the mattress, moments before the door opens and Tse walks in. He takes one look at me and shoos the dog off the bed, taking the vacant spot, and hauling me into his arms.

"You gotta calm down, Fee," he mumbles, rubbing a big hand up and down my back.

"What are you doing here?" I finally manage to calm myself down enough to say.

"Duff called me. Said you needed me."

I lift my head from his shoulder and look at him.

"And you dropped everything." It's not so much a question as it is a conclusion.

"Babe…" he drawls, an eyebrow raised.

I instantly feel ashamed for causing drama. He's been nothing but steady, despite my folks' constant presence and my mood swings.

"I'm a mess."

One side of his mouth lifts in a smirk.

"Yeah," he confirms with brutal honesty. "But you'll get your shit together. Give it time."

Even that—not offering to fix things for me, but trusting me to fix myself—is a testament to what a good guy he is.

"Thank you."

I lean in and brush his lips with mine, but when I pull back, his hand cups the back of my head and he deepens the kiss. We're lying in bed—wandering hands and legs and tongues tangled—it heats up quickly, and if Van hadn't let out a soft *woof* alerting us, Blossom walking in might've been embarrassing.

"We're heading out," she announces from the doorway.

I scramble from the bed and fling myself in her arms.

"Don't. I'm so sorry for snapping at you. I've not been—"

"Hush, baby-girl," she interrupts, placing a cool hand against my cheek. "Your father's been itching to get on the road and Bianca is starting to wonder what's keeping us."

Because it's still very early, I didn't want to announce my pregnancy yet. Not until I have a chance to get used to the idea myself anyway. Blossom may not have any boundaries, but is a vault when it comes to secrets. I hope she can keep my father in check, because if anyone's going to let it slip it'll be him.

"I'm sorry," I repeat.

"None of that. We'll swing back this way after we hit Vegas before the snow falls."

Only twenty minutes later I stand tucked under Tse's arm—a show of silent support I'm grateful for—waving as my parents' deathtrap on wheels rumbles down my driveway. When they disappear from sight, Tse curls me into his body and tips up my chin with a finger.

"Go get cleaned up, Fee. We've got a stop to make before I drop you off at work."

I'm grateful for that too. Not pampering me but instead steering me firmly to a familiar routine. I lift up on my toes and kiss him lightly. Then he lets me go and I head inside.

"Where are we going?"

Van's big head is sticking between the front seats, his eyes on the road ahead. He loves riding in the car.

"Brick called yesterday. He found a truck that checks all the boxes on my wish list at a dealership in town."

"He couldn't fix the old one?"

His dark eyes turn to me.

"Babe. That one was toast before it broke down. He's been keeping an eye out for a while, but I told him a few days ago to put a rush on it."

"Oh."

I glance out the side window. I'm not sure what it means. We've been doing fine with just the Jeep since he has his bike as well. Unless he's planning to go back to the clubhouse, which would make sharing a vehicle a bit of a challenge. I noticed last night his clothes are still in his duffel bag on the floor of my closet. I even made room for him, also freed up a couple of drawers in the dresser, but the bag remains on the floor.

"Stop." I swivel around to find him glaring at me. "Whatever's going around that head of yours, making you look like someone kicked your puppy. Just stop."

I try, I really do, but when we pull into the car dealership just half a mile up the road from the restaurant. I'm near tears. Again. If this is what pregnancy does to me—turning me into an emotional mess—I'm not a fan.

Tse holds my hand as we walk to the showroom when an older man intercepts us.

"You must be Tse?" he says, holding out a hand. "Brick said you'd stop by this morning. I'm Ted. It's right over here."

The 'it' he's referring to is a deep burgundy crew cab pickup truck with a Honda logo on the grill. Brand-new from the looks of it. It's very pretty—as pickup trucks go—and although not huge, like some monsters you see on the road, it looks roomy.

Tse lets go of my hand and walks around the vehicle before he opens the passenger door for me.

"Hop in."

I glance over at the salesman, who nods, before getting in. Tse rounds the front of the truck and gets behind the wheel, closing the door.

"Like the color?" He twists toward me, dropping his arm on the back of my seat. "They have one in black in stock as well, but Brick suggested I ask you."

"It's your truck. You should decide."

He reaches for the hank of hair that keeps slipping from behind my ear and tugs it.

"Don't care other than it's functional, a safe ride, and fits a baby seat. Your ass is gonna be in it a lot, so pick the color."

I'm such an idiot.

"Red. I like the red," I tell him, the first tear rolling down my face.

"Fuck me," Tse mumbles, tilting his head back to look at the ceiling. Then he leans in to brush a thumb under my eye. "Gotta stop doing that, baby."

"Then I guess you shouldn't have knocked me up," I snap, annoyed he makes it sound I'm doing it on purpose.

But I'm no longer crying.

Tse

"COOL TRUCK."

Elan walks up when I get out, eyeing my new ride.

I still haven't been able to get much out of Ravi, but his confidence seems to have grown over the past weeks. Yesterday when I suggested he check to see if some of the other kids wanted to come and help, he seemed open to the idea. Apparently, he didn't waste any time.

Elan's comment makes me realize I haven't been at the clubhouse for a while. I should rectify that, but since Blossom and Duff left, Sophia and I hit a nice, easy groove I don't wanna mess with.

"Picked it up last week. The old one was dead."

The kid grins, bending down to greet Van.

"Yeah, tell me about it. Brick had us rip it apart to salvage good parts. There weren't many."

I start walking toward the house that is actually starting to look like one. The wrapping is done, as is a lot of the interior framing. We're getting it ready for electrical and HVAC to go in next week, which means we'll be focusing on the exterior. At this rate we'll have it close to ready by the time the first snow flies.

In a few weeks it'll be September. Sophia is dead set on going to the Four Corners Motorcycle Rally, which always takes place the first weekend of the month. She heard about it from Lisa. I'm not so sure it's a good idea but she's been adamant. Says it may be the last chance she'll get to be on the back of my bike since by next summer the little one'll be here.

I caved, but I did insist she get the okay from a doctor first. Her first appointment is this afternoon so

I'm leaving early; despite her insistence she'd be fine on her own. She's been driving herself to work, but I'm still following her there and home—which earns me an eye roll every time—but I don't give a flying fuck. We continue to have eyes on the restaurant, so I know someone's looking out for her at work, but I'm not about to let her go to the clinic by herself. I promised her she wouldn't have to do this on her own, and that includes doctor visits.

I'll admit there are times I feel like the responsibilities are piling up on me, and I wonder if I'm cut out for this. Mostly at night when Sophia is snuggled up against me, trusting me to keep her safe. It's not just her life but also that of our baby. What if I drop the ball? Hell, I look at the boys at the club—at Ravi, at my own sorry history—and see the evidence of how easy it is to fuck up a kid's life.

I'm terrified I'll be that parent. The one who can't control his temper, who gets overwhelmed, and ends up hitting their kid. Or worse.

Fuck.

Here I am working on another man's house, when I should be worrying about my own living situation. I don't even have a proper place for my child to come home to.

I'm already screwing it up.

"NO MISTAKING THAT."

The doctor walks into the small examining room where we've been waiting. Sophia was asked to change into a gown and is sitting on the edge of the table.

"You are definitely pregnant. Have you been taking prenatal vitamins?"

Sophia nods. Her mother had picked them up in town that first day.

"Good. Why don't you lie back and let's see if we can get some more clarity."

Sophia grabs my hand as he scoots up the gown and puts a hand on her belly. I almost say something because the way he fucking digs his fingers in can't be comfortable, but she catches me glaring and sends me a little smile.

"So you said the first day of your last period was the end of June?"

"Yes. Uh, the twenty-ninth."

"Which would put your due date at around April fifth, give or take a couple of weeks either way. You're about six to seven weeks pregnant."

That confuses the fuck out of me, because it hasn't even been six weeks since Moab. I look at Sophia, who doesn't seem disturbed by this fact at all, and grins at me.

"They calculate from the first day of the last period."

Okay. It still doesn't make sense but what do I know? Only that by this time next year I'm gonna be a goddamn father. *Jesus Christ.*

"We may be a bit early but let's have a listen."

He pulls a contraption from his pocket that looks like a walkie-talkie with a microphone attached.

There's a swishing sound as he moves the little microphone over her stomach, until suddenly, I hear a distinct thumping. Sophia's hand twitches in mine.

"Good. I'd like you to set up an appointment for an ultrasound next week."

"Isn't that a little early?" I vaguely hear Sophia ask.

"You won't be able to see much yet, but it gives me a bit of a baseline."

The entire conversation sounds like it's taking place underwater.

Those steady thumps still echo in my ears.

A heartbeat.

Fuck.

23

TSE

"ARE YOU SURE?'

Her eyes flutter open and her lips stretch in a lazy smile.

"Positive…"

"It's not gonna—"

"It's perfectly safe. Please, Tse."

She's on her back, her ass on the edge of the mattress where I just ate her. I'm holding her legs spread wide and as eager as I am to hammer my cock into that hot slick pussy, the thought of harming her or that little thing growing in her is holding me back. Hell, it's been holding me back for weeks and I've started to worry my balls might fall off.

"Please…"

I position the tip at her entrance, the light brush already drawing an involuntary groan from deep in my chest. Then I ease inside her, my leg muscles shaking, trying not to pound into her, but that effort fails when I feel her pussy spasm around me and bury myself deep.

"That's it."

She wears a sly little smile as she tilts her hips a little more, grabs on to the bedspread, and hangs on for the ride.

I'm not gonna last.

"It's gonna be beautiful."

Sophia wanted to come see the progress on Paco's house and dropped in at the site. She's off today and was getting a little stir-crazy at home, so I told her to drive down. We're done for today and it's just Paco, Ravi, and myself doing some cleanup.

"Thanks," Paco, who just took her around inside, mumbles.

It is coming along nicely and after next week, when we can hopefully start hanging drywall, it's going to go even faster. He'll be able to move in before Christmas.

I'm happy for Paco, he's putting down some roots, but it also makes me painfully aware I'm living out of my duffel bag. No roots, no place to call my own, and nothing to offer. Instead, I'm shacked up in my woman's one-bedroom rental with a kid on the way.

That feeling of inadequacy I've been carrying around

gets a bit heavier with every day that passes. Sophia insisted we keep the pregnancy to ourselves a little longer, so I can't ask my brothers for advice yet.

"Hey, I was going to make tacos for dinner," Sophia says when we get outside. "You guys want to come over for a bite?"

"Yes!" Ravi is quick to respond, the smile is closer to the surface these days. Especially around Sophia.

"Sorry, kid. I've gotta get back to the clubhouse," Paco tells him.

"We can run him back after," Sophia jumps in. "Right, Tse?"

"Sure."

The kid hops into the Jeep with the dog and Sophia, and I follow them up the mountain in the truck.

At the house, Ravi disappears around the back with Van—probably exploring—and I corner Sophia in the kitchen.

"You're good with him," I tell her, my hands on the counter on either side of her, caging her in.

"He makes it easy. He's a good kid."

I can't deny that, but I know all too well that what he shows us on the outside is only part of the story. It's what he buries deep that should be cause for concern. I should know.

I rest my head on her shoulder and she runs her fingers through my hair.

"Are you okay, honey? You've been quiet these past couple of days. Something eating at you?"

Just like Sophia to be straightforward. Part of me

wishes I could unload on her, just lay it all at her feet. The other part of me is worried one day I will and she'll know what a fucked-up bastard she got herself involved with.

"I'm fine," I lie, pressing a kiss to the patch of exposed skin at the base of her neck before I lift my head. "I'm gonna grab a quick shower and I'll give you a hand with dinner."

"Actually, I was hoping you'd get Ravi to help you finish that firepit out back. I picked up some giant marshmallows when we did groceries a couple of days ago. I thought he might like to roast some for dessert." She turns her head and glances through the living room and out the sliding glass door, where Ravi is tossing an old Frisbee one of them must've found lying around for Van. "I was thinking maybe he never had that before. It's something we did with my parents all the time. You think he'd like that?"

I press my lips to the side of her head.

"I'm sure he'll love it."

I don't have the heart to tell her the boys devoured entire bags of roasted marshmallows when we were camping back in June.

By the time I get out of the shower and head downstairs, Ravi is sitting at the counter in the kitchen, watching Sophia chop vegetables.

"Ever hear the saying a watched pot never boils?" I ask him, as I ruffle his hair.

"I'm hungry."

Sophia swings around. "Why didn't you say

something?"

"Grab a banana to tide you over and come outside with me. Need a hand with something. "

I'd already started digging a hole for the firepit after Sophia's parents left. Duff had been satisfied just tossing down some rocks in a circle so I let him. But if his daughter wants a firepit, I want to make her a proper one.

"We've gotta get those stones and that bag of sand that's been in the back of my truck," I tell Ravi when we get outside, Van happily trotting out behind us. "We're making a firepit."

"Cool."

"I've already dug the hole but I want to line the bottom with some sand and those small pavers. Then we'll build up the circle with the stones."

It takes us maybe an hour to put the thing together.

When we stand back to admire our work, Ravi looks mighty pleased with himself. He's a smart kid with good spatial sense. He'll do well working with his hands.

Behind us the door slides open.

"It's perfect," Sophia says, coming down the steps.

She sits down on one of the four stumps the kid and I rolled over here to circle the fire. They'd been behind the woodpile, clearly intended to be used at some point. I plan to use them as the base for two raw-edge benches, but that's a job for another day.

"Can I build the fire?" the kid asks.

"How about you save that for after dinner?" she answers, grinning over at him. "Go wash your hands. It's on the table."

He doesn't have to be told twice and is off like a shot. Sophia gets to her feet and walks up to me, putting a hand on my chest.

"It really is perfect."

She lifts up on tiptoes and treats me to a sweet kiss.

"Glad you like it, baby."

The tacos are the shit, some with shredded chicken, the others with spicy sliced flank steak, and topped with some kind of chipotle sauce she threw together. Thank God she likes to cook and is damn good at it too, because everyone knows what a disaster I am in the kitchen.

We had a late start and by the time Ravi is shoving the last taco down his gullet, it's already getting dark outside.

"I'll clean up." I collect the dirty dishes and dump them in the sink. "You guys go ahead outside and start that fire before it gets too late."

It doesn't take much to tidy up, and I'm just about to head out back with the bag of marshmallows I found when my phone rings in my pocket.

Wapi's name pops up on the screen.

"What's up?"

"You need to get your ass down here."

"Where? What's going on?"

"Backyard. We've got a problem."

That's all I get before the line goes dead. *Shit.*

I see Ravi just got a nice fire going when I step outside.

"Did you find long sticks?" I ask him when he about snatches the bag from my hands.

"Yup."

He shows me a couple of nice long ones.

"Good. Don't give yourself a sugar coma," I caution him when he shoves three gigantic marshmallows on one stick.

Then I bend over Sophia, who is watching him with a smile on her face.

"I've gotta run, Fee. Something urgent's come up, but I'll try to be back as soon as I can to get the kid home."

She tilts her head back and asks worriedly, "Everything all right?"

"I'll let you know as soon as I do."

They're having a good time and I don't want to spoil their fun before I know what is going on.

"Okay. And don't worry about us. I can get Ravi to the clubhouse when were done here."

I hesitate for a second but then I remember the urgency in Wapi's voice, and drop a hard kiss on Sophia's lips.

"I'll call you."

SOPHIA

"No MORE FOR Van, kiddo. Too much sugar isn't good for him."

I don't bother cautioning Ravi that twelve marshmallows after he just ate five tacos might be pushing the envelope as well. From the way he presses his hand in his stomach, he's discovering that for himself.

"Okay."

I've been a little uneasy since Tse left abruptly, wondering what could have happened to make him rush out of here. It sounded urgent. As long as it's not dangerous.

I hope he'll call soon.

"Next time, if you want, you're more than welcome to bring a friend."

I'm trying to fill the deep pockets of silence. Ravi is the least talkative kid I've ever encountered. So unlike my sister's girls, who chatter nonstop. Especially Reagan, who is about to turn twelve, going on twenty. I bet she could talk Ravi out of his shell.

"That's okay," he mumbles. "I don't really have any."

My heart spasms in my chest. He sounds so sad. So lost. I just wanna wrap him up, but I'm afraid he'll bolt if I touch him. Tse told me about the incident at the clubhouse but Ravi never talks about it.

"How come?" I ask gently, and he glances at me, as if the question surprises him.

"I don't get along. I'm not like the other kids."

He says it very matter-of-factly, which makes it all the more heartbreaking. My pregnancy hormones are filling my eyes with tears as I furiously blink them back. I'm going to terrify the kid if I start crying now.

"You know," I start carefully. "I remember having a hard time adjusting when I went to college. You've met my parents. They're different. My sister, me, and my younger brother were all home-schooled. We lived in Arizona on a large piece of land with a bunch of other families. Grew all our own food, and never owned a computer. We had to go into town to use one in the library."

"You grew your own food? What, like vegetables?"

"Yup. It was like one big farm. We grew vegetables, had some livestock for milk and cheese, and sometimes meat, but mostly we ate vegetarian meals."

"You eat meat now, though," he points out.

"I do. I've changed a lot since I left home." I try to steer the conversation back around. "Still didn't really know how to make friends, though. When I was younger other kids teased me because I was different, and by the time I was grown up I was pretty used to being by myself. That's until I met Kelsey, Finn's mom. She and I grew to be good friends. She'd had a different kind of childhood as well and we understood each other."

I notice he's listening intently and then appears to get lost in thought as he stares into the dwindling flames.

"My mom made the best Naan," he suddenly says, his eyes still on the fire. "She had this big round heavy pan I had to help her lift on the stove. It would get so hot, steam would come off."

That explains some of his features. He looks at least part East Indian to me.

"I love fresh Naan," I prompt when he falls silent. "In fact, I love all Indian food."

"She loved that pan," he whispers, and I have to lean forward to hear him. "And then my uncle smashed her head in with it."

I couldn't have held back my gasp if I tried, but he doesn't seem to notice.

"He said she shamed the family honor and I had to go live with him."

Swallowing down the bile surging up my esophagus, I ask, "How old were you?"

"Nine." He lifts his gaze on me. "Do you think you can make me Naan some day?"

God, how I wish Tse was here. I'm terrified of saying something wrong and breaking his fragile offer of trust.

"I never have before, but I'm happy to try. Maybe you can help me?"

"Sure."

He picks up the Frisbee and throws it for Van, who happily jumps up from where he was lying and bounds after it. As if he didn't just drop the most heartbreaking story at my feet.

The buzzing of my phone has me almost jump out of my skin, and I rush to pull it from my pocket.

It's a message from Tse.

Gonna be a bit longer. Need you to take Ravi to clubhouse and wait for me there.

I check the time and notice to my surprise it's almost eleven. The boy should probably be in bed by now. The fire is almost out anyway.

Okay. Leaving now.

Ravi just nods when I tell him and quickly throws some sand on the fire like Tse told him to do, before he follows me inside.

"Are we taking Van?" he asks, when I grab my wallet

and my keys and open the front door.

"No. He probably needs a nap after all the exercise you gave him today. We'll be back soon enough."

I watch as he bends down and gives the dog a hug before he follows me out the door I lock behind us.

Just around the bend past Paco's property I see rear lights up ahead. A car is parked half on the road, half on the shoulder, with the driver's side door wide open. When I get closer, I notice something lying in the middle of the road. Not something, someone. They're not moving.

I stop the Jeep at a distance.

"Is she hurt?" Ravi asks.

It's only then I recognize it's a woman with blonde hair. Something about her is familiar.

"Stay here," I tell him.

I get out and am already pulling my phone from my pocket as I jog toward her.

"Oh no…Mandy?"

I kneel down on the ground beside her and brush the hair off her face, when suddenly her eyes snap open.

"I'm sorry."

It's the last thing I hear.

24

Tse

THERE ARE ALREADY five or so bikes parked in the back, except for one lying on its side.

I could see the flashing lights of emergency vehicles from the road and rounded the restaurant parking lot to the back. Three patrol cars and an ambulance are blocking my view of the back door.

Getting out of my truck, I rush toward the sound of angry voices to find Paco and Honon struggling with Kaga.

"What the fuck is going on?" I bark at Wapi when I spot him near the rear of the ambulance.

"It's Lea. She was heading home when someone took a knife to her in the parking lot. I was at the bar."

"Lea?"

Kaga's wife has been working at the restaurant now for a month or so. She's a sweet woman. She and Kaga have been together for probably close to twenty years and have a couple of teen boys. Kaga is our second in command, his calm and laid-back character a perfect counterbalance to Ouray's often more explosive personality.

Kaga is not so calm now.

"How is she?"

"I don't know, man. Emme went out to toss some garbage in the bin and saw her lying there. Yelled for me." He runs both his hands over his head and I notice they're stained red. "So much blood. She was lookin' at me but couldn't talk. I didn't know where to put my hands to stop the bleeding."

We both jerk our heads around when the ambulance suddenly tears out of there. Kaga's loud keening sets my hair on end and when I look his way, he's on his knees on the ground.

"We need to get him to the hospital," I announce, walking toward the small group, grateful I opted to drive instead of ride. "Get him in my truck."

At that moment Ouray comes walking out of the restaurant and marches straight up to Kaga, hooks him under the arms and hauls him to his feet. Then he takes the other man's face in his hands and leans close.

"Get it the fuck together, brother," he barks in his face. "You keep this shit up and they won't let you into the hospital either. Your wife needs you calm."

That last comment seems to resonate and moments

later we're putting him in my passenger seat. Honon and Ouray get in the back and I guess the other guys will follow later.

"Someone get me up to speed," I ask, as I steer the truck toward the exit.

Ouray explains how he, Kaga, and Honon were just coming back from the gym when Paco ran out of the clubhouse. He'd been checking the camera feed for the restaurant and saw the attack go down.

"We just took off. Didn't realize it was Lea until we got here. Paco actually thought it was Sophia at first, with the similar haircuts."

Never registered that before, but now that he mentions it, they both have short brown hair and are probably about the same height. Suddenly uneasy, I fish my phone from my pocket and toss it in the back seat.

"Text Sophia, tell her to bring Ravi to the clubhouse and stay there."

I don't want to waste time arguing over the phone with her, nor do I want to tell her what is going on until we know how Lea is doing. Otherwise, she'll insist on coming to the hospital and I need to know she's safe at the clubhouse.

"Good call," Ouray mumbles, and when I glance in the rearview mirror I catch his worried eyes on me.

"She's texting back," Honon announces and I sigh in relief. "Says she's leaving right away."

"I'm gonna kill him," Kaga mumbles beside me.

"You need to cool it, brother. Focus on Lea." Ouray leans forward and grabs a firm hold of his shoulder.

"Family first, then we'll talk revenge."

I get us to Mercy in record time, where we're directed to a waiting room while Ouray is trying to get information from the nurse at the desk.

"Any idea who it was?" I ask Honon.

We're standing off by the doors while Ouray sits down next to Kaga in one of the few available seats. The ER is busy. Every time a white coat walks in through the doors, the rumble of voices quiets and all eyes turn that way. Everyone is eagerly awaiting news.

"Paco said it was hard to make out on the screen. Fucker came at her from behind. Looks like he stabbed her first in the back and when she turned around, he repeatedly slashed at her front. Says she tried to fight him off."

"Jesus."

"All he could tell was the guy was maybe a couple of inches taller—not by that much—and had a slight build. Dark clothes, probably a hoodie, or whatever. Light-skinned."

"Where'd he go after? Did he see?"

"He was already on the phone with the cops when he watched him run across the parking lot toward the trees at the back."

I'm suddenly transported back a few weeks to the alley where I saw a figure of a similar description kick Sophia, who was on the ground, before taking off. I followed him through those trees and between two buildings, right across to the other side of the railroad tracks.

It would make sense. The feds had picked up a few of

the dealers before the sting went sour, but that particular guy had not been among them.

"Be back in a minute," I tell Honon, and walk down the hall and out the door to the parking lot to make a call.

"Yeah."

"Paco, it's Tse. I had a thought."

"Kinda have my hands full. Feds just showed up."

"Appreciate that, brother, but I may be able to help. That video of the attack. Can I access that from my phone?"

"Fuck, man, you don't want to see that shit. Trust me on this."

When I explain my suspicion it might be the same dealer from the alley, he immediately texts me a link and a password.

"Skip ahead to nine oh five," he says, staying on the line with me. "That's when she walks out. You can see the guy coming from the other side of the bin."

I watch Lea come into view, walking away from the restaurant. She's maybe twenty feet into the parking lot when you can clearly see a shape detach itself from the shadow of the dumpster. Crouched low, the figure sneaks up behind her.

I hiss sharply as I witness the brutal attack, but force myself to observe the figure instead of Lea's futile fight. The moment she drops to the ground, the guy backs away a few steps before he turns and starts running.

"Wait a minute," I mumble, stopping the feed and backing it up.

There, right as he crosses through the beam from the

light over the back door.

I replay it again to make sure.

"Nine oh seven," I tell Paco. "Guy is running, the light hits his right side. There's a name running down the sleeve of his hoodie. Pretty sure I saw something similar on the guy who attacked Sophia. He moves the same way too."

"Shit. Tell me she's safe, brother."

"Should be at the clubhouse. I've gotta go."

I end the call and immediately call the clubhouse where Brick answers.

"Did Sophia and the boy get there okay?"

A moment of heavy silence passes before Brick responds.

"She's supposed to be here?"

"Texted her half an hour ago. Maybe a little longer. Let me call her."

Hanging up, I dial her number and listen to it ring until it goes to voicemail. Maybe she's driving. I try again and leave her a curt message to call me right away, but it's not sitting well with me.

Running back to the waiting room, I fill Honon in when I catch Ouray's glance. He must've seen something in my face because he comes right over.

"Honon, go with him," he snaps when I explain the situation. "I gotta stay here, Luna is on her way here with Kaga's boys. Fucking find her and call me right away."

Honon follows me out the door and to my truck, already on the phone with the clubhouse before I pull away.

"Brick is leaving, heading toward her place as well. He'll keep an eye out on the road."

I hand my phone to him.

"Sophia's number is last dialed on my phone. Keep trying her."

I'm breaking every speed limit but the moment we hit the route she would've taken I slow down and keep my eyes peeled for any sign of her Jeep.

"Dark green Jeep Cherokee. Older model," I share with Honon, who is scrutinizing his side of the road.

There's nothing along US160, and once we hit the turnoff going up the mountain we have to slow down even further. There are no lights here other than my high beams.

"Either her battery's out of juice or she doesn't have the phone on her."

Honon drops my phone in the center console just as I see something up ahead.

"What's that?"

I hit the gas but never take my eyes off the vehicle parked on the shoulder up ahead. Honon leans forward over the dashboard, squinting.

"That's it. Jeep. Looks empty," he confirms.

Maybe there was a problem with the Jeep and she and Ravi walked back to the house. It's not that far. But the next moment that hopeful thought vanishes when Honon yells.

"Stop. Something on the road."

He's out of the truck before I can put it in park on the opposite shoulder, the high beams hitting the front of the

Jeep. He crouches down, picking something up off the road and holds it up.

I grab my cell and hit redial as I get out, hearing the phone in Honon's hand start ringing.

"Screen is cracked," he says.

Makes no sense.

I walk over to the Jeep, holding my breath for fear of what I'll see, but there's nothing other than her wallet in one of the cupholders between the front seats. Both doors are closed, but when I try the driver's side, I find it unlocked. The keys are dangling from the ignition.

She'd never voluntarily leave her keys, wallet, and her phone behind, but still I have to make sure. I start jogging back to the truck.

"Stay here!" I call at Honon. "Gotta check the house."

I keep my eyes focused on the side of the road all the way up to the driveway, hoping against hope to catch a glimpse. The outside light is on but the house itself is dark.

They're not here. I can feel it in my gut, but I still need to make sure.

Van is at the door when I walk in and find the alarm still set to *away*. I quickly disarm it and with the dog on my heels check every room in the house, confirming what I already know. Instead of leaving him behind, I clip the dog's leash on and load him in the back seat.

By the time I get back, Brick's truck is parked next to the Jeep, but there's no sign of Honon, and flashing lights are heading toward us on the other side of the road.

Brick's face is pale when I get out of the truck and I

imagine mine is not much better.

"We'll find them," he says, but he's not half as convincing as he tries to be.

Panic running like ice through my veins is making it hard to breathe.

"Someone took them. Should'a told her to stay put. Would've been safer." I feel myself become lightheaded and bend over, my hands on my knees.

Brick's large paw clamps on the back of my neck.

"We're gonna rip this fucking town apart until we have them," he growls by my ear, as I hear the crunch of footsteps approaching. "Not gonna lose anyone else, brother. Not gonna happen."

"She's pregnant," I croak.

"Say what?"

I lift my head and focus my eyes on him.

"Fee…she's pregnant."

SOPHIA

"I'M SORRY. I'M so sorry."

I wake up to a mantra of whispered apologies, but I can't see a thing.

It's dark and cramped, smelling like fuel, dirty clothes, and urine. I try to reach out my hand but my wrists are tied behind my back. My head is pounding.

"I'm so sorry."

"Mandy?"

I feel movement at my back like someone rolled into me.

"Oh thank God. I thought you were dead."

"Where are we? What's going on?"

"You've gotta keep your voice down," she whispers behind me. "We're in the trunk. He may be able to hear us."

"In whose trunk?"

"I don't know. I never saw his face. I'm so sorry, he had a gun on me, I had no choice."

It's really hard to try and fit the pieces together when you find yourself tied up in the trunk of a car, after getting knocked out. At least that's what I assume happened.

It all went so fast. One minute I was leaning over Mandy, the next I was out. I vaguely remember Mandy saying she was sorry then too. I have no concept of time or place, and I try hard to get a grasp as thoughts spin through my mind, but one I zoom in on.

Ravi.

"Did you see what happened to the boy?" I ask her urgently.

"Shhh," she hushes me. "I got a glimpse of him heading for the woods when you were being dragged to the car."

I squeeze my eyes closed against the sudden burning, praying Ravi got away.

Suddenly I feel the car swerve, rolling us into each other before it seems to straighten out again. I'm starting to feel evidence of being treated roughly all over my body, as we appear to be going over some rough terrain.

I'm on high alert when the vehicle starts slowing down.

"Mandy. There's two of us, one of him, right?"

"I think so."

"Two of us, one of him. We should be able to take him, together."

"You're crazy."

I've been called worse, but there's no way in hell I'm just going to let myself be taken without putting up a fight. I have so much to fight for.

"Roll on your back."

"I can't, my hands are tied behind me. It hurts."

"You have to. It's not that bad."

I feel her shift beside me as the car comes to a stop and I hear a door slam.

"Quickly, pull up your knees and when the trunk starts to open, kick out as hard as you can," I hiss at her. "We can do this."

I've barely got the last word out when I hear a click and see a crack of light on Mandy's side open.

"Now!" I yell, no longer caring if he can hear us as I kick up as hard as I can.

2 5

SOPHIA

"GODDAMMIT, SONOVABITCH!"

The trunk is wide open and I scramble to get my legs under me, but Mandy is in my way. I can only lift up my body so far before I'm wedged behind her.

I yell at her, "Get out!"

Before she has a chance to move, the long barrel of a rifle slides over the edge of the trunk toward my face.

"Wouldn't suggest it."

The deceptively calm voice sends a chill down my spine. I've heard it before. Mandy has too, and she whimpers beside me.

"Get the blonde one out."

Fuck. There's two of them. One must've been waiting.

A man I don't recognize, with blood streaming from a

cut under his chin, leans in and grabs Mandy by the hair, yanking her upright before she's hauled out by her arms. She screams and I hear a thud, followed by silence.

I'm afraid to move, the black barrel inches from my face.

"Now this one."

The same guy reaches for me and I don't fight him. Not when that rifle is still pointed at me. He's none too gentle when he unceremoniously tosses me on the ground beside Mandy, who seems too still.

"She's not dead," the familiar voice shares. "Not yet anyway."

I slowly turn my head and look up. He's backlit so it takes a minute before his features come into focus.

"You."

He grins, looking pleased I remember his ugly mug. Only difference is he's not wearing his ball cap with the Clover Produce logo now.

"Me. You're the only two who've seen my face and can connect me to the deliveries." He waves the barrel at me. "Knew where to find you the whole time, but I had to find that bitch first. Luckily, her sister isn't the smartest. Blabbed on social media…"

While he talks, I do a quick scan of my surroundings. I'm pretty sure we're not in Durango, judging by the desert-like surroundings. I have no idea how long we'd been driving before I woke up, but I'm pretty sure we're nowhere near the mountains.

This place looks like an old industrial park. The sparse buildings are old, run-down, most of the windows broken and others boarded up. Over time they've taken on the color of the dry sand around them.

"…made for a good distraction at the restaurant." He barks out a laugh. "Tweaker cut the wrong bitch, but it sure played into our hands."

"Restaurant? What happened at the restaurant?"

He leans down, grabs my upper arm, and roughly hauls me to my feet, almost dislocating my shoulder in the process.

"You pissed off a dealer." He laughs again as he starts pulling me toward a two-story building that looks like it may have been an old garage. "Stabbed the bitch right in the back. The idiot thought it was you. Watched the whole thing on camera and I knew this could be our chance. Sure enough, not five minutes later that piece of shit Tse gets in his truck and leaves you alone. Like I said, we've had eyes on you."

I almost trip when he tugs me into the dark building. I was scared before, but now I'm terrified. He talks about *we* instead of *me*. He's been watching the restaurant? My house?

A quick glance behind me shows the second guy, the one with the cut on his chin, heading this way with Mandy tossed over his shoulder.

So many bits and pieces of information are bouncing around my head, not helping the persistent throbbing.

"What do you want with us?" He ignores me, half dragging me up a stairway when I lose my footing. "Who are you?" I persist, but there's no answer.

He shoves me into a room and I stumble, hitting

carpeted floor, and scramble back until I feel a wall behind me. A few moments later, Mandy is literally tossed into the room with me. The door closes and I hear the sound of a lock turning. Then I hear two sets of footsteps go down the stairs, the low rumble of some words exchanged, and finally it's silent.

They've left.

The first thing I do is test the strength of the binding around my wrists. I think it's a zip tie. It cuts into my skin when I try to pull on it. Then I crawl over to Mandy and lean close to see if she's still breathing. I let out a sigh of relief when I feel her chest move and sit back, resting my head against the wall beside her.

I close my eyes and let the seriousness of the situation sink in. We're in deep shit and I wish I knew what they planned to do. Or maybe it's better I don't.

I replay the driver's words in my head, even the parts I pushed to the background. Like the part where someone got stabbed in the parking lot of the restaurant. I'm sure that was the urgent call that had Tse rush out the door.

Tweaker cut the wrong bitch.

That was supposed to have been me. The only person I know who even remotely looks like me is Lea. A sob breaks free.

Oh my God. She has kids.

The driver had laughed coldheartedly when he mentioned her. It's suddenly crystal clear he intends to kill us. The only thing I don't get is why he hasn't already. That would've been easier. Why go through the trouble of kidnapping us?

Something else is nagging at me. I could've sworn he mentioned Tse by name. In fact, he called him *that piece of shit, Tse*. Sounds like something you'd say about someone you know and don't like.

How?

I have no idea what time it is. I wonder if Tse already knows I'm missing. If he does, he must be out of his mind. I know he'll be looking, but I can't just sit here and hope he'll find me.

It's not just about me anymore; I have a tiny, brand-new life I'm responsible for.

And Mandy, I'm worried she hasn't come to yet. I have no way to know how badly she's hurt, but I'm definitely not helping her by sitting idle on the floor.

Time to get moving.

My eyes have had a chance to adjust to the dark room and I can make out a few more details. A window that looks to be blacked out, except for a tiny sliver near the bottom of the frame. Drawn by the small strip of light, I get to my feet and shuffle in that direction.

Bending over I try to peek through but the slit is too narrow to see anything. It looks like tape. I have to turn my back so I can reach it and start feeling for something I can grab on to. I pick and scratch at the slick surface until I manage to loosen an edge, pinch it between my thumb and index finger, and pull.

I stop when I hear a soft moan.

"Mandy?"

I wait but it's dead silent again. Doubling my efforts I yank at the piece of tape, managing to pull a little more up. Noticing more light in the room, I turn and see I've widened the gap. Now when I bend down I can see outside. Thank God this isn't one of the boarded-up windows.

There are no lights but the moon is still out, providing enough to see the two men out front. One looks to be smoking, the red ember glowing. The other guy has his back to me and I notice a large emblem on the back of his vest.

As I'm watching, the smoker turns his head and appears to look right at me. I scramble back from the window, my heart racing in my chest, waiting for footsteps to come running up the stairs. When none come, and my panic subsides, I realize it's not likely he would've been able to see me. The exposed patch of glass is no more than a couple of inches.

With better light in the room, I start looking for something I could use. Anything, a piece of metal, a sliver of glass, something heavy, but other than dirt and a few scraps of paper, the room is empty.

Dejected, I sit down on the floor beside Mandy, my back against the wall. Frustrated tears roll down my face and, exhausted; I eventually drift off.

I'm not sure how long I've been out when I wake up to the sound of rumbling engines outside and I rush to the window. I have to blink against the morning light before I can see a group of four or five bikers pull off the road and head this way.

Oh my God.

Tears start blurring my vision.

Tse.

Tse

"You've gotta eat something."

Lisa sets a plate with bacon and eggs in front of me, along with a mug of hot coffee.

It's been over seven hours since we found the Jeep.

It didn't take long for some of my brothers to show, and after that the cops and the feds. We spent most of that time searching the woods, knocking on doors, calling in favors, anything to try and get a sense of direction. Some kind of clue where to start looking.

The only thing we found was a small piece of fabric stuck on what looked to be a wild gooseberry bush. Same green color as the T-shirt Ravi was wearing. I tried taking Van, hoping maybe he'd pick up a scent, but he did little else than growl. Either because of the number of people, or the thick tension in the air, but the dog clearly felt threatened so I put him back in the truck.

The general consensus seemed to be Ravi witnessed something, managed to take off, and is hopefully hiding. But if Sophia had been out there with him, I'm positive she would've tried to go back for her vehicle, or at least her phone. No, someone took her. I could feel it in my gut.

Brick finally got me to agree to wait for morning light to go back out there—just a few of us—and try again with the dog.

I look out the window and notice the sky is lighting up a bit. Waiting and doing nothing has been hell. My imagination has had a chance to work overtime, thinking of Sophia, who has her, what's being done to her. Maybe I should eat a little because I can't fucking wait to go out there and do something.

Seven fucking hours.

"Just talked to Trunk." I'm just taking a swig of my coffee when Ouray walks into the kitchen. He's been holed up in his office, making phone calls, since we got here. "Lea is stable. They've inflated her collapsed lung, repaired the nicked artery, and stitched up the cut on her cheek and her forearm. She's expected to make a full recovery."

"Bless her heart."

This from Lisa, who was waiting anxiously when we got back to the clubhouse earlier. No one seems to have gotten a lick of sleep, other than the boys in the bunkhouse. I guess Trunk must've gone to the hospital to take Luna's place when she got called to the scene up on the mountain.

I'm grateful Lea's gonna be okay, don't get me wrong, but my fucking woman is still out there under God knows what circumstances. That is, if she's still alive.

"I talked to the Moab Reds, Mesa Riders, and the Amontinados. Had to call in a few markers, but they're keeping an eye open and an ear to the ground."

They're all clubs we were at some point affiliated with, sharing a thriving drug trade in the region back in the nineties. Arrow's Edge got out, but the others still have at least a partial interest in that business and might have an idea who we're dealing with.

"Anything from Luna?" I ask between bites, forcibly

swallowing the food down.

I haven't really kept track of what the cops and the FBI were doing, but there were still some cars at the scene when Honon drove us here.

"Yeah, she's on her way to the clubhouse. I was gonna let her tell you herself."

I shake my head. "Give it to me now, because in five minutes I'll be gone. Ravi is out there somewhere and he saw something. He's our best bet. I've gotta find him."

"Fair enough. They figured someone must'a been watching Sophia's place. She's not a stupid woman, so she would have to have had a good reason to pull over. That takes planning." Lisa hands Ouray a coffee and he takes a sip. "Found a wireless trail camera up in a tree across from the driveway. They could see anyone coming and going."

I slam my fist down on the table so hard the dishes rattle and my coffee spills.

"Easy, brother."

Honon, who's been quietly sitting at the table with me, puts a firm hand on my forearm. Probably a good thing, because I was about to hurl my plate at the wall.

"They've been waiting."

"Would seem so," Ouray confirms. "Probably saw the security cameras on the house and simply waited for a time she'd be coming down that mountain by herself. When they saw you leave—"

"They set a trap," I finish for him. "They're organized."

Ouray nods. "Yup. Luna says they're gonna try and access the feed. See if they can pin down an exact time she left."

"How the fuck is that gonna help?" I snap, my patience run out. "She's already gone. Why the fuck aren't they out there looking for her, instead of wasting their time on a goddamn camera?"

I forcefully shove my chair back from the table and get up.

"Time line," Ouray states calmly, blocking my exit. "They've got access to traffic cameras and such. If they know the time she was taken, it'll be easier to find and track the vehicle that took her. It could give us a fucking roadmap to where she is."

I nod at him. "I hadn't thought of that."

He claps me on the shoulder.

"Take Honon with you."

By the time I walk with Van out of the clubhouse to my truck, I don't only have Honon but Paco, Wapi, and Yuma following me.

In my hand I have a Ziploc baggie with a pillowcase from Ravi's bed.

Not sure if it's gonna do any fucking good, but I have to try.

ARROW'S EDGE MC

2 6

Tse

Hᴇʀ ᴊᴇᴇᴘ ɪꜱ gone.

A Durango PD SUV is parked in its spot.

I cross over the median and pull up in front of it. Yuma's vehicle does the same behind me.

As I'm getting out, two figures come walking out of the woods: Tony Ramirez and Jay VanDyken.

"Anything?"

"We just got here too," Ramirez says, looking behind me. "We've got how many? Seven and a dog? We make a decent search party."

Means a fuckofalot these guys are back out here at the crack of dawn.

"Thanks."

Nowhere near sufficient to describe my gratitude, but

I have a feeling they get the message.

VanDyken claps a hand on my shoulder.

"Hang in there," he mumbles under his breath.

"Here's my thinking," Ramirez continues. "The kid's how old? Fourteen?"

"Will be next week," Wapi answers.

I turn to him, surprised he knows and at the same time embarrassed I forgot. Not like the kid ever mentioned it. Not since the camping trip anyway.

Goddammit. If we get them back…No, fuck that… *When* we get them back, I'm gonna personally see to it Ravi gets the best damn birthday celebration he's ever had. I know all too well what it's like to go without. To have every year pass without anyone even noticing. If it's up to me that kid will remember every fucking birthday from here on out.

"And he's smart," Ramirez continues.

"As a whip," I respond this time.

"Then I don't think he's gonna have wandered too far from familiar territory. So here's what I suggest. We go in on this side and spread out parallel to the road about twenty-five yards apart. Head up toward the house, then cross the road, circle the house and make our way back here on the other side."

With everyone in agreement, we head into the woods. I bend down and let Van sniff the pillowcase.

"Find the boy, buddy. Find the boy."

I start walking, trying to stay level with Paco and VanDyken on either side of me as we make our way through the trees. Here and there the underbrush is heavy, snagging at my jeans, but I trudge ahead, only stopping to check the occasional fallen or hollow trees for hiding spots.

Every so often I let Van have a sniff of the bag I'm holding, but so far he hasn't given any signs of picking up a scent. It was a long shot, tracking dogs have trained noses and given the abuse this dog has seen in his life, I'm not even sure his nose works properly.

I've all but given up on the dog when he stops, one of his front paws pulled up to his chest and his snout in the air, standing on alert and furiously sniffing. I'm guessing we're almost level with Sophia's house. Van takes two steps forward and then suddenly veers to the right, toward the road.

"Dog's locked in on something," I call out as we cross right in front of Paco.

Ramirez, closest to the road, must've heard me because he's waiting.

"What's going on?" he asks, falling into step beside me.

"I'm not sure, but whatever it is he's eager to get at it."

The dog has his head down and is pulling on the leash. I'm almost running to keep up with him. He doesn't bother slowing down when we get to the road and almost yanks the lead from my hand when I try to. No cars, thank God.

I hear footfalls on the asphalt behind me as Van pulls me into the trees on this side. The farther he gets away from the road, the more worried I get he's on the trail of some animal, instead of the boy, and is taking us farther away.

But then we cross a path I've walked before. When Sophia and I went to look at Paco's place.

The leash is ripped from my hold when Van makes a sudden right and starts running down the path. Toward the new build.

It makes sense. Ravi feels safe in the unfinished house. He knows every nook and cranny since he spends almost all of his time here. He must've realized, other than the brothers, it's not likely many know about the place since it's not visible from the road.

"Paco!" I yell behind me. "He's at your place!"

By the time I see the house through the trees, I'm sucking air into my lungs and my legs are on fire. I'm out of shape and I fucking feel it.

The front door is in, but we haven't installed the sliding doors in the rear yet. I immediately head that way. Ramirez is first through the door and I hear a deep, fierce growl from inside.

"Tse…in here."

He's standing in the doorway to what is going to be the master bath. I look over his shoulder and see Van, the hair on his back up, his head low, and his teeth bared. In the corner behind him is Ravi, making himself as small as possible, his face turned into the wall. The smell of terror is thick in the air.

I recognize it.

It's been so long since I've lived on the edge of fear, I'd forgotten how paralyzing it can be.

"It's okay, Van," I coo at the dog, never taking my eyes off him as I ease Ramirez out of the way. "Ravi, it's me, kid."

"Tse?"

"Right here."

In a flurry of movement the boy is on his feet and running toward me, barreling into me so hard I stumble back and land on my ass. My arms instinctively close around him.

"You're okay," I repeat, over and over again, barely cognizant of the men filing in behind me.

"He took her." His voice is raspy but firm as his large brown eyes search out mine. "Sophia. He hit her on the head and put her in the trunk. The other one too."

"Other one?"

He nods. "The blonde girl that was lying in the road. She wasn't moving either."

That's why Sophia pulled over. The girl was a decoy.

"Did you get a look at who took her?"

I try to keep the urgent hope out of my voice, afraid to put too much pressure on him.

"Not the front, but I could see his back when he was putting her in the trunk. He had a leather vest like yours. A big patch on his back."

"A patch?"

Ravi looks over my shoulder at Paco who spoke.

"Yeah, something with flames."

My entire body seizes and I hear Paco's soft curse behind me before he asks, "Was there a name on the logo?"

"All I can remember is that it started with an A."

SOPHIA

DUST KICKS UP as the bikes round the building, heading toward the rear.

Then I notice the car that brought us here is no longer out front. Neither are the two guys.

I pull the tape up a little higher, hoping to see more outside, but there's no sign of any life. I hear a groan and turn to see Mandy blinking her eyes. I rush over and drop to my knees beside her.

"Hey…are you okay? Mandy?"

She seems a little disoriented but eventually her eyes seem to focus on me.

"Wha…"

I try to make out the rest of her words but her slur is so thick I can't distinguish anything she says.

"It's okay," I say stupidly.

Of course it's not okay. It's not okay at all.

I sink down on my butt, frustration threatening to overwhelm me, and once again I try to wrench my hands apart. It's no use; I can't get any movement. I remember once seeing a video of a girl using her shoelace to get out of zip ties binding her wrists. Unfortunately, I'm wearing sandals and even if I had a shoelace, I can't remember how she did it.

I can't believe they just drove by. Maybe I should've tried to break the window, gotten their attention. Hell, I'm starting to doubt that was even Tse at all.

The room slowly turns brighter as outside the sun climbs higher in the sky. Waiting for something to happen is driving me crazy. What if I could break the window? With my hands tied behind my back I can't hold on to anything. I'd have to jump and there's no chance in hell I'd come out of that in one piece.

A faint scraping sound draws my attention and I turn my head slightly to hear better.

There it is again. Is someone here? Maybe they didn't leave.

The thought has barely formed when I hear distinct footsteps coming up the stairs, and in the next instant I'm on my feet.

"In here!" I make my way to the door and kick it as hard as I can. "We're in here!"

Suddenly I can't hear anything anymore and press my ear against the surface. There's rustle of fabric, then a soft jingle and the scratch of metal on metal as someone slides a key in the door.

It takes me only a second to clue in it's not likely someone who is here to rescue us has a key ready. I'm already backing away when the door opens.

"Hola, Mamacita."

I press myself into a corner as he saunters into the room, barely glancing at Mandy, his focus on me. The other guys scared me with their anger, but much more terrifying is the smile on Tse's former friend's face. I thought I had this figured out, but now I'm more confused than ever.

"What do you want with us?"

He looks down at Mandy.

"Nothing with her. She was a means to an end and now she's useless." Then his eyes slowly track up my body and I start to shiver. "Now you're a means to an end."

"I don't know what you're talking about."

He chuckles and leans in, sniffing me. It turns my stomach.

"You're the prize, *hermosa*. Already your fear smells like victory."

"I d-don't understand," I stutter, the shaking making it hard to speak.

Manny steps back and starts pacing the room.

"You will. Once my *brother* shows up, you will."

He almost spits out the word, brother, like it leaves a filthy taste in his mouth.

"Are you talking about Tse?"

I've got to keep him talking, distracted from whatever he has planned. I watch him pace the room and every time he moves away from the open door, I look at the hallway beyond. But there's no way I could get to the door before he'd catch up with me.

"Did he tell you we grew up together?"

He glances over and I nod.

"In foster care."

He snorts derisively and closes the distance. "I'd hardly call that care. Did he tell you our so-called foster father liked boys?"

Oh, Jesus.

He sees the shock on my face and smiles.

"Yeah. She liked the extra money and turned a deaf ear. But I heard; the beatings and the…"

He shakes his head, as if to clear it, before he leans so close I can feel his heavy breath on my skin.

"Ben promised to protect me but he didn't. Then he told me he'd always have my back. That was a lie too."

I'm having trouble breathing, the monstrosities he describes sending bile up my throat. Then the horror turns to fear when it dawns on me: this is revenge. I'm bait and he…he's going to kill him.

"He was just a kid too. He's a good man, please don't hurt him."

He braces a hand on the wall beside my head and his body crowds mine. I feel like a caged animal.

"Waited years for a chance to pay him back. Killing him was never enough. Death doesn't scare him. But I knew the moment I saw him with you in that parking lot—that look on his face—you meant something to him. I could've taken you then, but as luck would have it, we'd just set up a new distribution line that involved the Arrow's Edge restaurant."

He barks out a laugh.

"That was a thing of beauty. Stickin' it to those fucking bastards and they didn't have a clue."

I shudder when I feel his free hand run up the side of my body, squeezing my hip before moving it higher.

"We had a good thing going for a while, but this is even better. We'll be killing two birds with one stone."

When his hand reaches the swell of my breast, I whimper as he kneads it roughly.

"No one left to tie us to the drugs…"

He grinds his hips into me and I'm horrified to feel his erection pressing against my stomach.

"But best of all, I get to destroy my brother when I make him watch me kill you."

Suddenly he ducks his head and bites down on my breast so hard I scream.

"Yeah. My mark on you now."

His head snaps up and he turns to the window.

"They're here," he whispers. "And we're ready for them."

I hear it then, the rumble of motorcycles.

ARROW'S EDGE MC

27

Tse

"YOU'RE NOT GOING in alone," Ouray says. "We're gonna be smart about it."

If Ravi hadn't been there, scared out of his mind, I would've already been barreling down the highway to the Amontinados compound just outside Farmington.

And I would've driven straight into a trap without knowing it.

After finding Ravi, we hauled ass back to the clubhouse where Ouray was waiting with the news that he'd just received a tip. From none other than Manny Salinas. He pointed to a location north of Farmington, not too far from the Amontinados compound. A group of abandoned buildings, used frequently for drug deals, where he said a woman was seen hauled from a car into one of the buildings.

"You don't get it," I tell Ouray, feeling a sense of urgency. "This is about me."

"Doesn't matter," he answers calmly. "Luna's on her way there. FBI is already on it. They plan to send up a drone to get a lay of the land. We're not going in blind."

"Fine," I grind out. "But we've got a fucking hour's drive to get there. Let's get going."

He nods at Honon and Yuma to step aside. They've been blocking the door, ready to take me down should I try to leave.

"All right. Let's arm up and roll. We rendezvous with law enforcement in the Mountain Bike Trailhead parking lot at the end of Foothills Drive. Better fucking dust off your vests."

The next five minutes is chaos, digging up and donning bulletproof vests that haven't seen the light of day in over a decade, and stuffing as much ammo and weaponry as possible in pockets and saddlebags. We're ready for battle by the time we get on our bikes.

Brick, who is staying behind with Shilah and Lisa to look after the kids, walks up to me and puts a hand on my shoulder.

"Trust you to bring her home, brother, but lead with your head, not your heart."

I nod, even though I'm not so sure I'll be able to deliver.

Ouray pulls out, then Paco, and I follow with the rest of my brothers filing in behind me.

The longest fucking ride of my life, but at least Ouray

set a good pace.

We roll onto the parking lot just north of Farmington barely forty-five minutes later. A large van and a couple of unmarked vehicles are parked at the far end. I see Gomez and Luna, as well as a guy I don't know, breaking away from a group gathered beside the van.

"Special Agent in Charge Wainer," the stranger introduces himself when they reach us, and doesn't waste time waiting for a response before he lays it out for us. "Five buildings total. Two on the right and three on the left when you pull in from the road. Seven bikes and a car parked at the back of the complex. Three guys with long rifles on the roof. Second building on the right, second and third building on the left."

"We figure at least eight guys there, though," Gomez interjects. "Which means we don't have a bead on five of them."

"Four, actually," Wainer says. "We watched one of them go into the center building on the east side. He's still in there. I have three of my agents already on the ground standing by. Only way in without alerting them was on foot. My guys can take out the three snipers on the roofs, but they're gonna need a distraction. That's where you guys come in."

Manny and his guys are expecting us, so Wainer wants us to ride in, but stop at the entrance and make a ruckus while his agents disable the first three and take over their positions on the roofs. He's hoping we draw the others out and his guys can pick them off. At the same time Luna, Gomez, Wainer himself, and one other agent will come up behind us.

Too many loose ends for a watertight plan but we're running out of time. Fuck, Sophia is running out of time.

I manage to talk Ouray—with the help of his wife—into letting me take the lead, since I'm convinced Manny has plans for me that don't include shooting me on sight.

I've always known part of him blamed me for what happened—fuck, *I've* blamed me—but he was good at hiding it. For a while there brotherhood won out, but since he broke away from Arrow's Edge his resentment for me has only grown. It probably didn't help that I turned him down when he asked me to go with him.

Guess the time for reckoning has come.

My heart is pounding in my chest when I lead the pack into the abandoned complex. My eyes dart around, hoping to see some movement, anything to alert me to their locations. As agreed, I stop, the other guys pulling up as close as they can behind me, reducing the target.

"Salinas! Show your coward face, *hijo de puta!*"

I pull my gun and aim it in the air, shooting off three rounds. The agreed upon signal to the agents. Behind me a volley of shots go off as my brothers do the same. Immediately there's return fire from a main floor doorway on the far right. There was bound to be at least one nervous trigger finger in the bunch.

I aim at the doorway and fire back. Chaos ensues and I crouch down using my bike for cover as bullets start flying from all directions.

At the sound of glass shattering, I look to my left. Shards are still sticking up from the frame of a window on the second floor of the center building.

"Hold your fucking fire!" I hear Manny's voice.

I see her first, her eyes large in her pale face. Then I notice the arm around her throat and the knifepoint to her cheek, and an angry roar bursts out of me.

"There it fucking is!" he yells. "That's the pain I've craved to hear for so goddamn long."

Getting out from behind my bike, I start moving toward the building, my eyes locked on Sophia's.

Manny laughs.

"That's it. Come closer, I want you to see this."

When I'm standing right underneath the window the arm around her neck suddenly moves as he yanks her shirt down, exposing her tit. A trickle of blood runs from a perfect bite mark down past her nipple.

"I marked her."

"I'm gonna rip you apart," I grind out.

It takes everything for me not to run in there. I want Manny exposed at the window. There are guns trained on him, waiting for the slightest move, the narrowest margin, to take him down.

"You can try, but not before I rip her apart."

That's when he makes his mistake. So eager to see me suffer, he pokes his head over her shoulder.

The next moment Sophia screams as a shot rings out.

I'm already running as gunfire breaks out all around me. My only thought is getting to her.

I take the stairs two at a time and burst into the room where I saw them. Sophia is on her knees on the floor by the window, next to the body of Manuel Salinas. There's little left of his head.

"Tse…" she whispers through the blood she's covered with.

"Oh, Christ, baby…"

SOPHIA

"THERE. ONCE THAT heals it'll be as good as invisible. Now, we should probably get you a tetanus shot."

The doctor discards the suture needle and puts a Band-Aid over the stitches on my face.

Just three, where Salinas's blade nicked me when he was shot. The bite mark on my chest was cleaned and bandaged.

I turn my head to look at Tse, who's been a stoic presence by my bedside. He carried me into the hospital in Farmington and despite staff's efforts to get him to leave the room, he's been here the whole time. Other than yelling for help when he picked me up off the floor in that room, he hasn't said a word.

"Left or right?" the doctor asks, holding up a syringe. "Your arm could be a little sore after."

"Left," I tell her, but at the last minute I pull my arm back. "Wait." I dart a quick glance at Tse. "Is this safe during pregnancy?"

The doctor's eyes bulge in surprise.

"You're pregnant? How did you not mention that before?" she scolds me.

Before I have a chance to answer Tse responds gruffly.

"No one fucking asked."

The woman presses her lips together and lightly shakes her head as she rubs an alcohol wipe on my upper arm.

"It's perfectly safe." She gives me the injection, gets rid of the needle, and leans over the side of my bed, her face stern. "From what I understand you've been assaulted, kidnapped, bitten, cut, and generally tossed around. If I'd known you were pregnant, I'd have started with an ultrasound."

Now she's pissing me off. I notice Tse moving like he's got something to say, but I give his hand a squeeze, this one's mine.

I push myself a bit more upright in the bed, forcing her to back up a little.

"As you said, I was assaulted, kidnapped, bitten, cut, and tossed around, so forgive me if I didn't follow protocol to the letter. However, I *am* pregnant, and I *would* appreciate knowing the baby is all right."

She looks at Tse, who stares back hard, before she turns to me.

"You're right. I'll get the portable in here. Drink that cup of water for me."

While we wait I try a few times to get Tse to talk to me, but he keeps telling me to rest. I don't want to rest, I'm afraid the entire past twenty-four hours are going to play on repeat the moment I close my eyes.

I eventually give up and almost sigh in relief when the bitchy ER doctor is back with the ultrasound.

"We'll have a quick look, but I'll also have the attending OBGYN pop in for a quick consult. Just in case."

She plugs the ultrasound unit into an electrical outlet and starts it up. Then she asks a few questions and feeds the answers into the machine.

"Have you had an ultrasound before?" she wants to know, rolling a protective sheath over the wand before squirting it with gel.

"No. Not since I got pregnant anyway. But I did have one scheduled for this coming week."

"Pull up your feet as close to your bottom as you can and let your knees drop to the side," she instructs, lifting the sheet up from the bottom. "That's it. Any particular reason why so early? I mean, you're barely even eight weeks pregnant."

"I don't know. He just said he wanted a baseline."

"Where the hell are you going with that?" Tse points at the wand.

"This early in the game we won't be able to see much with an abdominal ultrasound," the doctor explains. "We have to use this transvaginal probe to get a closer look."

"It's okay, Tse," I reassure him. "Trust me there are worse things women have to put up with on a regular basis."

He looks at me with a deep frown grooving his forehead, probably trying to gauge if I'm serious or not.

"Ready?" I look at the doctor and nod. "Take a nice deep breath in and slowly let it out."

On my breath out, she slips the wand inside. It's not exactly comfortable but my body quickly adjusts. I feel pressure when she starts probing around and clamp onto

Tse's hand.

"This can be a little uncomfortable with a full bladder, but it helps make the fetus more visible this early on."

I just hope I don't pee myself for the second time today. The first time was earlier, as I found out after Tse loaded me in the back of the FBI vehicle. It must've happened when Manny was shot. I swear I could feel the bullet that hit him moving right past me.

"Mmm," she mumbles, pulling out the wand. "Is this an IVF pregnancy?"

"IVF?" Tse pipes up.

"In vitro fertilization. It's when——"

"I know what it means and hell no. I planted that baby there myself."

I don't know whether it is the shock on the doctor's face, an abundance of nervous energy on my part, or the insulted tone of Tse's response—likely a combination of all three—but I burst out laughing so hard the tears are running down my face.

"Jesus, Fee," Tse mumbles worriedly, as he leans closer and with his free hand wipes at the wetness on my cheeks.

"I'll be right back."

She darts out the door, probably thinking she has a lunatic on her hands as I have a hard time controlling my hilarity.

"Are you okay?" he asks when I finally get myself in check.

"I'm——"

The door opens and the doctor walks back in, followed

by a friendly-looking older man who introduces himself as the OBGYN.

"Well, let's see what we have here."

He takes his colleague's place and picks up the wand with one hand, while turning the screen for us to see. He reapplies gel and slides the wand back inside. I'm not sure what I'm looking at until his hand stills and I see a small shadow pulsating on the screen.

"Is that a heart beating?"

"Sure is. Now look from this side."

He moves his hand slightly, angling the wand a little more as he presses deeper. There it is again, a steady heartbeat…and second one beside it.

"Wait…that…is that?"

"Any twins in the family tree?" he asks, a kind smile on his face.

"Twins?"

My mouth drops open as Tse suddenly leans forward to get closer look at the screen.

"There's two?" he asks.

"Congratulations."

I start crying as Tse sits back in his chair and presses the heels of his hands against his forehead.

"Holy fucking hell."

28

TSE

"HEY."

Sophia's hand squeezes my knee and I turn to look at her.

We're in the back of Gomez's SUV driven by Luna, who is taking us back to Durango. Honon is sitting in the passenger seat. He got a round in his thigh. I hadn't even noticed he got shot; I'd been so focused on Sophia.

Through and through, thank God. He was lucky and came limping out around the same time Sophia was released.

Quite a bit of law enforcement in and around the hospital, with one FBI agent shot and two of the Amontinados injured. Worst of was the girl, though— Mandy. From Luna we heard she was taken in for emergency surgery to relieve pressure on her brain.

"You've been so quiet. Are you okay?" she asks softly.

"Am I okay? Babe, you're wearing scrubs because your clothes are covered in blood. *Fuck*, you still have blood in your hair, I should be asking you."

Except I haven't asked. Because I'm a coward.

I'm afraid to hear what Manny shared with her. Scratch that, I already know because I know Manny. He wouldn't have passed up on the opportunity to paint me in a bad light; especially to the woman I love.

She drops her head to my shoulder.

"I'm good now. I knew you would come, but I was hoping you wouldn't."

"What?"

She snuggles in closer, ignoring my bark.

"He wanted to make you watch him kill me and then it would've been your turn."

I take a deep breath and clamp down on the resurgence of the rage I felt seeing him use her as a shield. I wish I'd killed him myself. I have to find a way to get rid of some of this angry energy or I'm going to explode.

Luna takes us through Durango and up to the compound where my truck is still parked. The brothers made it back, all their bikes are lined up in front of the clubhouse. My bike is still in Farmington along with Honon's. Gomez said he'd make sure they get back to Durango.

Brick is standing out front when we roll up and has the back door open the moment the vehicle stops.

"Son of a fucking bitch," he hisses under his breath

when he catches sight of Sophia's face.

"I'm all right, Brick," Sophia soothes, as she slides out of the car and gets swallowed up in Brick's embrace.

He looks at me over her head and mouths, "*Thank you.*"

Fuck. He's thanking me when it was because of me she was put through this in the first place.

As I get out my side of the vehicle, Lisa comes flying out the door of the clubhouse and makes a beeline for Sophia. Seconds later she's wrapped in a big hug and then Lisa leads her into the clubhouse. Honon and Luna follow them inside but I hesitate.

"You okay, brother?" Brick asks.

"No. I'm not fucking okay. I need to hit something."

He takes in my hunched shoulders and clenched fists and nods.

"The old punching bag is hanging in my shed. I also have a pile of new wood that needs splitting behind the cottage. Have at it."

I start walking but stop after a few steps and turn to Brick.

"Sophia…"

"We've got her. Lisa has Ouray's bedroom made up for y'all. For tonight anyway. Go, get it out of your system."

SWEAT IS POURING down my body and my hands are slick with blood from my split knuckles.

I don't know how long I've been in here, taking out my anger on the bag, when I feel a hand on my shoulder.

"*Shee-it*, Tse. Done a number on yourself," Trunk rumbles behind me.

All of a sudden, the last of my energy drains and I lean into the bag. When a bottle of water appears in front of me, I grab it and drink the whole fucking thing down.

"She's pregnant. He cut her, bit her so hard he drew blood, and she's fucking pregnant. You know what she's thinkin'? She's fucking worried about me. *Me*." I draw back my hand and punch the bag but there's not much behind it. "Carrying my fucking babies, listening to the filth coming from that bastard's mouth, and she knows he's gonna kill her. Those big eyes staring down at me were wide with fear for *me*."

A sound I don't recognize rips out of me, and the next thing I know Trunk is holding me up.

"You're okay, brother. I've gotcha."

When we finally walk out the night is already dark, but my step is lighter. I left a heavy load in that shed.

My pace increases as we head for the clubhouse, suddenly eager to see Sophia.

"So…twins?" Trunk rumbles beside me.

"Yeah."

I actually manage a smile.

"*Shee-it*."

Pushing open the door my eyes immediately scan the space, looking for her. A group of brothers is hanging around the bar and Lisa, who was sitting at the large dining table with Nosh, gets to her feet when she sees me.

"Where is she?"

"Ouray's office with Luna," she says, but when I try to walk past she grabs my arm. "First you need to look in on the boy."

I know instinctively she's talking about Ravi and a wave of guilt washes over me. I dumped him here early this morning and took off without a second thought.

"Shit."

"Yeah," Lisa mumbles. "Been hiding in your old room all day with that dog. Brick and I tried to talk to him, get him to come out for something, but that damn dog wouldn't let us get close."

Okay, change of plans.

I head down the hall and pause outside the door, knocking lightly. A soft growl can be heard on the other side of the door.

"It's me, boy. Easy."

I open the door slowly. The dog is standing at the foot of the bed, his body squared up and almost vibrating with tension. He turns his head to the bed before looking at me again, clearly torn between greeting me and protecting the kid.

Ravi is curled up on the far corner of the mattress, still in the clothes I found him in this morning. He hasn't even had a shower.

I ease the door shut behind me and hold out a hand for the dog, who sniffs the air but won't budge from his spot.

"It's okay, Van. Come here, boy," I whisper.

He takes a tentative step forward, but stops when

Ravi's voice sounds from the bed.

"Tse?"

"Yeah, kid."

In a flash he's off the bed and plows into me. His spindly arms wrap around my waist for a tight hug before he releases me and steps back. I bend down to greet the dog, who now feels secure enough to approach.

"She okay?" I can hear the anxiety in his voice. "Brick came to the door and said you found her."

"Yeah, we found her, kid. And she's gonna be just fine. Just got banged up a little."

"Where is she?"

"Getting cleaned up." The dog is whining by the door. "Has he been out at all?"

The guilty expression on the boy's face is answer enough. Poor dog has to be about to spring a leak after being locked in for probably close to twelve hours.

"Tell you what. You take Van and give him a chance to do his business; I'll go check in with Sophia. You can come see us in Ouray's office after."

"Okay."

He darts out of the room, Van glued to his side, and I'm starting to wonder who that dog belongs to.

SOPHIA

I TAKE THE last sip of tea Luna brought me; although I'd much rather have a swig of something stronger.

Lisa whisked me through the clubhouse, through Ouray's office, and straight into the surprisingly nice suite right beside it. I lost sight of Tse, but when I mentioned I was worried about him, she said Brick had him. She had clean towels for me in the bathroom and I took a long shower, despite the doctor's suggestion I wait a day. I had to scrub my body and wash my hair several times to get the stench of death off me.

Lisa was waiting with a clean change of clothes from her own closet when I got out. She suggested the stitches on my face would heal better exposed to the air and helped me change the dressing on my chest. She did it with tears in her eyes, and I badly wanted to cry with her but was afraid if I started I wouldn't be able to stop.

I knew Luna wanted to talk to me and I preferred getting that part over with sooner rather than later. So, for the last hour or so I've gone over the past twenty-four hours, telling her what I know. Unfortunately, other than my trip in the trunk of that car, I remember everything in great detail.

"Any word on Mandy?" I ask her.

"I actually just got a message from Gomez," she says, running her finger over the screen on her phone. "Uh, she's out of surgery. Brain bleed, but they relieved the pressure and she's stable for now. "

"Almost the same as Bernie," I comment.

Something flashes across Luna's face as she tucks her phone away.

"What?"

She blows out a breath through pursed lips and her eyes make it up to mine.

"They found Bernie and his sister."

There's something about the way she says it that has my breath get stuck in my throat.

"Oh, no…" I manage.

"When local feds flew the drone over the grounds, they spotted a patch of earth behind the complex that looked freshly turned. This afternoon they dug up their remains."

I surge to my feet and rush to the bathroom, when the cup of tea I just finished makes its way back up. Luna follows me and has a wet washcloth ready when I'm done tossing my cookies.

"I'm sorry," she mumbles. "I didn't want to tell you, at least not yet, but I don't want to lie to you either."

"It's okay." I wipe my mouth and face. "I think part of me already knew."

"You know, you're right though, one of the Amontinados we took into custody had a makeshift sap tied to his belt. No more than a tube sock with a pool ball tucked inside, but an effective and potentially deadly weapon. We think he's the one who attacked Bernie at the Backyard—we're starting to hear rumors he may have been skimming some of the drugs for his own profit—and Mandy in Albuquerque, likely with that same weapon. I haven't talked to Ravi yet to confirm, but I suspect that same guy may have been the one who knocked you out."

"Did he have a cut on his chin?"

Luna looks surprised. "He did. How—"

"When we kicked open the trunk of the car, it connected with his face. That's the guy who took me."

I toss the washcloth in the sink and head out of the bathroom right as Tse comes walking into the bedroom. I stop in my tracks and take in his dirty, sweaty shirt, and the bloodied knuckles of his hands.

"I'll leave you guys to it," Luna mumbles, slipping past me and out of the room.

"Sorry I disappeared on you," he starts, his eyes never leaving mine. "I needed to blow off some steam."

I walk up to him and take one of his hands, studying the damage.

"I see that. I need to clean these but you need a shower first."

He looks at me funny but then nods and walks past me into the bathroom, yanking his shirt over his head on the way. I hear the shower turn on as I grab the first aid kit Lisa used on me and set it on the bed, getting some disinfectant and pads of gauze ready. Then I pull open a few drawers in the dresser, looking for something clean for him to wear. I'm sure Ouray won't mind.

I find a shirt and a pair of sweatpants and carry them into the bathroom just as the water turns off. His showers are always fast, but this one probably broke a record. I hand him a towel when he steps out and he doesn't waste time toweling off.

"Didn't think you want to borrow a pair of Ouray's boxers," I tell him.

"You'd be right," he grumbles.

I watch as he puts on the sweats commando, and almost feel guilty for wishing he'd just stay naked for my viewing pleasure. I love his body. Big, solid, strong, with just the right amount of padding to make it comfortable. I'm disappointed when he tugs the shirt down.

"Now let me have a look at those hands." I give him a little shove into the bedroom and he takes a seat on the edge of the bed. "How is the other guy?"

I try to make light of the situation, because truthfully, the way he's looking at me makes me a little nervous. I carefully dab some gauze soaked in disinfectant on his raw knuckles but he doesn't even flinch. I can feel his eyes on me the whole time.

"I love you."

His voice is raspy and so soft, I'm not sure I heard him right.

My hands still as I search his face.

"What?"

"Never used those words before. They feel a bit strange on my lips." He takes my hands in his and pulls me between his legs, his warm eyes aimed up at me. "I love you, Fee," he says a little stronger, and his words—aided by my pregnancy hormones—have my emotions well up. "Not gonna lie, I've had a lifetime of second thoughts about this just in the last couple of hours. I'm not sure if I can be who you need, and I'm scared as fuck, but when I think of a future that doesn't include you all I see is a black hole."

"Baby…" I take his face in my hands.

"I don't have the logistics worked out yet," he continues, obviously not done yet. "We're gonna need a bigger place for sure, but I've got money socked away. I can afford to look after you and the babies—"

I cut off the flow of his words with my mouth, kissing him deeply and putting all my feelings into the kiss.

"You are everything I need," I whisper against his lips. "Just as you are. I've never trusted someone this completely, and I love you so much."

A knock sounds at the door, interrupting our moment.

"Shit. Ravi," Tse mumbles. "He wanted to see you. He's been worried."

"Go, let him in." I step out of his hold. "I'm gonna wash my face and be right out."

I head to the bathroom when I hear him call my name.

"Never heard those words either," he admits when I turn my head. "Feels good."

When I walk into Ouray's office a few minutes later, Van is so excited in his greeting he almost knocks me off my feet.

Ravi is more cautious in his approach and stops a few steps away, staring at the mark on my face.

"I'm sorry."

My narrowly regained composure threatens to crumble again, but I hang on. These guys are gonna have to stop apologizing or I'll be blubbering the next nine… wait…seven months.

I close the distance and fold him in a hug.

"Sorry? Are you kidding me? If you hadn't gotten away, you wouldn't have been able to give Tse the information he needed to find me." I set him back and look him in the eye. "You saved me, kiddo. You and Tse both."

The smile is barely distinguishable, but I see it. Just a

slight tug at the corner of his mouth as he ducks his head and turns to the dog for distraction.

I meet Tse's eyes and smile. His mouth doesn't move but I read the smile in his eyes.

These guys break my heart. Both so closed off, yet I see all of them.

"I'm hungry."

A chuckle escapes me. Typical teenage bottomless pit.

"I could eat something too," I admit.

"Then let's go see if we can raid Lisa's kitchen," Tse suggests.

Before he has the door all the way open, Ravi darts past him, Van Gogh on his heels.

ARROW'S EDGE MC

29

Tse

I STARTLE AWAKE when Sophia suddenly shoots up straight in bed.

I stroke a finger over her arm and she almost jumps out of her skin, her eyes wide when she swings her head around.

"It's just me."

Recognition washes over her features and I gently pull her down on top of me.

"Ugh."

"Nightmare?"

She groans in response.

I reach over to flick on a light on the nightstand and check the clock. It's after four in the morning.

"Wanna talk about it?"

I stroke a hand up and down her back, trying not to notice she's not wearing panties underneath an old T-shirt of mine she's using as a sleepshirt.

"Not really," she mumbles against my chest.

It's the second night we're staying at the clubhouse. After the attack on Lea and Sophia's abduction Thursday night, Ouray shut down the restaurant for a 'family emergency.' It'll stay closed today, tomorrow being Monday it would've been closed anyway, and the plan is to reopen on Tuesday. Sophia is determined she'll be back at work then.

If it were up to me she'd take more time, but yesterday she announced she wanted to get back to normal. That included heading back to her place and being at the restaurant on Tuesday when it opens. We compromised. She's going in to see her own doctor on Monday and if he gives the all-clear, we'll head back to her place tomorrow night and she opens the restaurant Tuesday morning.

We dropped in to see Lea yesterday, who is recovering well but has to stay in at Mercy until after the weekend. Something she was not that happy about. Sophia was a mess when she saw her, feeling guilty she'd been attacked but Lea waved it off. Told her it was the best compliment she'd received in years, being mistaken for the younger—and according to Lea, prettier—Sophia.

I'd kind of hoped, maybe after seeing Lea, Sophia would've been able to relax enough for a good night's sleep. Instead, another nightmare.

"It may help, Fee."

She lifts her head and rests her chin on her hands, a sly little smile on her face as she wiggles her pelvis against my fast-awakening cock.

"You know what would help?"

I grab a healthy handful of her bare ass cheek.

"What's that, Fee?"

She drops her legs on either side of my hips and I can feel the heat of her pussy against my bare skin.

"Do I need to spell it out?"

"You sure that's a good idea?"

She answers by leaning forward, licking at my lips with the tip of her tongue. With a hand I cup the back of her head to keep her still and open my mouth, sucking her tongue inside. *Fuck, yeah.* I shift my grasp on her ass and dip my fingers between her legs. Slick, warm, and ready for me.

Her moan is muffled when I play with her, rolling the pad of my finger over her clit before slipping one, and then two digits inside her tight pussy.

She tears her mouth from mine and pushes herself up, reaching between her legs to take my cock in a firm hold.

"Make me forget, Tse," she whispers, as she brushes the crown along her wet crease.

She's beautiful, her lips swollen and eyes heavy with lust. My gaze drops to her full tits and—ignoring the bite mark—slides down to her belly, which I swear already looks a bit more rounded.

She looks wholesome and ripe, and the need to claim her erases any lingering concerns as I grab on to her hips, plant my feet in the mattress, and power up inside her.

Her mouth falls open and she drops her head back, the long lines of her neck exposed. I grunt with the effort, lifting my shoulders off the bed so my mouth can close around a dark pink nipple. The moment I suck deeply, her hands clamp on to my head as she grinds down on my cock.

It's uncontrolled—wet, hot, and wild—and we're not exactly quiet about it either. When she comes she cries out, and with her body still pulsing around my cock, I follow not long after on a roar.

Still connected, she collapses on my chest, both our bodies slick with sweat as we catch our breath. She whimpers when my softening cock slips out of her.

"I should clean up," she mutters, suddenly sleepy again.

I tighten my arms around her.

"Later. Close your eyes."

I don't have to wait long for her breathing to deepen as she succumbs to sleep.

Sleep eludes me but I hold her safely in my arms while she grabs a few more hours.

I use the time to plan for our future.

"We got the dealer. The suspect in the attack on Lea. Picked him up yesterday."

"Where is he?" Kaga growls, instantly on his feet.

We're crowded around the big table in Ouray's office. Gomez, Luna, Ramirez, Sophia, and most of the brothers.

"Sit your ass down," Ouray barks. "Last thing Lea needs is a fucking husband behind bars."

Kaga turns on him.

"He. Cut. My. Wife."

I feel him. Fuck, what I wouldn't have given to kill that bastard, Manny, myself. Instead, I have to live with the knowledge he still haunts my woman in her dreams. For that alone I'd like to have seen him suffer. At least I have some comfort in knowing his brains are splattered all over that room where he kept her.

"Karma will get him eventually," Ramirez promises. "It's inevitable with lowlifes like him."

Gomez just briefed us that the FBI was able to lay charges against nine members of the Amontinados, not counting Salinas. Some of the names are familiar, despite not being in the same line of business anymore, we've continued crossing paths with the club over the years. Mostly at rallies, like the one in Moab.

Most of the charges are drug related—the feds found a cache of illegal narcotics during the execution of a search warrant at their clubhouse—but there are also several charges for murder, attempted murder, conspiracy to commit murder, kidnapping, and assault.

In short, the Amontinados have been decimated, with the bulk of the brotherhood facing lengthy prison terms.

Can't say I'll be mourning the loss.

SOPHIA

"LET ME DO something."

Lisa looks up from the dough she's kneading on the flour-dusted counter when I walk in.

Tse just left with Honon, for the FBI office, to pick up their bikes Gomez had arranged to be towed back to Durango. I voiced concern for Honon to get on the bike with a fresh gunshot wound to the leg, but he just laughed it off. Told me he'd had injuries worse than a little hole in his leg.

These guys, so tough and casual when it comes to their own well-being, but they treat their women like precious cargo. Kaga's reaction at yesterday's briefing by law enforcement was evidence of that.

As a further case in point, when we got back from my appointment with the doctor this morning, Tse's overprotective side came out in full force. Dr. Cairns told me to be prepared to need more rest and take some extra naps where I can. Apparently carrying twins takes a lot out of you.

Tse interpreted that to mean I have to take naps and therefore can't go back to work full time. That resulted in a doozy of an argument when we got back to the compound. I'm sure anyone anywhere in the clubhouse would've heard us, because despite being behind closed doors in Ouray's bedroom, we weren't exactly quiet.

Tse stormed off and I felt it prudent to hide out in the bedroom a little longer. Especially since I didn't want to walk into the clubhouse with those damned tears I seem to be shedding at the drop of a hat still damp on my face. When I felt it safe to come out, Tse and Honon had already left, as Wapi informed me.

I'm thinking when Tse goes back to work on the house tomorrow and I start at the Backyard, we'll soon be able to find some normalcy back. At least I hope so.

"Can you handle rolling meatballs?" Lisa asks, pointing at a large metal bowl with a massive amount of ground beef. "I've already spiced it."

"Yeah, of course I can."

I wash my hands at the sink and dive in.

"Hmmm."

I glance at Lisa.

"What?"

"No nausea? No weird aversions?"

Shaking my head I tell her, "No. Why?"

"Some pregnant women don't have the stomach for it."

I drop the ball I was shaping onto the tray and turn to face her.

"You heard."

She snorts and rolls her eyes.

"Honey, don't think there was anything living between here and the city that could'a missed *that*. But I already knew. Not from *you* mind you." She wags a dough-covered finger at me. "Had to find out from Brick."

Right away my eyes well up. *Dammit.*

"He didn't get it from me," I assure her. "Look, Lisa, I would've told you before anyone else, but we agreed to keep it to ourselves a little longer. At least I thought we did. It was a surprise—"

"Oh, I bet it was," she scoffs, but she does it with a twinkle in her eye.

Thank God.

"I'm only eight weeks. I…I mean *we* weren't even sure and so much happened. We've barely had a moment to let it sink in. I just wanted a moment to get used to it myself before making any announcements."

Lisa bursts out laughing.

"Well, honey, I have news for you. By now the entire club knows you're having twins. These boys are like old wives the way they talk. Trust me, the word's already spread far and wide." She gestures at the big bowl of meat I have my hands in. "Why do you figure I'm making twice my usual? That clubhouse is gonna be full tonight. Everyone's gonna be flocking in for dinner and congratulations."

Of course that breaks the dam and I end up sobbing on Lisa's shoulder. She assures me the tears are better than morning sickness—which I seem to have been spared, at least so far—and that I'll get back to my normal self soon enough.

God, I hope so.

I finished rolling eighty-seven large meatballs, and am tossing the second of two salads when I feel Tse's lips on my neck.

"You're on your feet," he rumbles against my skin.

Despite the sweet kiss and the endearing concern, his words annoy me.

"Let's make a deal," I snap, turning around. "How about you let me decide when I'm tired and need to get off my feet. I understand it'll become tough soon enough, but I'm not about to lie in bed for the next seven months, give or take. If you think I have a temper now, I'll be downright violent then."

I hear Lisa chuckle and notice Tse is grinning as he pulls me to him.

"Glad to see that bite hasn't suffered," he shares before laying a wet one on me.

He makes me forget my surroundings as I wind my arms around his neck.

"Excuse me, I'm trying to cook dinner here," Lisa grumbles, bumping my hip with hers.

Tse grins against my lips.

"Love you, Fee."

I smile into his soft eyes.

"Love you back."

"Well, good Lord Almighty, my teeth hurt with all that syrup. Ya hafta do that here?"

Tse chuckles as he releases me and turns to Lisa instead, planting a big smooch on her cheek.

"You're a shit liar, Lisa," he teases her. "You love it."

She pushes him off and swats him with a dish towel.

"And you're a menace," she taunts back with a sparkle in her eyes. "Go on—out—both of you!"

SHE WASN'T LYING.

The entire club turned out—brothers, wives, children—there's no room left to sit.

We end up having to order a couple of pizzas for the younger kids, because not even the eighty-seven meatballs I rolled are enough to feed everyone.

I didn't have a chance to ask Tse what kept him so long this afternoon before they started filing in, but it'll wait, he's over there laughing as his brothers rib him. Every so often his eyes drift my way and he winks, or smiles, making me feel important.

I've never received so many hugs, kisses, and congratulations in a day, and already I'm overwhelmed with the offers for secondhand clothing, and cribs, and toys. At this rate we won't have to buy a thing.

I snuggle Finn on my lap, sniffing his hair—the same color as Kelsey's—which smells like baby shampoo. A wave of sorrow hits me as I remember when she found out she was pregnant. Our circumstances were very different, but she'd been equally surprised. She'd grown to look forward to that baby and let me share her excitement every step of the way.

I wish she were here to share this with me.

"You miss her."

Brick's voice pulls me out of my head and I shoot him a watery smile.

"Yeah."

He bends over and kisses my forehead.

"Didn't know my daughter that well anymore, but I'm pretty sure she'd've been happy for ya."

I watch him make his way to the bar and know I'm not the only one who feels her absence.

"Quit hogging the baby," Tse says when he walks up.

My guess is he caught that little interaction and is checking in on me, without appearing to do so. He's so transparent it makes me smile.

"I'm not hogging him. I've barely had a chance."

He plucks him off my lap anyway, and I have an immediate visceral response when he settles Finn in the crook of his arm.

"Now that you've claimed him, you claimed that poopy diaper too. He probably needs a change." I smirk at his horrified expression. "Lord knows you're gonna need the practice."

After dinner I'm chatting with Jaimie, Trunk's wife, when I notice Ravi disappearing down the hall. As is becoming the norm, Van follows right behind him. He's been quiet all day and I wonder what is going through his head.

I excuse myself quickly and head after him.

The door is already closed when I get to his room, so I knock.

"Hey, Ravi? It's Sophia. Can I talk to you for a minute?"

From inside I hear a muffled, "Okay," and push open the door.

He's sitting on his bed and watches me while I greet Van, who behaves like he didn't just see me minutes ago.

"Can I sit?" I indicate the bed and he nods.

"Guess you heard I'm having a baby, right?"

"Two," he corrects me with a serious face, making me smile.

"So it seems. Which is why I wanted a word with you," I start, hoping I can find the right tone. "You see, I was kinda hoping you'd be able to help out with the dog.

Things will probably get busy and I'm sure there'll be times we have our hands full. It would really help a lot to know he has someone looking out for him. And maybe for the babies too, when the time comes."

I may be imagining it, but he looks like he's sitting a little taller.

"Sure."

He ducks his head but can't hide the pleased expression on his face.

"Good, that makes me feel a lot better. Thank you."

I get up to leave but stop at the door.

"Oh, and, Ravi?" He lifts his eyes. "I haven't mentioned to anyone what you told me, that's up to you, but maybe if you ever needed someone to talk to, Tse would be a good person. I think he'll understand better than anyone."

I'm afraid he'll shut down on me but instead he surprises me by nodding.

"Maybe," he mumbles, but it's enough for me.

30

Tse

One month later.

"Tse! Visitor!"

I'm brushing off some of the drywall dust I'm covered in as I make my way outside.

VanDyken is talking to Paco—who just hollered for me—when I walk up.

"Jay."

"Talked to Meredith," he shares with a grin, wasting no time. "She's ready to get the wheels rolling."

"Fuck, that's great news."

What a relief.

I was trying for the past month to find us a place. Something big enough, with a few extra rooms in case

Sophia's family comes to visit, but she's been resistant. Last week that turned into an argument ending in her teary confession that with everything that happened she'd barely had a chance to enjoy her new life, her new house, and with the babies on the way she felt overwhelmed and out of control.

I know that's been a big issue for her—the lack of autonomy over her life—but the need to look after her and secure a future with her has been mine.

I didn't get much sleep that night, but by morning I had the raw outlines of an idea, which could be the perfect compromise, if it worked out. That was the problem, because it wasn't just up to us. I spent most of the week fine-tuning my idea on paper, sorting out timelines, logistics, talking to the guys at the worksite, and even touching base with Brick.

Didn't particularly enjoy keeping Sophia in the dark, but I didn't want to get her hopes up when ultimately it all hinged on one thing.

Looks like I just got my all clear.

"I've gotta go," I announce to Paco.

I slip the tool belt off my waist and hold it in one hand, while I offer VanDyken the other.

"I'll give you a call," he says, clapping a hand on my shoulder, which sends a dust cloud up in the air.

Instead of rushing to the restaurant I should probably have a shower first, but I need to drop Van off at home anyway.

"Appreciate you, my friend," I tell Jay.

Then I whistle for the dog and toss him and the tools

in my truck before I tear out of there.

We've been making major strides on Paco's place. During the week it's mostly been him and me, with a couple of guys from Jed's crew popping in occasionally. With the kids back in school, Ravi's been out here helping on the weekends, proudly wearing his own tool belt Sophia thought to get him for his birthday last month. A couple of times Elan showed up to lend a hand as well. Those two seem to have forged something of a friendship.

Unfortunately, if Sophia is on board with my plans, it would mean finishing Paco's house would be on hold for at least a couple of months. By then it'll be winter but he's assured me a few times since the work we have left on his place is mostly inside, the weather won't matter.

I bring Van inside, feed him, and have a quick shower while he eats. Then I take him out for a quick pee, lock up the house, and head down the mountain.

It's Wednesday and although not as busy as on the weekends and still fairly early, the parking lot of the Backyard Edge is more than half full. I pull around back where most of the staff parks and find the spot beside Sophia's Jeep empty.

They've had to hire some new staff for both the kitchen and the dining room. Lea was back at work since last week, something Kaga had not been too pleased about, but she announced she was going stir-crazy at home. Sophia suggested training Lea so they can eventually share management of the restaurant. Ouray had been on board, and Kaga was satisfied knowing his wife wouldn't be on her feet all day.

As for me, I'm happy there'll be some relief for Sophia. She has a tendency to push herself and I suspect the time will come when work will become too much. Already she gets tired quickly.

I slip in the back door and find her in her office, her head resting on her arms on the desk. Softly closing the door behind me, I drop the papers I brought with me on the desk and bend down to press a kiss to her neck. Startled, her head snaps up and she would've clipped me in the chin if I hadn't taken a quick step back.

"It's only me."

She swings around her chair and looks a little disoriented.

"Shit. Was I sleeping?" She doesn't wait for an answer and immediately follows it with, "What time is it?"

I take her hands and pull her to her feet, looking down at her belly, which is getting quite pronounced. I love watching her grow with my babies. Everything about her is getting fuller. *Fuck*, it makes me want to beat my chest and howl at the moon. Sinking down to my knees, I put my cheek to the soft swell.

"What are you doing here?"

She sounds like she's smiling and I feel her fingers comb through my hair.

"Can't I come say hello to my girls?"

I tilt my face up and catch her shaking her head at me.

"How do you know it's not boys?"

"You never had morning sickness."

She laughs at me, as she often does these days.

"And what is that supposed to mean?"

I shrug and get to my feet. "I read somewhere that means it's a girl."

"You know you can't believe half of what you read on the internet, right? It's an old wives' tale. There's another one that says exactly the opposite. If you really want to know we can ask when we go in for the next ultrasound."

She snuggles in my arms and I inhale the shampoo I massaged into her scalp this morning. If my brothers could see me—washing hair, rubbing lotion on her skin, massaging her feet when she gets home—hell, they'd never let me live it down, but I like taking care of her in any way she'll allow.

"Maybe not a bad idea," I mumble in her hair. "We'll know what color to paint the room."

She leans back and looks up at me suspiciously.

"Room? What room? I thought we'd agreed we'd let it rest for a while."

I gently turn her to the desk and unroll the plans I've been drawing up.

"What is this?"

"It's the A-frame. With an addition."

I point at the single-level add-on cutting into the slant of the roof on the west side of the existing house. I drew five different versions—all adding three bedrooms and one bath—but this one will be easiest to complete. It also leaves the option of eventually bumping up one more level should we decide we need more room.

"Honey," she says putting a hand on my chest. "It looks amazing, but you can't just build on to a house we don't even own. And I know for a fact the reason Meredith rented it out in the first place is because she's not ready to let it go."

This is where I get to flash my shit-eating grin.

Because she's wrong.

SOPHIA

Two weeks later.

"I STILL CAN'T believe this."

I'm sitting on the back deck with Meredith, watching her dog, Beau, romping around with Van Gogh. The boys—Tse, Jay, and Ravi, who spends quite a bit of time here—are cooking today. Most of it is being done on the big new grill Tse came home with a few weeks ago, thank God. But to be on the safe side I hid some frozen pizzas in the bottom of the freezer yesterday. Tse does not have a great track record in the kitchen.

Fortunately, according to Meredith, Jay is pretty handy with the grill so I've been able to relax and get to know her a little better.

We signed the paperwork on the house four days ago and on Monday construction on the addition will start. Tse is determined to have everything done before Christmas so we can have my family over. I'm still walking on clouds.

Meredith chuckles.

"You say that now, but you may get sick of finding me on your deck."

That had been her only request when she agreed to sell us her house; she could pop in on occasion to sit on the deck when she had a craving for the peaceful mountains.

"Doubtful." I put a hand on my blossoming baby bump. "I look forward to it and once these two are here, I imagine I'd enjoy some adult company even more."

The house is ours. Both our names are on the deed, something Tse surprised me by insisting on, even though three-quarters of the funds came from him.

"Sorry to be nosy, but are you planning for a big family?" she asks. "I couldn't help notice the three additional bedrooms with the option for further expansion."

"No plans." At least not on my part, I'm not sure how I'll manage with the two; I haven't dared think that far ahead. "But I do have family we'd like to have room for when they visit. In fact, one of my nieces was supposed to come this summer, but the circumstances were never right."

"And the boy?"

"Ravi?" I look over at him.

He's starting to fill out a little and his voice seems to have settled on a lower octave. He even smiles more these days. I'm not sure if he ever talked to Tse—that's between them—but it wouldn't surprise me. Ravi is much more at ease with both of us.

"Yeah. I was just wondering, not that it's any of my business, but he seems to fit in well."

I press my lips together to prevent myself from smiling too big.

The truth is, Tse and I were just talking about the possibility of Ravi moving here with us, once the addition is done, just a few days ago. Tse brought it up and didn't have to sell me on the idea. Both of them deserve a loving family after having the start in life they did.

Over the summer I've grown to love the kid and, eventually, once the babies are here and we've all had a chance to get used to each other, I'd like to look into the possibility of adopting him. Only if he wants that too, though.

"He does," I admit, looking over at the men and noticing Van hovering around, waiting for scraps to fall. "Even the dog is more loyal to him than he is to either one of us."

Suddenly the dog's single ear perks up, he barks, and then he takes off running around the side of the house. Ravi runs after him, trying to call him back.

Tse looks over at me.

"Were you expecting anyone else?"

I shake my head and get to my feet.

"Would you excuse me?" I tell Meredith, but before I can take a step I hear a voice.

"Surprise! Look at you! I swear you've grown a foot!"

My groan is apparently loud enough for Meredith to hear and she promptly starts laughing.

"Nothing like unexpected visitors."

I bulge my eyes at her.

"You don't even know the half of it."

Blossom comes sailing around the side of the house, scarves billowing in her wake, almost obscuring my father with his arm around Ravi, who follow behind her. She hugs and kisses Tse, who is used to her exuberance, but then she turns to Jay, who appears to freeze when she opens her arms to him as well.

Beside me Meredith can't seem to stop laughing, and I'm mortified watching my mother ignore every physical stop sign Jay is throwing off as she wraps him in a one-sided hug.

"Blossom! Please don't manhandle my guests!" I cry out.

"Chill, baby-girl!" she yells back. "The man clearly needed a hug."

I quickly make introductions, hoping to spare Meredith from my mother's assault, but to no avail. Once Blossom is on a roll...

I can feel my blood pressure rising—once again my folks arrive unannounced—but when I look over at Tse with his arm hooked around Ravi's neck, both of them grinning wide, the roaring in my ears dims. Tse glances over and winks at me, and I can't help but smile too.

To my surprise, Meredith and my mother hit it off. They apparently have an interest in organic living in common, and Meredith doesn't seem to mind when Blossom probes her for gory stories related to her job. Hardly appropriate dinner conversation. That doesn't seem to bother Ravi, who has made his way over to our little group and seems equally fascinated with the morbid details.

Duff is keeping the men company, discussing the merits of grilling with the lid open or closed. Despite the conflicting opinions, the food gets cooked and we're able to sit down for dinner.

We sit at the old picnic table I picked up for a steal a while back and spruced up. Tse had called it scrap wood, but I loved the way previous users had carved initials and names into the weathered boards. By the time I had lightly sanded it down, preserving as much of its carved history as I could, and given it a couple of clear coats of polyurethane, even he had to admit it looked good.

The night is beautiful and Meredith and Jay stay long enough to enjoy the fire Ravi builds us, until I start nodding off on Tse's lap. Suddenly everyone gets up at the same time and within ten minutes the house is empty, except for Ravi, who opted to crash on the couch when Tse offered.

Tse grabs a pillow and some sheets for the kid while I head upstairs and get ready for bed.

"That was a good night," Tse rumbles when he crawls into bed behind me.

His body curves protectively against my back and one of his big hands immediately finds my belly. This has become our new way to sleep, now that the baby bump is getting in the way.

"It was," I mumble, feeling his lips on my neck.

I cover his hand on my stomach with my own and snuggle a little farther back. I'm already drifting off when I hear him whisper.

"Best thing that ever happened to me."

ARROW'S EDGE MC

EPILOGUE

Tse

January.

"WHERE IS SOPHIA?"

I watch Mel Morgan—a lawyer the club sometimes uses when dealing with Child Protective Services—walk toward me. A stunning woman, with long silver hair, a do-not-give-a-shit-what-anyone-thinks attitude, and tough as nails. She also dresses like a recalcitrant teenager, in ripped jeans, old concert T-shirt, worn hoodie, and Chucks on her feet. The latter only because it's cold as fuck outside, otherwise she'd be in bare feet or wearing flip-flops.

Mel's daughter, Lindsey—also her legal assistant—is more appropriately dressed for a law office. I'm pretty sure Mel must've had her when she was still a kid herself, seeing as Lindsey is probably mid to late twenties and Mel can't be a whole lot older than me.

She may not look the part, but she is sharp as a tack and is helping us get guardianship of Ravi. We'd initially planned to wait until after the house was finished, but with Sophia now ordered on bed rest—the result of high blood pressure—and more early snow than normal, work on the house has slowed down. Unless I can convince her to stay at the clubhouse for a bit so she's looked after while we finish it, I'm not sure when it'll get done.

The plan is to get this paperwork ready and I'm keeping my fingers crossed it'll be enough of an incentive for her to get on board with the temporary move to the compound. Although, I can't really blame her for digging her heels in, she's already had to deal with a Christmas that didn't turn out exactly as she'd hoped.

"She's home. Bed rest."

"Well, that sucks, but we're gonna need her John Hancock as well."

"I know, but I was hoping I can take it with me. I'll get her to sign it and can bring it back."

"Sure. That'll work. Just remember I told you I'm gonna have a hard time getting a judge to sign off on it if you don't have room for the kid. How's the house coming along?"

I give her an update and my promise that as soon as I can get Sophia out from underfoot, I should have it move-in ready at the latest by mid-February.

Twenty minutes later, I walk out of the office with the

paperwork I hope is going to do the trick.

I already know I have my brothers' support, and last weekend we sat down with Ravi. Not gonna lie, it wasn't just Sophia tearing up that time. The kid was afraid to believe us at first, which killed me, but we were eventually able to assure him we were serious.

Now I can show him how serious. Transferring guardianship from the Arrow's Edge MC to us is only the first step, but it's a big one. Once the house is done and our family is complete, we'll set the wheels in motion to make it permanent.

When I get home, Van appears to give me a quick sniff before he heads back for the couch. That's where he's spent most of his time with Sophia, lying on the floor at her feet with his eye on the door.

I kick off my boots and tiptoe in; I don't want to wake her up if she's sleeping. Sophia is lying on her side—wrapped around the body pillow Lisa got her—her eyes on me.

"I thought you were sleeping."

I sit by her feet and rub her leg.

"I was, but I heard you come in. What is that?"

She points at the manila envelope where I dropped it on the coffee table and I grab it. Figures she'd zoom in on that.

"I stopped by to see Mel."

Her eyes grow big as she pulls herself up to a sitting position.

"Mel?"

"Yeah, guardianship papers were ready for our

signatures. Mine's already on there, it just needs yours."

She smiles big and holds out her hand but I pull the envelope from her reach.

"Let me sign it."

"Not so fast." Her face instantly looks mutinous. "There's a catch. She says no judge will sign off on it if we don't have an appropriate space to offer him. Which means this house needs to get done." I point at the temporary wall we've had to put up between the addition and the A-frame when winter struck. "And we both know what that means."

She falls back on the couch, her forearm covering her eyes.

"I hate this," she mumbles, her voice wobbly.

I lean down and pull up her sweater to kiss her stomach.

"I know you do, Fee. We don't really have a choice. If I could take over growing those babies for you I would, but what I can do is get this house ready for all of us. It'll just be for a few weeks. Maybe a month."

More like six weeks, but I'm not going to push it.

"You'll have Lisa and Brick around when I'm working, and you'll see Ravi after school every day." She wipes her eyes with her sleeve and struggles to get upright, so I give her a hand. "Think about it," I add. "You won't have to eat my cooking attempts anymore."

"Fine," she grumbles through a faint grin. "Get me a pen."

When she's signed the papers, I tuck them back in the envelope and move to the other side of her so I can pull her back against my front. She drops her head back on my shoulder.

"After these two are out and Ravi is ours, no more babies. I'm done."

I bend down and kiss the tender skin at the base of her neck.

"Okay, babe."

She tilts her head up and glares at me.

"I mean it."

I smile and drop a kiss on her lips. Not the right time to bring it up, but now that I've had a taste I wouldn't mind a big family.

But that's a discussion for another time.

"I know, Fee."

SOPHIA

February.

"Do YOU HAVE to go? I'm bored out of my mind."

He bends over the bed and presses a kiss to my pouting mouth.

"Baby, I'll be a few hours, that's all. I've gotta get those rooms painted, but Ravi and Elan are helping so it shouldn't take us too long."

I snort before wincing a little when the babies move. I rub a soothing hand over my now impressively distended stomach.

Six weeks to go. I can do this.

"Can I get you anything to eat before I go?"

"No. I'm fine."

For once I don't feel like eating. A little too late, I'm already as big as a house. With my luck I'll never get this baby weight off.

"Call me if you need me."

One last kiss and he takes off, leaving me in bed with just a big-screen TV and Van for company.

I grab the remote and click on Netflix. I have three more seasons of Homeland to watch, that'll keep me busy for another day or two and then I'll have to find something new again.

But first I need to pee.

I'm barely through the second episode of the day when I need to pee again. I pause the show and swing my legs over the side of the mattress, just as the door opens and Mel Morgan pokes her head in.

"Are you decent?"

"Yeah, come in. What are you doing here?"

I try to scoot back in bed but it feels like my bladder is going to burst.

"I come bearing good—"

"Hold that thought," I interrupt her and ease off the bed. "I need to use the bathroom."

The moment my feet hit the floor and I stand up I feel a trickle down my leg.

Wonderful.

I do a quick shuffle toward the bathroom, hoping she doesn't notice I peed myself when a large gush leaves me standing in a puddle on the threshold.

"Oh shit…"

"Right." Mel immediately jumps into action and squeezes past me in the bathroom, pulling towels off the rack and dumping one at my feet. "Back up on the bed with you. Right now."

She leads me to the bed and puts the other towel on the mattress before helping me lift my feet up. Then she hands me my phone.

"Call your doctor, tell him your water broke, ask him if he wants you to go to the hospital on your own or call an ambulance. I'm gonna grab Lisa."

Then she's gone and I'm trying not to have a panic attack.

I'm not an idiot, I know twins can come early, but this is six weeks early. That can't be good.

I dial and am quickly put through to Dr. Cairns, who tells me to get myself to Mercy right away and try to stay as horizontal as I can. I'm just hanging up with him when Mel storms in, followed by Lisa and Paco, of all people.

"He told me to get to the hospital but stay as horizontal as I can."

Lisa starts opening dresser drawers and pulling out clean clothes, and Mel turns to Paco tossing him a set of keys he deftly catches.

"Pull my vehicle up to the front door and find someone who can help you carry her out."

"Tse. We need to call Tse."

"First we get you cleaned up and out of here," Lisa says, heading into the bathroom.

She comes back with a couple of pads and a washcloth.

I feel oddly comforted with these two women who clearly know what they're doing, when I can barely remember to breathe.

"You'll be fine," Lisa assures me as they help me get into clean clothes. "Those babies too. Don't you worry."

Mel is on the phone talking in a low voice. When she hangs up, she turns to me.

"Tse will meet us there."

"Wait. What were you about to tell me? Earlier?"

She grins at me.

"The judge signed off on your petition for guardianship. Congrats, it's a boy," she jokes.

Ravi is ours and these babies are intent on arriving the same day. Emotions well up and spill over.

I'm still crying when Paco and Brick walk in a few minutes later to help me to the car.

Lisa kisses my cheek when I'm deposited on the back seat of Mel's SUV.

"Brick and me gotta take care of a few things here, but we won't be far behind you. You'll be fine, honey."

To my surprise, Paco jumps in the driver's seat, earning a dirty look from Mel.

"It's my car, I drive my car."

"Get in, Mel," he grumbles.

"I will, as soon as you get out," she argues.

I groan when I'm overwhelmed by a surge of pressure low in my belly.

"Fuck, you're a pain in my ass. This woman needs to get to the hospital or she's having those babies in your goddamn back seat."

"Pressure, Mel," I manage to get out.

"Shit. Don't you dare push, Sophia." She hops in the passenger seat. "Drive!" she yells at Paco, who takes off like a bat out of hell.

I can't remember the drive. All I know is I'm huffing like a madwoman, trying to keep from pushing, while feeling like the guy from Alien when that creature clawed its way out of his body. Except I have two aliens.

Paco barely comes to a stop in front of Mercy when the back door is yanked open and Tse sticks his head inside, taking one look at me. Then he reaches in and lifts me out. I cling on to his neck helplessly, unable to control my body's actions.

"I've got you, Fee."

Four hours later Tse pushes my wheelchair into the NICU where Wyatt and Ella De León are being monitored for a day or two.

They're so tiny.

Wyatt came barreling out less than thirty minutes after we arrived here, and Ella followed seven minutes later.

Tse hasn't been able to stop smiling.

TSE

RAVI COMES RUNNING outside the moment we pull up to the house. Behind him Blossom stands in the doorway.

Sophia opted to stay at the hospital these last few days until the babies could come home, while Ravi and I scrambled to get the house in order.

I would've liked a few days with just my family at

home, but I wasn't going to turn Sophia's parents away when they showed up unannounced yesterday.

Blossom makes a beeline for her daughter, while Ravi helps me take the babies out of the car.

"Can I carry her inside?" he asks, holding Ella's baby seat.

"Okay, but remember, precious cargo, kid."

He grins at me, "I know," and leads the way inside.

Duff takes Wyatt's carrier from my hands in the doorway and I turn around to wait for Sophia. Blossom goes ahead and I fold my woman in my arms on the doorstep. She lifts her face and smiles tiredly as I gently kiss her lips.

"A full house, a full life, and a full heart. You gave me everything, Fee."

THE END

ABOUT THE AUTHOR

USA Today bestselling author Freya Barker loves writing about ordinary people with extraordinary stories.

Driven to make her books about 'real' people; she creates characters who are perhaps less than perfect, each struggling to find their own slice of happy, but just as deserving of romance, thrills and chills in their lives.

Recipient of the ReadFREE.ly 2019 Best Book We've Read All Year Award for "Covering Ollie, the 2015 RomCon "Reader's Choice" Award for Best First Book, "Slim To None", Finalist for the 2017 Kindle Book Award with "From Dust", and Finalist for the 2020 Kindle Book Award with "When Hope Ends", Freya continues to add to her rapidly growing collection of published novels as she spins story after story with an endless supply of bruised and dented characters, vying for attention!

www.freyabarker.com

CPSIA information can be obtained
at www.ICGtesting.com
Printed in the USA
BVHW081949070521
606760BV00004B/1293

9 781988 733623